BEAR CAT

Raland J. Patterson

General Creighton Abrams, while commander of all US forces in Southeast Asia, said of the 1st Cavalry, "The big yellow patch does something to an individual that makes him a better soldier, a better team member, and a better American than he otherwise would have been."

CHAPTER 1

Captain Johnny McKay leaned forward in his seat and looked out the window of the Pan Am 747 bound for Vietnam. He and more than one hundred other soldiers had boarded the long flight from Fort Dix, New Jersey, to Saigon. The young soldier seated next to him was obviously scared to death. His nerves caused him to talk incessantly, and McKay discovered the only way to stop him was to keep leaning forward to look out at the countryside passing thirty-five thousand feet below them. The question that had him craning his neck this time was, "Sir, are you scared?"

McKay thought about it for a minute and realized he wasn't. For some reason he felt a calmness about what was before him. His mind began to zoom back over his army life. As he remembered the main events, he couldn't decide if it had been fate or his own desire to improve his station in life that had determined his path so far. He knew fate caused him to crush his little finger the first year he'd been in, but he wasn't sure if the decision to amputate it was what had motivated him to apply to flight school. He had certainly pursued the aircraft maintenance officer course (AMOC) on his own by volunteering for Vietnam. He had to question his real motivation for volunteering—was it to attend AMOC or the fact that every officer in his company wore a chest full of medals, and he, as a captain, only had a national defense ribbon?

He leaned back in the seat and quietly said to the soldier, "My grandmother used to say worry and fear are like a rocking chair. It gives you something to do, but you don't get anywhere. My advice is, just do your job as best as you can, and you'll be okay."

Surprised at his wisdom, the soldier said, "Thank you, sir. Believe it or not, that actually makes me feel better." Then he tilted his seat back, and within minutes, he was sleeping like a child.

McKay couldn't sleep. Without all the questions, he was left with nothing but his own thoughts and concerns. They had been in the air for over six hours, but this was the first opportunity he'd had to take in his surroundings. The plane seemed huge, but he had little experience to base such a judgment on, as he had only been on an airplane a few times in his life. This plane must have been modified to accommodate transporting soldiers to an unpopular war. There were three seats on both sides of the aisle, from the front of the plane to the rear. Obviously, there were no first-class seats available on this flight. McKay turned to look at the seats toward the rear of the plane. It appeared the passengers were all strangers to one another; nothing like the stories his father and uncles had told him about how things were when they entered WWII. Their stories all involved strong units of men they knew well and had lived and fought with for long periods of time. McKay just kept searching for a familiar face—he'd been in the army for four years, so surely there was someone on this plane he knew. He got up and walked toward the bathrooms in the rear. By the time he got there, he was almost sorry he'd made the journey—so many of the soldiers stared back at him with tired, empty eyes, obviously fearful and apprehensive of what was to come. He'd heard fatigue makes cowards of everyone. *The brave man is not without fear but does his job in spite of it.* He realized if the parents of all these men could see the heroes they had raised, they wouldn't worry anymore. McKay had been drafted, but he figured about two-thirds of the men onboard had volunteered for service. They may be showing some fear now, but if they made it through, they would come back men. Even with all these thoughts in his head, he knew he was no longer the skinny farm boy who wasn't good enough to associate with the girls who lived in town. He'd always been quiet and shy at home, but he was realizing now that some women saw that as a challenge. Who would have ever thought a

2

bashful man was a turn-on for women? With those thoughts, he was finally able to fall asleep.

The closer the 747 got to its destination, the quieter the passengers became. As they landed at the Tan Son Nhut airport in Saigon, everyone strained to look out the windows at their new home. McKay and the other passengers were directed to pick up their duffle bags and head toward a waiting bus. It seemed everyone wanted a window seat. As they exited through the airport gates, they entered a small Vietnamese village. The soldiers were like kids at Disneyland. They'd yell out every time they saw something new, "Look, there're five people on that bicycle." "Look over there! I've never seen anybody carry a ladder on a bike before." Once they were in open country, there were new sights. "Look how big that water buffalo is!" "You think those straw roofs leak?" When McKay saw a farmer's home; or as the American GIs called them, hootches, he was reminded of a little old lady who lived on Sugar Creek. Every single day she'd take her broom outside and sweep her front yard. It was as level as a pool table—a red pool table, from all the red clay. This hootch was as spotless as the old lady's. McKay was impressed with how much of the area was devoted to farming. When they arrived at the gate that opened to the 90th Replacement Center, they all scrunched their noses at the unexpected smell. It was an odor that would become a part of life until they got back on the freedom bird: the strong smell of burning diesel and human feces.

The next morning, after a class on how often to take malaria pills and how to brush their teeth with fluoride, a roster was posted with the names of the soldiers and their future units. Captain Johnny McKay had been assigned to the 1st Cavalry Division. That evening he was called to the orderly room, and a sergeant asked if he was an aviation maintenance officer. When he replied affirmatively, he was told he wouldn't be going to the week of Vietnam orientation. Instead, he was informed, there would be a helicopter at oh-eight-hundred to take him to the 1st Cav headquarters, and he'd better be ready.

The pilot was ready and waiting the next morning. He must have been there awhile, as the helicopter was at flight idle. When he saw McKay approaching, he began to add power in preparation for takeoff. The cargo doors were pushed back, so McKay could look out over the countryside as they flew. He was amazed at how many small streams and rivers there were and how green everything was. It was hard to believe a war was going on, but reality set in when the pilot set down on the helipad at Phu Vinh. Fifty feet from the pad were two acres of grass and weeds completely surrounded by concertina wire and posted warning signs—*Beware: Mine Fields.* McKay retrieved his duffle bag and watched as the pilot pulled pitch and left; then he walked toward the 11th Aviation Group Headquarters entrance sign. As he pulled the tent flap back, a major looked up and read his name-tag. "Captain McKay, welcome. Just a minute—the brigade commander, Colonel Roberts, said he wanted to see you as soon as you arrived." The major knocked on the plywood door and announced him. Upon receiving permission, McKay entered.

"Captain McKay, welcome to the 1st Cav."

"Thank you, sir."

"I'll bet you're wondering why you're here. Well, it's because I asked for the next AMOC graduate. Is that you?"

"Yes, sir. I graduated five weeks ago."

"Looks like you were first in your class. How'd you like to work right here for me?"

"What would I do?"

"Keep up with my charts and update me on the status of all of our aircraft. The battalions will provide you with the information every night at midnight, and then you'll update me and/or ADC Bravo at oh-eight-hundred hours. It's an important job, and it appears you're up to the task. What do you say?"

Even though McKay realized the job he was being offered would be one of the safest in Vietnam and one most men would jump to take, he didn't think he'd be comfortable working at that level. His farm-boy upbringing told him he hadn't yet earned the right to work directly with an O6 colonel. He knew he needed to feel like he'd proven himself before taking on that challenge.

"Sir, I'm honored, but I'm not sure I'm your man."

"Tell me then, Captain. What do you want?"

"Sir, I'd like to be down at a lift company, where I might make a difference."

The colonel quickly stood, and so did McKay. "S-1, send this young captain down to one of our lift companies so he can get to work." The colonel stuck out his hand, and as they shook, he said, "Good luck, son. Keep your head down."

Within an hour McKay was on another helicopter in route to Bien Hoa. His new unit was Charlie Company, 229th Aviation Battalion.

CHAPTER 2

When he walked into the Charlie Company orderly room, McKay was surprised to be introduced to Captain Jenkins, the company commander. Usually that was a major's slot. Even if Jenkins was only a captain, however, it was obvious he was in charge. He drawled, "Captain McKay, you're an unexpected surprise. Our maintenance officer doesn't DEROS for four more months. That's really good, though, as we usually only get a couple of weeks of overlap. What I require from my maintenance officer is to personally fly every type of mission our pilots get. It's important that you know what the pilots actually put the aircraft through. I'll have operations make a list of the different kinds of missions, and you can check them off as you get them done."

McKay agreed it was a good idea and started to head towards operations.

Jenkins raised his hand. "Whoa, buddy. Let's find you a place to sleep first." He led him to the maintenance area and introduced him to CW3 Nicholson, who indicated he wanted to be called Nick.

Jenkins asked, "Do you think you could find this guy a bed?"

"Roger that. Follow me, sir. Let's take care of that first, and then I'll give you a tour of our maintenance area." As Jenkins left them to it and returned to the orderly room, Nick laughed and said, "Looks like the old man is going to work on his tan."

Confused, McKay asked, "What do you mean?"

Nick started walking as he explained, "He will DEROS in six weeks and wants to be looking good for his fiancé." He pointed to the two Conex containers next to the orderly room. "He's always there every day around noon."

They approached a well-constructed building, and McKay commented, "Nice-looking hootch."

"Yeah, civilian contractors built it last year. They only built the sides and the roof. We had to fill and stack the sandbags around the sides. We had a couple of pilots who'd been contractors before the army, and they fixed up the insides. It cost us a case of Johnny Walker Red to get the plywood from the Seabees."

Once they entered, McKay looked around, impressed. It was partitioned into cubicles; each was about ten feet wide and twelve feet deep. They were similar to the one he had in OCS. His cubicle had two army bunk beds, a foot locker at the end, and a place to hang clothes on the back wall. He was pleased, because he'd expected to live in a tent the entire year, like he had at Fort Stewart while on field exercises. "Nick, this is really classy."

Nick looked smug. "Wait until you see the bar. You'll be roomies with CW3 Woods. He's our IP and will give you the in-country check ride. He's out on a mission now, so we'll plan on catching him at the bar later."

For the rest of the afternoon, Nick took him through the area and introduced him to the multiple maintenance teams assigned. McKay was impressed—they were organized exactly how they had recommended in AMOC. When he met Captain Rogers, the maintenance officer he was slotted to replace, McKay was surprised to learn he'd never attended AMOC. He had been a Huey crew chief who'd come up through the ranks. Rogers had gray hair and wrinkles, and McKay decided he must be really old—at least thirty-one. Nick interrupted his thoughts when he noticed Mr. Woods walking away from a nearby revetment. He called out, "Woody, come meet your new roommate, Captain McKay. He's Captain Rogers' turtle."

"Nick, we call our replacements turtles because they usually take so long to get here. I don't think 'turtle' fits McKay. Maybe Speedy Gonzales would be better," Woody replied. He came over and stuck out his hand. "Welcome, Speedy McKay. Did Nick tell you I'm the company IP?"

"Yeah, he did. I'm ready."

"Have you got your flight gear from supply yet?"

Nick cussed under his breath, "Nah, I forgot to take him."

"Well, come on." Woody waved his hand. "We'll go to the supply room and get your gear and operations to set up a check ride for tomorrow."

McKay turned to Nick. "Nick, guess I'll see you at the bar. The first drink will be on me."

"New guys always buy," Nick teased.

When they finished in operations, Woody suggested, "Let's head to the mess hall for some hot chow. Hope you like orange Kool-Aid, because that's all we've got right now."

"Are you serious?"

"Yeah, that's right, kid. Makes you remember you're in a war zone. They're promising we'll have coffee in the morning."

By the time they got to the bar that evening, it was standing room only. Music was coming from someplace, but for the life of him, McKay couldn't figure out where. Woody steered him toward Captain Rogers' table. Nick was there with another warrant officer. McKay noticed Nick was tipsy and feeling no pain as he stood and introduced the other warrant officer. "Captain McKay, this is Mack the Knife."

McKay noticed Mack's name tag read "McIntyre" when he stood to shake his hand. Rogers laughed. "Just ignore Nick. He's drunk already."

McKay asked, "You're not drinking?"

"No, Mack and I need to do some test flights tonight. Nick had his turn last night. We take turns being sober."

"Makes sense; looks like you guys have a handle on things."

Rogers laughed. "Just you wait."

McKay's first night in his new home was more than he'd expected. His hootch was located next to the concertina wire that surrounded Bien Hoa. There were a couple of guard posts nearby; one was about thirty yards away and the other about seventy yards. All night long the two posts would randomly take turns firing their M-79 grenade launchers. McKay would hear them shoot, and a couple of seconds later he'd hear the round explode. After enduring this for a couple of hours, he had just about fallen asleep when the guard post nearest him fired its launcher. McKay kept waiting and waiting for the explosion. The longer he waited, the more awake he became. It was a long night, and by the time he finally drifted off, he had only gotten a couple of hours of sleep. He was embarrassed that he hadn't been able to get any sleep and hoped Woody hadn't noticed.

He put on his new gear and asked his roomie, "What do you call these things again?"

Woody just laughed. "Don't you know? You're sporting the newest and greatest in flight suits: Nomex. Not only are they comfortable, they're fireproof—but I don't suggest you check that part out."

"I have to admit, they feel better than those grey cotton ones we wore in flight school."

"Trust me, after you've worn them for a while, you'll love them."

After breakfast they headed to the flight line, and Woody observed McKay doing his preflight. When they got in the aircraft, Woody took over, and McKay was just a passenger for a while. Woody was a great instructor and very professional. He seemed to complete a checklist in his head before he let McKay take over. He began by climbing to the north and keyed his mike. "Sir, get the logbook, and we'll get the DEER check out of the way."

"What's a DEER check?"

"I thought all you maintenance guys knew about that; after all, you're the ones who thought of it."

"Guess I must be a dumb one then; so how about explaining it to me?"

"I'll try. Huey engines seize when they get up to around five hundred hours. A smart maintenance guy noticed the engine temps start to creep up just before they actually seize up. So they started having pilots log daily engine temps and had maintenance plot them on a board. When the temperature starts to climb more than a few degrees, they'd change out the engine. It must work, because we haven't had an engine fail since we started

10

doing it. Captain Rogers has us pull twenty-five pounds of torque, climb to two thousand feet, increase or decrease speed to maintain that level, fly for two minutes, note the EGT gauge, and then note the engine temperature in the logbook. Our two minutes are up, so how about noting the temp and logging it in?"

"That makes sense to me, but what does DEER stand for?"

Woody thought for a moment and then just chuckled. "I don't have a clue. I know that's not a good answer coming from an IP, but it's an honest one. If you find out, how about letting me know? Why don't you take the aircraft?"

As soon as McKay said, "I have the controls," Woody cut the throttle and asked, "What are you going to do now?"

McKay just instinctively dropped the collective and, with the cyclic turned into the wind, calmly said, "See that open area straight ahead? That's what we're going to shoot for. Would you come up on guard and give a mayday call?"

Woody nodded in satisfaction. "Di Wee, looks like this isn't your first rodeo. I think you'll do. I have the controls."

As they climbed back to two thousand feet, Woody pointed to the river just north of them and said, "See the sharp bend in the river? That's what we call the top hat. On the map it looks just like one. While we're at it, we'll check out some of the other areas you'll be seeing a lot of." After they flew for a few more minutes, he pointed to a built-up area. "See that? That's Phu Loi. It's the headquarters for 15th TC Battalion, your direct support maintenance. Got a feeling you'll be seeing a lot more of that place than you'll want."

Then he turned south and said, "Now, let's go to a fun place—Hotel 3 in Saigon."

Even though Woody couldn't be a day over twenty-one, by the end of the day, McKay respected his professionalism. As they completed their post flight, Woody turned to him and said, "I have a resupply mission scheduled tomorrow. If it's okay with you, I'll have operations put you down as my co-pilot."

McKay quickly agreed. "That's fine with me. Captain Rogers wants me to fly each type of mission, so I guess yours will be my first. Woody, I really appreciate this."

"No problem, just doing my job. That's what we do."

CHAPTER 3

After an early breakfast, McKay tried to anticipate what Woody might need, but without any experience, he just ended up following him around like a puppy. It wasn't until he was introduced to the crew chief that he realized he could finally help. The chief and the door gunner had more than they could carry—two machine guns, ammunition, a case of C-rations, two helmet bags, and a few other small bags. Without a word, he grabbed up the C-rations and two helmet bags and asked, "Which aircraft is ours?"

He smiled when he noticed the two enlisted men's reaction to his help. Woody just pointed to one of the aircraft in the last revetment. McKay threw the rations and helmets on the deck and immediately began the preflight. He finished about the time the machine guns were mounted and ready to go. Woody had them move to the side for the mission briefing. "Guys, this is Captain McKay's first mission in Nam. Now be easy on him. Captain, this is Sandy Sanders. He's our crew chief and a surfing king from Huntington Beach, California. Our door gunner is Slim Barker, a grunt who got tired of walking in the jungle and decided to hitch a ride. They're the best crew in the company."

McKay could see the two men beam with pride at the compliment, so he just listened as Woody continued, "Guys, we've got a resupply mission today. It may be a hover-down. If it is, keep your eyes open and talk to me. You're my eyes out there, so don't let us hit anything. Now, let's go have some fun."

Woody made the call to Castle Tower and told them where he was and that he'd be departing to the northeast. When they cleared him, he keyed his intercom, "Sir, take the controls, climb to two thousand feet, and maintain a heading of forty-five degrees."

McKay asked, "Are we doing a DEER check?"

"Yeah, but there's a more important reason to fly at two thousand. When you're flying over here, fly below fifty feet—we call it nap of the earth—or go high, fifteen hundred feet or above. Fifty to fifteen hundred is the dead zone. A lot of good pilots learn the hard way and die just because nobody told them." His voice sounded serious as a heart attack when he warned, "Don't ever get complacent and fly in that zone. In fact, don't ever let yourself relax out there while flying. That's killed more pilots than enemy fire. If you don't hear anything else today, remember that."

He realized he was sounding too serious, so he said, "Okay, school's over. Let's go out and play. We get to fly a helicopter all we want, the gas is free, and they even pay us to do it."

Sandy came on, "And they give us free ammunition."

McKay laughed. "You guys have obviously been over here just a little too long."

When Woody landed at Firebase Nancy, a three-quarter-ton truck drove up to meet them. Woody watched as a major got out of the passenger seat and said, "This mission must be serious. That's the battalion S-3. We usually get our orders from a captain."

As the major discussed the mission with the two officers, Sandy and Slim edged closer to listen. While he was talking, they saw the driver and a couple of privates began to load their aircraft with water, rations, ammo, and a replacement radio. As soon as the major finished, he got back into his vehicle and went back up the hill to the operations tent. Woody walked back to the aircraft, confirmed it was loaded, and assumed his crew chief had supervised the process. "Sandy, untie the rotor blade, and let's go to work."

A minute later Woody yelled, "Clear!" and pulled the starter switch. He made a call to field control that he was on the go. When he tried to come to a hover, only the rear end of the aircraft seemed to come off the ground. It was way out of center of gravity limits, so much so that an inexperienced pilot would have flipped the aircraft. Concerned, McKay asked, "What's wrong?"

Woody answered, "The CG is too far forward." As he brought it to flight idle, he looked back at the cargo and immediately saw the problem. "Sandy, why'd you let the privates load the aircraft like a truck? They have all the water bottles against my seat."

Looking back, McKay asked, "That's what those things are? I thought they were rations. They look like five-foot-long rubber bologna casings. In fact, they're even the same color."

"It's an easier way to carry water. Soldiers just strap them to the back of their packs. It might have been okay to put some of them up here, but eight are too many. Sandy, move them back against the transmission wall. You let me down. Don't let that happen again."

Considering it was McKay's first ride with them, Sandy was mortified and quickly mumbled, "Yes, sir."

On this attempt Woody made a smooth rise to a three-foot hover. As they departed, he had McKay tune into the patrols frequency and pointed to a gauge in the center of the panel. "Let me show you a quick way to find people in the jungle. Watch that needle and tell me which way it moves." Then he made a radio call to the team leader and asked for a slow count.

As the count began, the needle moved. McKay said, "It moved left."

Woody began to turn the aircraft in that direction and instructed, "Tell me when it's centered." He kept turning until McKay acknowledged. Woody looked at his compass and saw it was 185 degrees. "We'll fly this heading for a while."

The team leader on the ground came over the radio, "I can hear you coming."

McKay looked at Woody and said, "The needle is a little to the right."

Woody said, "Sandy, Slick, start looking for a big hole in the jungle; we're getting close."

Slick yelled, "It's at one o'clock."

Woody smiled. "These guys did a good job. Looks like they've cut four or five trees for us. Our rotor blades are forty-eight feet from tip to tip. Some of the grunts cut holes only big enough for the fuselage, which is nine feet. They forget rotor blades aren't designed to cut down trees."

McKay looked down and thought it looked like giants had been chewing on the end of some matchsticks. "What on earth did they cut them with?"

"C-4 and det-cord."

Realizing he'd asked a stupid question, McKay said, "Guess it would be hard to carry a chainsaw in your backpack out here."

Woody went into instructor mode. "The trick to coming to a hover above this opening is to pull a little more power than you actually need. That will prevent you from settling with power."

McKay intently watched Woody's hands, but he was so skilled at his job, it was hard to detect movement. It was as if his thoughts were flying the aircraft. Woody kept his eyes straight ahead, and Sandy would tell him to move right or left. The aircraft seemed to just automatically drift to the correct position. About fifteen feet off the ground, a soldier directed them with hand signals. Woody responded, but warned McKay, "Always be careful following these guys. They think this is a flying truck, and if you don't watch them, they'll land you on a stump."

When Woody landed, he kept the RPM up in case they needed to depart quickly. It seemed like ants were approaching from all directions, the way people swarmed the scene; within minutes, the aircraft was completely unloaded. Four men came out of the jungle carrying a folded poncho, and a man carrying a backpack followed them. He handed it to Sandy, and the four men slid the poncho across the deck. In that instant McKay realized there was a body inside. When Woody saw the expression on McKay's face, he rushed to explain, "That's why the S-3 came in person. This guy was killed on the first day. The major was adamant about getting him out of here today, because the morale of the team had hit an all-time low. They've been carrying that body for three days."

As Woody talked, the wind shifted, and a smell like McKay had never experienced hit his nose. Woody said, "There's nothing worse than the smell of a decomposing human body. Let's get this one to Phu Vinh, so they can take care of him."

On the way back, McKay noticed that every once in a while, Woody would push in the pedal, causing the aircraft to fly out of trim. This would create a crosswind in the cargo compartment, which would temporarily remove the smell. This wasn't Woody's first rodeo, either, and McKay's respect for him continued to grow.

When they landed at Phu Vinh, two men with a stretcher approached and retrieved the body. No one said anything all the way back to Bien Hoa. Instead of going to refuel first, Woody landed near the wash rack. Sandy was spraying water on the deck before they even shut down.

McKay just watched the team move like a well-oiled machine and realized he wasn't quite a part of it yet. He threw up a silent prayer: *God, I've got a lot to learn. Help me live long enough to learn it.*

In operations, he checked on his next mission. The operations officer, Captain Kerns, was surprised to see him so early. "Mac, how'd your mission with Woody go?"

"There was a lot more to it than I'd expected."

"It takes a really good pilot to do those hover-downs."

"Yeah, that's true, but hauling that body to Phu Vinh was kind of creepy."

"Trust me; it doesn't get any easier, no matter how many you haul."

Brushing off the memory of the flight, McKay compared his list of required missions from Captain Jenkins and asked, "What's next?"

"It's a little slow right now, but we have a nine-bird troop insertion mission in four days. Looks like Woody has already penciled you in as his copilot. Guess you southern boys like to stick together."

Shocked, McKay asked, "Woody's southern?"

"Man, how can you miss that accent of his?"

Truly perplexed, McKay stared at him. "What accent?"

Jenkins came through the door, and Kerns laughed. "Sir, come over here. McKay here doesn't believe Woody has an accent!"

Jenkins laughed. "Didn't you know? The southerners all think it's us Yankees that have an accent. McKay, Woody tells me you seem to have a cool head up there. That's a fine asset for a maintenance guy. Good on you!"

"Thank you, sir," McKay replied. "And your accent isn't too bad."

Everyone in operations began to laugh. It was a good tonic, considering the sights they saw on a daily basis. Normally they only let go in their little bar after a drink or two. The operations NCO and specialist standing on the other side of the counter just grinned at each other—it was looking like the new guy might help lighten things up a little.

Jenkins brought them back to earth. "When's your next mission?"

"Kerns said four days from now."

"The insertion mission? That's a good one. They're our bread and butter. This down time will give you a chance to get to know your team."

"I agree; I'm headed over there now. Have a good morning, sir."

The morning briefing in maintenance had just gotten underway when McKay entered the shop. The sergeant was standing in front of a board with six aircraft butt numbers written on it. He went through each, one at a time, and explained why they were down, the requisition numbers for parts, and when they were expected to be flight ready again. McKay just listened and was impressed at how Rogers ran the meeting. He was just listening and observing as each of his men gave updates as needed. In awe, McKay realized from the body language and actions of the attendees that this approach made everyone feel important and a part of the team. His previous experience had been that the maintenance officer did all the talking, and everyone else just asked questions. It reminded him of what his grandfather had always preached—*if you have to tell someone you're the boss, then you're not really the boss*. Rogers didn't need to say it. He was the best boss McKay had ever seen. One thing he knew for sure: he wasn't going to change the system when Rogers DEROSed.

When McKay left the shed, he noticed a group of enlisted men arguing among themselves and moved close enough to pick up bits and pieces of the conversation. One of them said, "I know it's him! He was one of my instructors. I thanked God when I got my orders to leave Fort Eustis and come to Nam. At least it got me away from Sergeant Rock."

Curious, McKay just blurted out, "Sergeant Rock?"

When the group saw he was a captain, they all snapped to attention. He waved his hand, "At ease, men. I'm going to be here all day—in fact, for the rest of the year. I couldn't help but overhear you, and I'm just wondering what this Sergeant Rock looks like. He must be one hell of a man."

One of the men was eager to explain, "He was one of my instructors at Fort Eustis. He's so gung-ho, he bleeds olive-drab green."

Another one objected, "Ah, he can't be that bad."

One of the two remaining men scoffed, "Oh, yeah? Remember that safety wire you put on the Jesus nut? Well, he made me redo it eight times before he'd finally pass me!"

The last guy groaned, "Oh, my God! And I thought I was the dumb one. He made me remove and retie the safety wire on the engine governor four times before he'd sign off. I thought that was bad!"

The three who had been students just looked at each other, laughed, and yelled in unison, "*This* is not a test! The real test is on the aircraft that men must fly."

One just laughed and rubbed his stomach, "God, if I heard that one time, I heard it a thousand. I thought I'd left hell, but it's found me again. Rock is in Bien Hoa."

McKay couldn't help but laugh at them. "Relax, guys. He was just trying to make you better maintenance men. I'm sure he's soft as butter since he's gotten here." He just shook his head. These guys were more afraid of Sergeant Rock than the VC. If he was going to be the maintenance officer, he'd better meet this guy.

He went straight to the orderly room to see the first sergeant, "Top, did we get a new maintenance NCO this week? Some of the guys are calling him Sergeant Rock."

The first sergeant laughed. "Sir, they must be pulling your leg. Sergeant Rock is a comic book character. You and Staff Sergeant Williams are our only two new guys this month. Trust me, Williams is a little guy. They're pulling some kind of joke on the new guy."

Not convinced, McKay asked, "Where is Sergeant Williams?"

"You might find him in the supply room."

As he entered the room, he saw a guy about five feet eight inches tall and weighing about 140 pounds. He called out, "Sergeant Williams?"

The man turned quickly. "Yes, sir?"

"I'm Captain McKay, the incoming maintenance officer. You work in maintenance?"

"Yes, sir, for almost fifteen years now. I was a maintenance instructor at Fort Eustis for the past three years."

McKay's eyes widened. "Is your nickname Sergeant Rock?"

"Sounds like some of my old students must be here," Williams said wryly.

"Is that going to be a good thing?" McKay asked, grinning.

"Well, at least they know what's expected," he grumbled.

"They say you have a saying."

Williams just smiled in response. "That the real test is on the aircraft that men must fly."

"That's the one. Can I walk with you over to the maintenance area? It should be fun."

"Yes, sir, just let me put this stuff in my hootch."

On the walk over, McKay asked, "Where do you call home?"

"LA."

McKay snorted. "Yeah, right. I can tell from the way you talk that LA must stand for 'lower Alabama.'"

"How'd you know?"

"My best friend in OCS was from LA—Evergreen, Alabama."

"I know exactly where that is. I'm from Troy, which is about twenty miles away."

When they entered, McKay had to hide his smile as he noticed the difference in the way the enlisted men acknowledged Williams. They were quick to call out, letting him know they were former students, and eagerly refreshed his memory if he didn't seem to recognize them. There was one thing for sure—McKay would never have a problem getting his guys to do maintenance strictly by the book.

CHAPTER 4

It was an exciting morning for McKay. He hadn't been around this many running aircraft since the last training exercise at Fort Stewart. Woody began to explain some of the tricks in flying. "The mission commander wants us to fly in a trail formation all day. I've found the best way to hold position is to fly close to the aircraft in front of you, then put his tail light in his engine exhaust. That will keep you above his rotor wash."

He purposely dropped below the aircraft in front, and as he did, the bird began to bounce around from the turbulence. When he climbed back into position, lining the taillight up with the exhaust, the turbulence stopped. Their mission that day was to insert two platoons into the middle of enemy territory. Because they knew the Viet Cong could hear the helicopters coming and see them landing, they decided to fool Charlie and make two landings. The first would be a false insertion, and then the troops would dismount on the second touchdown. As they approached the area of operation, rain clouds were moving across their final landing site. The mission commander elected to make a slow right-hand turn to let the storm pass. As they completed the turn, and the AO came back into view, the MC alerted the artillery. McKay had a ringside seat for the operation. For about twenty minutes, artillery went off in front of them. Then he saw two bright white rounds explode.

The MC announced, "Those are the white phosphorus rounds. The artillery is through. Gunships go to work." Immediately, the two Cobras flying on the flanks of the formation made a run at the false insertion landing zone and expended a few rockets.

Woody went back into training mode. "Each aircraft has a mission. The mission commander flies the lead aircraft. The second aircraft is responsible for all radio calls to the airfield and towers. As last ship, it is up to us to make sure the formation is tight: if anyone goes down, we follow them and provide assistance."

In the first LZ, McKay could see a few artillery holes still smoking. The real excitement came when Woody directed Sandy and Slick to open up with their M-60s. Theirs was the last aircraft to hit the ground. As soon as Woody reported to the MC that he was on the ground, the MC gave the command, "On the go."

All aircraft came back up into a perfect V formation. The second LZ was about two kilometers to the north. As the formation started on its final approach, the Cobras rolled in, expending rockets on both sides of the LZ.

McKay could see this LZ was where the artillery had hit the hardest. Trees a foot in diameter were cut down about six feet above the ground. Others looked like chewed toothpicks.

Again Woody directed, "Chief, open up. Spray those trees good. They're getting off here." Looking at all the destruction, McKay wondered how anything could have lived through that. The aircraft had just hit the ground when the MC commanded, "On the go."

Again they climbed out and went into a V formation. As they cleared the trees, McKay saw an amazing sight. Only one hundred yards from the LZ was a five-hundred-pound bomb crater at least a month old with a small pond of standing water in the middle. At the edge of the pond stood four deer, drinking. Only one even looked up at the passing aircraft. All that destruction, and they hadn't even scared the deer. As he was thinking how ineffective their weapons were, there was a radio call from one of the Cobra pilots. "This is Tiger 1-2. I've gotta go. My twenty-minute fuel light just came on."

The MC acknowledged with, "Roger that. See ya in the bar."

"Roger, I'm gone."

Two minutes later another call came in. "Too late. My engine just quit. We're shooting for the clearing just south of you."

Woody keyed his mike. "Tiger, I've got you in sight. We'll follow you down and give you a ride home."

McKay watched, as if in a trance, as the Cobra settled to the ground. On the intercom, Woody said, "He's shooting too long. He could go in that stream."

Sure enough, the aircraft landed right on the edge of the stream. As the rotor blades almost came to a stop, the bank gave way, and the aircraft flipped upside down into the fast-moving water. Woody landed just twenty feet away and yelled at McKay to take the controls. He and Sandy ran to the Cobra to give assistance. They began to desperately bang on the Plexiglas. Even using his .38 as a club, Woody couldn't break away enough to get them out. Helpless, they watched both pilots drown. Visibly shaken, he came back to the aircraft and relayed the events to the MC, who then instructed him to stay until the recovery bird could be sent.

Silently observing all that had happened, McKay couldn't believe how quickly two lives were snatched away. They were surprised when one of the other aircraft left the formation and landed next to them. The pilot had what looked like a hammer, with which he made short work of the Plexiglas. McKay watched as they pulled the bodies from the aircraft and tried to revive them. When they failed, he could see Woody banging his fist on the ground. Woody and Sandy helped load the bodies on the second aircraft. When Woody came back, he told McKay and Slick the other group would take the bodies to Phu Vinh. "We'll wait until maintenance comes for the Cobra." McKay looked down at his hands; his leather gloves were falling to pieces. They were a couple of years old, and the sweat from his hands had made them hard and brittle. His squeezing the controls as he watched was more pressure than the gloves could take. Looking for a reason to change the subject, he held up his hands and said, "Look, my gloves have had it, and they don't have any in the supply room. I asked."

Sandy heard what he said. "No problem, Captain Mac, I have an extra pair you can use until you can get some new ones."

"Sandy, I appreciate that. You're alright; I don't care what Woody says about you."

CHAPTER 5

The next day, Woody approached McKay in the maintenance area. "We've got a mission tomorrow you're going to love. We're hauling donut dollies to a couple of firebases."

"Donut dollies? What on earth are they?"

"They're volunteers for the American Red Cross! They send college girls over here to boost morale. You'll see. We'll pick them up in Ben Hoa tomorrow at oh-eight-hundred."

"It sure will be nice to have a little fun for a change."

McKay grabbed his helmet bag after breakfast the next morning and darted for a shortcut to the aircraft. By climbing a small hill, he'd shorten his walk by nearly a hundred yards. The path began behind a Conex container, where maintenance stored ground handling wheels and panels for the aircrafts. As he ducked behind the container, the bridge of his nose connected sharply with the side of a four-by-eight piece of sheet metal sticking out about two feet that someone had placed on top of the container at eye level for his six-foot-one-inch frame. Stunned, he tried to shake it off and continue up the hill to the aircraft. When Woody noticed him, his mouth fell open, "What did you do to yourself?"

Irritated, McKay said, "I hit something when I came around the corner of that Conex container."

"Man, you're bleeding like a stuck hog. Let me take you to the medics and let them take a look at it for you."

He pointed to the hootch next to the orderly room. "That's the aid station. I've got to go to Operations and get me another copilot. You can't fly like that."

The medic began cleaning the cut and put two butterflies on it in place of stitches. He told McKay, "There's no real damage, but it's going to be sore as hell for a couple of days."

When he went to enter the maintenance shed, he realized he was more embarrassed than hurt. Rogers laughed when he saw him. "Looks like you stood up when someone told you to shut up."

McKay tried to smile, "Something like that. Is there anything I can do, since I'm stuck here today?"

"I think Mack the Knife has a test flight later. You can ride with him and see how it's done."

McKay didn't mention he'd taken a weeklong course on test flights at Fort Eustis. He was already embarrassed and remembered what his daddy used to tell him—*when people think you're a fool, don't open your mouth and remove all doubt.*

From the beginning of the test flight until the end, McKay was concerned. He could remember that when he was taking the course, they always said, "We test fly, not stress fly." They'd always emphasized that if anything was going to go wrong, it would probably be within the first thirty minutes. Mack's technique was to make quick, jerky movements instead of the slow, smooth maneuvers McKay had been taught. The biggest surprise and disappointment was that Mack had all four maintenance team members onboard. Until that point, McKay hadn't seen anything he would have changed with Rogers' maintenance program, but he made up his mind right then that he'd either change the way Mack the Knife did his maneuvers or stop him from doing them all together.

That night Woody rubbed in what a wonderful mission McKay had missed that day. "They were five of the most beautiful women you've ever seen. One had long, blond hair with blue eyes that took your breath away. And you know what the best part was? She's a toucher!"

"Enough, Woody. You've made your point. I already feel bad enough as it is."

"Okay, let's go to the bar, and I'll buy my little man a root beer."

When Woody saw McKay's two black eyes the next morning, he let out a yell, "Wow! I suggest you wear sunglasses for the rest of the day."

Puzzled, McKay asked, "Why would I do that?"

"Look in the mirror. You look like a raccoon."

He walked over to the mirror and just shuddered; it was looking like it might be a long year for him in Nam. Reluctantly, he headed to the maintenance shed. He could only imagine how they would tease him. He took a deep breath before entering and reminded himself their time would come. As he approached, he heard a few of them snicker, but Rogers was the only one brave enough to speak up. "Nice shiners you got there. What's the other guy look like?"

McKay just smiled in response. With only two aircraft in for repairs, it appeared it was going to be a slow day. At noon, everything changed when Nick came running in from operations and exclaimed, "Captain Mac, go get your helmet. We've got an aircraft down. We've got to go rig it so they can sling it back. We'll be taking 7-8-1."

Mac was pleased with his new nickname. He knew it meant the men were slowly accepting him. While doing their preflight, Nick said, "The pilot said it was running a little hot. We may as well check it out while we're there."

Two men came rushing out of the maintenance shed, carrying footlockers. They placed them on the deck and strapped them down. The crew chief and door gunner mounted their machine guns and began to prepare for the flight. Mac took the right seat and strapped in. He tried to slide forward the protective plate on the right side of his seat but discovered it was stuck. After banging on it and shaking it for a while, it finally slid into place.

Nick suggested, "Why don't you fly, and I'll take care of the radio calls and find out where we need to go? It's up north someplace, so take a heading of twenty degrees. When we get to fifteen hundred feet, we should be able to talk to the pilot on the ground."

Mac asked, "Do you want to go ahead and get the DEER check out of the way?"

"Thank God you remembered. Captain Rogers would kick my butt if I missed it again."

Mac kept his power pulled and climbed to two thousand feet quickly. He pulled in twenty-five pounds of torque and flew his two minutes. Nick entered the temperature into the logbook. "They're right, it is getting hot. The DEER check today is ten degrees hotter than it was yesterday. I'll write it up when we get back."

It was a forty-minute flight to the downed bird. The crew chief spotted it and yelled, "There it is at eleven o'clock, twenty yards past the stream in that elephant grass."

Maintaining his two thousand feet, Mac began a right turn to get a lay of the land and figure out the best place to land. He noticed movement on the south and east side of the LZ. After looking intently, he realized they were American soldiers hiding behind the downed trees. He asked, "Nick, is this a hot LZ? Sure seems to be a lot of downed trees and craters around here."

"Not sure how hot it is now, but the aircraft was shot down, and the copilot was medevaced out."

Mac continued to survey the area, and he couldn't believe the height of the grass. It was as tall as the top of the doors on the aircraft. He decided to make a steep approach and land short of the downed aircraft, as he wasn't sure if the LZ was still hot. He kept flying his right turn until he could land into the wind. About a quarter mile away, he began his descent. With his final crosscheck, he realized the EGT gauge was climbing into the red. "Chief, stick your head out and see if any of that grass is getting into the inlet vents."

"Roger that, sir," He looked out quickly and replied, "It's clear, sir. What's wrong?"

"Engine's getting hot. It's already in the red."

Suddenly there was a loud banging noise in the engine, followed by a huge WHOOSH. Then a loud, high-pitched WHOOP, WHOOP, warning buzzer filled his earphones, letting him know he was losing engine RPM. He knew if he was losing that, then he would lose rotor RPM quickly. His training kicked in, and he began to act by rote. He pushed the collective down and quickly assessed the situation, knowing at his height of one hundred fifty feet and his speed of sixty knots, his reaction time was nonexistent. It was imperative that he keep the aircraft level. All of a sudden, the crew chief added to his nightmare, yelling, "We're on fire! The entire tail boom is burning!"

Mac couldn't worry about that problem right now; his main concern at present was getting them to the ground safely. At about fifty feet, he started adding collective, which put pitch on the blade and forced the rotor RPM down. It worked—his descent began to slow. He was still worried he might pull too much pitch and stop the rotor blades. Normally, with eighty knots of airspeed, he could flare the aircraft, which would build the rotor RPM back up, but that option had expired seconds ago. He held the collective steady until they were brushing the tops of the waving elephant grass and then smoothly pulled all of collective he had left. It had been one of the softest landings he'd ever made, and he laughed in relief.

As soon as the skids hit the ground, the crew and Nick abandoned the aircraft. The emergency seemed to have slowed time for him, and he just sat there in amusement as he watched them trying to run in tall elephant grass. It reminded him of his beagle puppies trying to run in the tall meadow grass below his family's farm. But humor changed to panic when he tried to push back the armor plate on the right side of his seat. It was there to protect him from small-arms fire, but now it was preventing him from exiting the burning aircraft. Looking around, he noticed his crew chief crawling through the grass headed straight for his door. *Thank God, he's coming to help me.* But when the chief opened the door, he didn't help McKay—he grabbed the fire extinguisher that was located at the base of the pilot's seat. Now Mac was pissed—*He didn't come back for me, but to save this damn aircraft.* He quickly pushed his way past the chief and hit the ground.

Once everything settled down, Nick asked, "What took you so long to get out?"

"I couldn't get the door open."

"Why didn't you pull that T handle in front of you? The door would have just dropped off."

He ducked his head in shame, "I didn't even think of it. Guess they're right when they say if you don't plan for emergencies, you won't be prepared. Let's keep this between us, if you don't mind. What do we do now?"

"Well, before, it was a simple process, but we just screwed it up."

"What do you mean, simple?"

"Normally, with a downed bird, we fly out, rig it to be airlifted back to maintenance, then call the 228th Aviation battalion—the Chinook unit. When one of them finishes their mission at the end of the day near our downed aircraft, he'll just come by, pick it up and drop it off in maintenance. It works just that slick. But now that we're down, too, they need to send two Chinooks and someone else to pick us up. That's what I mean by having screwed things up."

After both aircraft were rigged for transport, the crew chief and door gunner moved their M60 machine guns up top, so they could see better for protection. Then all they could do was sit and wait to be rescued. By this time the troops that had been inserted had moved deep into the jungle, leaving behind the two crews and their birds that wouldn't fly. It was a long, tense four hours until the first Chinook showed up. Everyone was afraid to talk or move and alert the VC to their presence. Mac held his .38 pistol on the ready. He shook his head in disgust at his stupidity. After another tense hour, he decided he'd never go on another mission so unprepared. He'd bet the enemy wouldn't be shooting a .38.

CHAPTER 6

August had arrived before McKay had realized it, and he was four weeks into his tour. He'd finally gotten used to the M-79s being fired at night. It was funny what a man could get used to. By now it was just normal routine. Another habit he'd developed was hanging out with the TIs as they inspected aircraft for the scheduled maintenance after one hundred hours of flight time. It didn't take long for him to realize that small problems could easily snowball into major ones if not addressed early. AMOC had taught the fine art of the paperwork needed when components were changed, but they had been weak on the best preventive maintenance needed to slow down the need to change them. He'd begun to see it as a big puzzle, and he loved it. One of the TIs was asking him what to do with the data from a DEER check when Captain Jenkins tapped him on the shoulder. "Mac, the battalion commander wants to see you in his office at fourteen hundred hours. My driver will take you there."

Startled, he asked, "Sir, do you know what it's about?"

"All he said was he had a problem, and he was hoping you could help him with it."

Mac went straight to his hootch, got out his cleanest flight suit, and took a cold shower. As soon as he was dressed, he asked the commander's driver to take him to the PX so he could get a haircut. When they returned to the company area, the driver began to rush him. Captain Jenkins had made it clear if they were late, he'd reassign him to a firebase, and he had no desire to sleep in a foxhole for the remainder of his tour. Stalling, Mac stated, "I just have one more thing to do, and then we can go." He took off at a dead run and quickly grabbed his display boots from OCS. They were Cochran jump boots that had helped him pass inspections on a regular basis, and he'd only worn them a few times. They almost sparkled as he walked back to the jeep.

The driver sighed in relief when they arrived almost ten minutes early. Mac just chuckled and headed to the battalion headquarters. The XO met him at the door. "Captain, I'm glad you're early. The colonel is waiting." He quickly ushered him into the office and closed the door behind him.

Mac started to salute, and Colonel Baxter said, "Forget the formalities. I've got a problem, and I'm hoping you're just the man to fix it. Pull that chair over here, and let's talk."

When McKay sat down, the colonel began, "My Bravo Company is located at Quan Loi. They have eighteen UH-1s, and the problem is, only one of them is flyable. The company is flat on its ass. Alpha and Charlie Companies have been carrying the load, but now that's not enough. I had to go to brigade for support. My orders from Colonel Roberts personally were to fix it. You've impressed Captain Jenkins; and based on his recommendation, I need for you to take over as the maintenance officer of Bravo Company. I need fourteen birds every day. If you can do that for me, I promise I'll give you a max OER. To help you, you can have any NCO in the battalion."

"Sir, you've got a deal. I'd like Sergeant Rock from Charlie Company."

The commander opened the door and yelled, "S-1, get in here."

Instantly, a captain was standing in front of him.

"Cut orders moving Captain McKay and Sergeant Rock from Charlie Company today."

The captain looked puzzled, "Sergeant Rock?"

Mac laughed, "It's Staff Sergeant Williams. The enlisted men call him Sergeant Rock."

The colonel smiled. "Sounds like you'll have all the help you'll need."

"Sir, we'll do our best."

"Son, I can't ask any more from anybody. Good luck to you."

That night, when Mac hesitantly began to explain to Sergeant Rock what he'd volunteered him for, he was surprised when Rock's entire face lit up, "Sir, I've been on the sidelines all my life. I was too little to play football, so they made me a manager. When I joined the army, they made me an instructor. You've put me on the field, and I won't let you down."

"Rock, you're my quarterback. You can call your own plays if you want to. All I ask is that you tell me first, so I don't embarrass myself."

Rock grinned gleefully. "Captain Mac, I can't wait until tomorrow."

Mac was packing his duffle bag when Woody and Nick knocked on his partition. "Captain Mac, your chariot awaits," Nick announced.

They both smiled, and Woody added, "We just need to know where you live, in case anything turns up missing after you leave."

Mac started to respond and realized he was emotional. He was relieved that Sergeant Rock happened to stick his head in and ask, "Sir, are you ready?"

Mac knew there was nothing to say. They were army men and knew how the system worked, so he just turned and said, "Let's go, boys, the war won't wait."

He and Rock sat in the rear, looking out as the countryside passed below them. Rock asked, "Do those red clay dirt roads make you feel like you're back home?"

Mac laughed. "Believe it or not, they do. If only they had a few fences and some cows."

"Guess you'll just have to settle for water buffalo, sir."

Woody's voice came over the intercom. "Well, guys, look out the left side, and you'll see your new home. You are now a Killer Spade. That's the call sign for Bravo Company." They could see a grove of trees on the right side of a hundred-yard-long runway. On the west side, it looked like there were twenty revetments. It was strange to see all of them filled with aircraft at this time of day. They were used to seeing them empty. Woody pointed to the helicopters and said, "See the ace of spades on the pilot's door?"

Woody landed about halfway down the runway, and as soon as Mac and Rock retrieved their duffle bags, he was gone.

Mac watched him leave in relief. He had worried the entire way there how he was going to say good-bye to his new friends. He dropped his bag near the closest revetment. "Rock, why don't you go down that way and I'll go this way and we'll see what's wrong with all of these aircraft," he said.

They had only been there a few minutes when a young CW2 came out and saluted. "Can I help you sir?"

"You sure can. What's wrong with that aircraft behind you?"

"It's got a damaged tail rotor."

"How about the one next to it?"

"It took a round through the transmission."

"Why don't you take the blade off of it and get the one behind you ready to fly?"

He looked offended. "We don't do maintenance like that around here, sir."

"Well, you do now," McKay informed him.

"You're our new maintenance officer, aren't you?"

"You're right. I'm Captain McKay, and that's Staff Sergeant Williams."

He read the soldier's nametag and continued, "Mr. Dixon, do you work in maintenance?"

"Yes, sir."

"Go get somebody to change out that tail rotor. Do you test fly?"

"Yep, me and Mr. Palmer."

"Well, where is he?"

"He may be in the bar." Dixon flushed as he realized what he'd revealed.

"Is it a normal thing for him to be in the bar at ten hundred hours?"

The soldier just shifted and continued to stare straight ahead. At that moment Mac began to consider the possibility that he might have bitten off more than he could chew. If he didn't get the support of the company commander soon, it would be his replacement coming in. "Mr. Dixon, let me know when you finish the test flight. Which way to the orderly room?"

Dixon pointed to a bunker. "It's underground, and the door is behind those sandbags." Then he turned and fled.

Mac headed down the stairs. It was much larger than he'd expected and was divided into two sections—flight operations and the orderly room. He asked the first person he saw, "Do you know where the company commander is?"

Behind him, he heard, "Right here. I'm Captain Fitzgerald. Are you my new maintenance officer?"

"Yes, sir, I'm Captain McKay. I brought Staff Sergeant Williams with me. He's well qualified, sir. He was an instructor of aircraft mechanics at Fort Eustis."

"I know all about him. Colonel Baxter called me last night and told me his nickname is Sergeant Rock."

"Yes, sir. I'd like for him to only report to me for a while, until we find the weaknesses in our program."

"Sounds logical; you're the expert, and I'll give you all the support you need."

"Thank you sir, I'm probably going to need it. What do you expect from me?"

"The same thing Colonel Baxter wants—fourteen birds a day. I'd also like for you to be there every morning when they take off and when they come back in the evenings."

"Sounds fair. Can you tell me what kind of pilots Dixon and Palmer are? I met Mr. Dixon, but he said Palmer might be in the bar. I didn't get a good feeling about that."

"The old maintenance officer thought they were awesome. Mr. Palmer is a CW3 and will get you up to speed ASAP. He's my man. Come on, and I'll show you the maintenance officer's hootch."

Fitzgerald led the way to the maintenance officer's hootch; Mac tossed his bag inside and returned to the maintenance area. He found Sergeant Rock in the maintenance tent and was amused when he got to watch the instructor side of the sergeant come out, as he was identifying to the crew which aircraft could be made flyable first. Then he asked for volunteers to make it happen. Mac almost laughed out loud at their response. They began to wave their hands in the air like little kids trying to give their favorite teacher the answer. He realized right then that this crew had pride and didn't like feeling like losers. He could use that, if they wanted to get the job done and wanted to do it correctly. He thought they just needed a little incentive. All he and Rock needed to do was show them how.

Shortly after noon, CW3 Palmer came strutting into the maintenance area. When he noticed McKay, he said, "Hello there, Di Wee. You must be the old maintenance officer's turtle. The old man told me to bring you up to speed. Don't worry; I'll keep you out of trouble."

Mac's answering smile didn't quite reach his eyes. "And you must be Mr. Palmer. Where've you been all morning?"

"The civilian maintenance techs have a poker game going on in the bar. I just had to take some of their money. I knew there wasn't anything I could do around here until we got some parts. If you'll follow me, I'll show you how we get things done around here."

Mac gritted his teeth in an effort to control his temper. "No thanks. Mr. Dixon did a pretty good job of that already."

"Dixon's okay, but he's a new guy. He's still learning. Where is he, anyway?"

"He's on a test flight."

Palmer exploded, "That little bastard. He was supposed to come get me if we had one. Where did he get the parts?"

"Off the aircraft with a bad transmission."

"He knows better than that! Captain Chase and I don't allow any cannibalization."

Mac just looked at him with one eyebrow raised, "I authorized it."

Sensing he was on thin ice and not sure how to proceed, Palmer stuttered, "Well, I guess you didn't know. Around here we do maintenance by the book."

"That's great to hear. Do you have your helmet? The 3-5-7 needs a test flight. I authorized another cannibalization."

"I'll test fly it, but you know you're going to be in trouble with the old man."

"Let me worry about that. I have a feeling he'll understand why I did it."

Three hours later, Green, the operation officer, asked, "What's this?" when Mac walked into operations.

"Here's a list of aircraft you can fly tomorrow."

Astonished, Green crowed, "We've got six aircraft?"

With a grin, Mac proudly replied, "You betcha, Red Rider."

"This is great. Excuse me, but I've got to call the battalion S-3 and let him know we can take missions again."

Rock was grinning when Mac returned to maintenance. "We've got two more ready. You want to tell operations?"

"Let's keep that under our hat, in case one of them goes down in the morning. Oh yeah, I need you there in the mornings when they crank at oh-four-hundred hours."

Rock shook his head. "And, sir, I was just beginning to like you."

CHAPTER 7

By the time Mac returned to his hootch that evening, he could hardly stand, and then he got the surprise of his life. He had the entire hootch to himself. It seemed the previous occupant had built a bunker in the center of the small room. Sandbags were stacked six feet high and four feet thick. On top of that he'd placed PSP that was normally used to build runways. He had layered four more rows of sandbags on top of that. Inside the bunker was only one bunk, and it was dead center. Mac began to wonder if he'd been worried about the VC's 122-mm rockets or his own men fragging him; however, tired as he was, he decided he'd worry about it another day. Oh-four-hundred would be here before he could blink. He was mentally and physically drained as he sat down on the bed to remove his boots. It felt so good, he had to just lean back for a moment. He was still dressed when he woke the next morning. He shaved and brushed his teeth and went to look for Rock.

They began walking the line of aircraft exactly on time. The crews of the six flyable aircraft were doing their preflight and mounting machine guns. As they approached the third aircraft, the crew chief looked up in recognition and said, "Sergeant Williams, you finally made it over here. My name is Finley, and I was in your first class in 1969."

Rock didn't skip a beat. "I remember you. You couldn't tie a safety wire worth a crap. I thought I failed you."

"Nah, but you almost did. Check out that safety wire on the forty-five degree gearbox. I just did it yesterday."

Rock looked at it and asked, "Why didn't you do it this well in school?"

Finley grinned broadly. "Guess I'm a slow learner."

"So am I, son; glad you're here. We really need good men."

As they walked on, Mac asked, "Did you really remember him?"

Rock just smiled. "There's no way I could remember all of them."

"Then how'd you know he had trouble with the safety wires?"

"Good guess. They all do—some worse than others; but trust me, it takes practice before they get it right."

"Rock, has anyone ever told you that you're kind of sneaky?"

"All the time."

At the end of the line they stood and looked at the only aircraft that had been flight ready when they arrived. A tall, lanky man was checking the engine, and a kid who looked young enough to be in elementary school was on top, checking the rotor hub. They were both carrying rags and were wiping down the old aircraft like it was a brand-new Thunderbird.

On their way to the maintenance shed, Rock said, "They love that old bird. Bet that's the reason it was the only one that would fly."

"We've got to get the other pilots to feel that way about their aircraft."

They watched as all six birds departed without incident and then headed to the mess hall for breakfast. There wasn't a crowd at oh-four-thirty, so it would be quiet until the morning shift was about to begin. They grabbed their trays and approached the food line. Mac filled his tray with powdered eggs, SOS, bacon, sausage links, and toast. The cook nodded in satisfaction when he noticed the new captain was enjoying their hard work and had sampled something from each station. They stayed and drank coffee until the company formation broke up and then walked back to the maintenance shed.

Mr. Palmer was already occupying the maintenance officer's desk, barking out instructions. Mac just stood in the doorway and listened. *He still thinks he'd the head rooster in this barnyard.* He stepped forward to correct him and then he remembered what his grandfather always said—*If you have to*

44

tell someone you're the boss, then you aren't really. It would be a waste of time to confront Palmer; besides, he had a better idea. He pulled Rock outside so they wouldn't be overheard and said, "The way they run this shop is like a motor pool, where the motor sergeant assigns each mechanic to a job. We've got to come up with something better; maybe getting back to the school solution."

"What do you need me to do?"

"Figure out which ones are the best mechanics. I want to build three periodic inspection teams of three to four men each. We've got a real problem coming. Over half the aircraft are within twenty-five hours of scheduled maintenance. If we don't do something fast, we'll be back where we were the day we got here."

"What can we do? You know Palmer will fight anything we try."

"The quickest way is to get some of the hangar queens back up and flying. Four of them came in for scheduled maintenance and never came out. One has been dead lined for five months, which is certainly long enough for it to qualify as a hanger queen. But most units only have one of them. Rock, that's your number one priority. Let me know what you need to get it flyable—and for Pete's sake, don't let Palmer know what you're doing. His loyalties are still with the old maintenance officer."

Rock shook his head. "I get being loyal, but I don't understand being stupid."

"Why don't you speak your mind?"

When the six aircraft returned from their mission, one was only three hours from its allotted one-hundred-hour cutoff for maintenance. That meant tomorrow's mission would put it back in the shop.

When Rock came to him with the news that the hangar queen needed a new engine and main rotor blades, McKay made a career-changing decision. "Do you have your list of best mechanics yet?"

"Yes, sir. Gibbs, Sheridan, and Sawyer."

"Good. What do you think of making a four-man periodic inspection team and pulling 4-7-4 in for early PE? We'll pull her engine and put it in the hangar queen. With us not needing to put the harness on a new engine, and using the main rotor, hub, and blades from the damaged transmission aircraft, we should be able to test fly it by the close of business tomorrow."

Rock looked at him and laughed. "I like it!"

"We'll need to give our reserve aircraft to operations in its place. Then we need to have a little meeting with our first PE team. Which of the three do you suggest?"

Rock didn't hesitate. "Sawyer; they call him Tom."

Mac shook his head. "Tom Sawyer? That would make sense. If anything makes sense over here."

In less than thirty minutes, Rock had the first team standing in front of Mac by the hangar queen. Mac could see the anticipation on their faces. When he'd finished explaining his plan, Tom and his men moved off to the side and huddled for a few moments. Mac and Rock just looked at each other and waited. The men came back, and Tom said, "If it's okay with you, we'd like to get started right now."

Mac was thrilled at their attitudes. "That's fine with me. Anything I can do to help?"

Tom lowered his head, already anticipating a negative response to his question, "Could you get the mess hall to make us some egg sandwiches, so we won't need to break for chow?"

Rock said, "How many, and when?"

Mac looked to both sides and whispered to the group, "Let's keep this between us kids."

Tom, feeling frisky, said, "And especially Mr. Palmer, right?"

Thrilled they were all on the same page, Mac said, "Roger that, Tom."

The team moved off to gather their tools, Mac he whispered to Rock, "We need one of the TIs to be there, so he can sign off on their work as they complete it."

"Way ahead of you, sir."

Mac couldn't sleep that evening; he was more tired when he got up the next morning than when he'd gone to bed.

In the afternoon, Tom came into the maintenance shed. Mac and Dixon were the only ones there. "Sir, 1-7-4, the hangar queen, is ready for a test flight."

Smiling, Mac turned to the pilot. "Mr. Dixon, you heard the man. Let's go test fly 1-7-4."

Dixon cranked the aircraft. Mac noticed he appeared to be a little leery and couldn't decide if it was because he was test flying the hangar queen or if it was because he was doing it with his boss onboard. He liked Mr. Dixon's approach. He didn't seem to be overly anxious to get in the air. He hovered for almost thirty minutes, doing pedal turns, climbing up to ten feet, and slowly descending to three feet. He had Tom standing off to the side, looking for leaks. After thirty minutes he nodded to Tom, who returned the gesture with a thumbs-up. Dixon called the tower, and away they went on a one-hour test ride and tour of the area. By the end of the flight, Mac had decided Dixon was one of the good guys.

"Mr. Dixon, I'm going to ask you a question, and I need the truth. I've noticed the other pilots avoid me like I've got the plague. What's up with that?"

Dixon shrugged. "It's Palmer. He doesn't like it that you've changed everything about the maintenance program that he and Captain Chase set up. He's telling the other pilots you won't be here long and to steer clear of you."

"I guess I need to explain why I'm having a difficult time working with Mr. Palmer. When I was a PFC, I worked for a supply sergeant at Fort Sill. His supply room was absolutely spotless; all of his paperwork would easily pass the toughest IG inspection. He had brand-new sheets and blankets on the shelves, but he refused to issue them to soldiers. His cabinets were filled with toilet paper, cleaning materials, and everything else authorized by supply. I worked there for almost a year, but as a supply clerk, I wasn't allowed to issue any of those items to the soldiers, even though they were in stock. Periodically the sergeant would order more toilet paper and cleaning stuff for the troops to use, but when we ran out of those, I was instructed to tell the soldiers we didn't have anything left to issue."

Mr. Dixon sat there in shock. He couldn't believe what he was hearing. "Even toilet paper?"

"Especially toilet paper. Somewhere along the line, the sergeant started to think his mission was to have a spotless, well-stocked supply room, not to take care of the soldiers. Mr. Palmer seems to have the mistaken belief that his mission here is to keep a spotless maintenance area. The company pilots actually flying helicopters interfere with his goal. Like my old boss, he feels it's more important to justify keeping the aircraft on the ground, because that way they can't sustain any damage or be lost on missions. As soon as I met him, I recognized that, just like my old sergeant, Mr. Palmer wasn't going to change, and I'd need to just work around him until he can be forced to leave. You know him better than I do; so tell me, does that describe him? Has he succeeded in convincing all of the other pilots to be afraid of me?"

"Like a rattlesnake," Dixon said, laughing.

Mac couldn't believe it. "You're afraid of me, too?"

"No, sir. I believe I understand you now. You just want to get the job done. I didn't know what mission-oriented meant until I met you and Rock."

"Thanks for your straight talk. Maybe someday the others won't think I'm such a bastard."

CHAPTER 8

Tom's team had brainstormed and suggested they pull 5-0-6 in for its scheduled maintenance. Because it was one of the better aircraft, it would be an easy PE and could probably be in and out of the maintenance area within two days. Mac quickly agreed and offered his assistance. Tom was quick to respond, "Could you give us some stick time? I think I might go to flight school."

"Tell you what, if I can test fly it in less than forty-eight hours, after I sign it off, I'll let each of you fly for twenty minutes. How's that?"

"Can Pappy Golden inspect it for us? He's the fastest and best TI."

McKay cut his eyes over at Rock. "Well, what do you think?"

Rock nodded. "Sounds like a plan. I'll go to operations and see when it'll be back from its mission."

"Tom, your time will start as soon as Pappy completes his inspection."

When the aircraft returned, Tom and his team were pushing Pappy to hurry. He had a clipboard with 2404 inspection sheets. As he filled out the sheets, Tom taped them to the cargo door. When he finished, they blanketed the cargo door from one side to the other. When McKay saw what a huge task it was going to be, he whispered to Rock, "Think they've bitten off more than they can chew?"

"Sir, don't ever underestimate desire."

"Hope you're right. Let's go look at the other hangar queens."

"Already have, sir. Two need stack bearings for the tail rotor drive shaft. It's the one thing we can't cannibalize. Every time we've tried in the past, when we take them off another aircraft, they're worn out of tolerance, and we end up putting down two aircraft instead of one."

"Got any ideas?"

"How about calling Nick and seeing if we can get some from him? We could return them when supply fills our requisitions."

Mac headed straight to operations and got Nick on the landline. Nick had just what he needed, but they weren't going to be free. Nick needed a starter/generator. Luckily, it was the one thing Captain Chase had kept in his PLL (prescribed load list, or parts for the aircrafts). Once they agreed on the deal, Nick volunteered to bring the stack bearings to him.

Later that day, Mac saw a helicopter land near the maintenance shed and assumed it was Nick. When he and Rock approached the aircraft carrying the starter/generator, they were shocked to see Brigadier General Boyd exit and walk toward them. Mac whispered to Rock, "Run and get the old man."

Mac quickly reported to the general and asked if he could help.

"Captain, I'm the ADC-Bravo. Heard you're getting the company back on its feet. I came to see if there's anything I can do to help you," replied the general.

"No, sir, it looks like we just need to keep our heads to the grindstone."

Sergeant Rock came running back and saluted. "Sir, Captain Fitzgerald is flying a mission. I'm sorry."

"Don't be; he's doing what he should be doing. Now, show me what you're doing and tell me your plan to get this unit fully operational."

The visit lasted almost an hour. When his aircraft departed, Nick came out from behind a revetment, grinning. Mac turned quickly. "How long have you been there?"

"Almost half an hour. Why didn't you tell me the general was here? If he'd seen me, he'd know exactly why I was here. I don't need another lecture on how to make the supply system work."

"He was a complete surprise. In fact, I didn't even know who he was."

"He's hands-on; look forward to seeing him often," Nick warned, speaking from experience.

"That's all I need."

As they were making their parts exchange, Rock's attention was drawn to the maintenance tent. When Nick flew out, Rock and four men approached Mac.

"Captain Mac, Sheridan and his team have a proposition for you."

Sheridan spoke up. "Tom said if they got the PE for 5-0-6 done early, you'll give them some stick time. Can we have the same deal?"

Mac looked over at Rock and winked. "Tell you what, if you can get one of those hangar queens ready for a test flight by close of business tomorrow, when I finish the test flight, you'll each get twenty minutes of flight time. Do we have a deal?"

When he stuck out his hand, Sheridan looked puzzled. He didn't know what to do. Rock laughed. "Shake the man's hand," he said. "Isn't this what you wanted?"

"Yes, but I didn't know I could shake a captain's hand."

Rock said, "He's a man, and that's what men do when they make a deal."

Sheridan grabbed McKay's hand. "Captain Mac, we won't let you down."

Mac was caught off guard; for the first time since he'd arrived here, he felt like he was beginning to fit in. He'd been an outsider for so long—the pilots feared him, the commander was worried he wouldn't get the job done, and the maintenance officers felt they'd be ostracized by the other pilots if they were friendly with the new guy. For several weeks he had felt like he was on the outside looking in, almost like a new student transferring into a small-town high school. He guessed it had been good in some ways, as he filled his time with work, but after a few weeks it had gotten old, and he'd longed to be just one of the guys. Maybe this challenge would be what was needed to thaw the ice.

CHAPTER 9

After weeks of hard work and long hours, the goal of fourteen flyable birds was reached. Rock asked, "Well, when do we tell operations we have sixteen mission-ready aircraft?"

"We don't. The battalion commander only wanted fourteen a day, and that's what we'll give them," Mac said. "We'll save the other two in case one goes down on crank in the morning. I have a question for you. Have you ever seen Captain Fitzgerald in the maintenance area? There's something strange about that. Captain Jenkins used to check in every day."

"From what the first sergeant said at the NCO bar, he just might be afraid."

McKay smiled. "Oh, you're running with the big dogs now."

Rock just shook his head at how naïve this guy still was. "Captain Mac, you *are* the big dog."

"What's that mean?"

"From what I hear, when Colonel Baxter came up to see Captain Fitzgerald, he told him he'd relieved the maintenance officer this time, but if the unit didn't start meeting mission requirements, Fitzgerald was next. I think he's scared to death you'll screw up what you're doing if he comes out here."

"Are you sure? I still feel Mr. Palmer gives him a complete update every night."

"Unfortunately, so do I. Palmer still thinks he's God's gift to maintenance. He quotes the FMs and TMs like they're Bible verses."

"You know, I've noticed that, and I wondered why the maintenance teams don't have their own TMs."

"I asked Mr. Palmer, and he said mechanics only get them dirty and rip them up. He also mentioned he doesn't think they're smart enough to use them." Rock's face turned red, and he was gritting his teeth in anger. "By God, if they were in any of my classes, they better know how."

Mac laughed and said, "Whoa, will the real Sergeant Rock please stand up?"

"Sir, you don't even want to know what I'm thinking right now."

"I can guess, but confronting him now won't get us anywhere. Somehow we've got to get him out of the ivory tower Fitzgerald put him in."

"I guess you're right. The company commander thinks Mr. Palmer's farts don't stink."

The next morning Mac sat in and listened to Mr. Palmer as he began his maintenance meeting. When he heard the supply tech saying the chains for triple six were here, Mac began to listen with a laser-like focus to what Palmer was saying. On two of the aircraft Mac had test flown, the tail rotor was rigged incorrectly, and he ran out of left pedal when he came to a hover. On one he had to cut the power and auto-rotate to gain control of the aircraft. When he heard Palmer direct Ensley and Jonesy to get their toolbox and meet him at triple-six, he noticed Palmer had paused to see his reaction. Ensley was on Tom's team, and Jonesy was on Sheridan's team. The two mechanics looked in his direction, expecting him to object. Instead, Mac backed out of the door and went to his footlocker. He pulled out his TM 55-1520-210, which was well highlighted, tabbed, and dog-eared from use. It was the one that the instructors at AMOC issued him when he began the class. The students were instructed to tab, highlight or do anything to the book that would assist them in locating information. They made a point to the students that they would be taking the TMs with them to their units in Nam. Mac smiled in satisfaction. *Today I'll show Rock what sneaky is really all about.*

He turned to the page in the TM that described how to correctly place the chain on the sprocket wheel, so the pilot would have plenty of left and right pedal. He noted the page number, paragraph number, and the caution and wrote it on the palm of his hand. Watching from a distance, he saw Mr. Palmer and the two mechanics begin work. As Mac approached, Palmer spoke up in a loud, clear voice, "Boys, according to the TM 55-1520-210, page forty-two, paragraph forty-eight, you place the chain on number seven link on top of the new gear."

Mac put a puzzled look on his face as he stepped closer. "Chief, are you sure about that? I know that's the correct TM, but I think the instructions are on page one-twenty-eight; and if you'll recall, the caution says if you don't rig it correctly, the pilot will run out of left pedal."

Everyone there could see that Mr. Palmer was pissed. How dare Captain McKay question him! "Sir, I've been doing this longer than you've been in the army. I know you went to flight school, but all they did was teach you how to fly them. I know how to work on them."

Mac froze and got extremely calm. "I hear you, Mr. Palmer. But, humor me. Why don't you get the TM and let's see?"

By the time Palmer made it back with the TM, a small crowd had begun to gather. Palmer smiled evilly. "I was right, it is on page one-twenty-eight."

Ensley objected, "But Mr. Palmer, you said page forty-two and paragraph forty-eight. I wrote it down. And you didn't mention anything about cautions."

Captain McKay took the TM and handed it to Ensley. "Give this to Tom. Tell him if I see his team working on an aircraft without using this book, I'll kick his butt." Then he quickly turned and departed. He could hear the buzz behind him and decided it was time to go get some coffee from the mess hall.

That night, when he carried the list of aircraft for the next day's mission to operations, he found Captain Green surrounded by pilots. All Green could say was, "I'm sorry. That's what I get from the S-3; we can only fly what they give me."

The group was still mumbling as they pushed by McKay. He handed the list to Green and asked, "What was that all about?"

"Ah, they're pissed about the ash and trash missions we're getting from the S-3. One guy hauled ice cream and Cokes all day…but I understand why the S-3 doesn't give us any real missions, like an insertion. We've proven we're not dependable. On the last one, we could only send three aircraft for a five aircraft mission. All I can say is forty-seven and a wake-up."

"You're DEROSing?"

"Date of Expected Return from Over Seas. If they'd put that to music, it would replace the national anthem." When he saw the expression on Mac's face, he continued, "I'm sorry. You just got in-country."

"That's okay. If you look at your list, you'll see you've got fourteen birds. If it will make it a little easier for the next forty-seven days, you'll always have fourteen birds."

Green was stunned and couldn't believe what he was hearing. "You promise?"

"That's what they pay me to do. In fact, I haven't had the first drink since I've been here because of all the test flights. So tell me, where is this bar I keep hearing about?"

Green laughed. "You walk by it every morning on your way to maintenance. It's that long building between maintenance and your revetments."

"I thought that was a mess hall."

"It may have been, when it was first built."

Mac left to go check the mail room to see if there was anything for him. He was disappointed his mail hadn't caught up with him yet. Then he remembered the last letter he'd written his parents had his Charlie Company address listed, and he realized he'd need to send them the new address.

McKay found the bar and the four civilian techs. It didn't take long for him to figure out that being sober around a group of drunks was not his idea of fun, so he opted for a good night's sleep instead. Even though it was a little cooler than normal, he still stripped down to his shorts and t-shirt. When the clock went off the next morning, he felt better than he'd felt in months. He wasn't sure why he had slept so well, but he was grateful.

When he located Rock, he blurted out, "You look like crap! What happened to you?"

"Charlie carrying satchel charges came through the wire last night. Sounded like the fourth of July all night. Didn't you hear it?" Rock asked incredulously.

"I didn't hear a thing. I slept like a baby."

"You slept through all that noise?"

Mac smiled. "You know, that's it. I haven't been able to sleep because it's so quiet up here. Guess I was missing explosions all night long."

"Sir, sometimes you just amaze me."

When the last aircraft departed on its mission, Mac and Rock walked to the mess hall. As they walked through the company area, McKay noticed the latrine, which was located about fifty feet from his hootch, had taken a direct hit from a 122-mm rocket and had been completely demolished. Rock just stared at him in disbelief. "You didn't hear any of that?"

"Honest, I didn't hear a thing."

The noise level was high in the mess hall. Everyone was talking about the zappers caught in the concertina wire. One VC had been killed in the culvert next to the POL point. One soldier was overheard saying, "Charlie was only ten feet from having a successful mission."

Rock shook his head and whispered, "And my boss didn't hear a thing."

Mac wandered around the rest of the day like he was lost. Rock could see he was upset but made the decision to let him stew for a while. About fifteen-thirty the first of the aircraft returned from their mission. Mac walked toward the revetment, and Rock hurried to join him. They could see 3-2-7 come hovering down the runway toward its revetment. When Mac looked at the pilot, he said, "Look at him. They look like they're both on pogo-sticks. That's the worst one-to-one vibration I've ever seen. We're going to fix that, you hear me?"

"Yes, sir. I can't believe how much they love that old bird, considering how it's beating them to death."

When they shut down the aircraft, Mac climbed up on the side and opened the pilot's door. "How'd it go today?"

"No problems, sir. We had two oil samples due, but the chief has already taken them. We don't have anything you need to worry about."

"What about that one-to-one vibration?"

"It's always been there, sir. Mr. Palmer said nothing can be done."

"Well, he's wrong. Leave her with me tomorrow, and let me check it out."

As they returned to the maintenance shed, Rock said, "You know, if we fix 3-2-7, Mr. Palmer's ivory tower just may come toppling down."

Mac just grinned. "That would be nice, but more importantly, the crew deserves a smooth ride. And by the way, I decided I need noise to sleep."

Rock just grumbled, "Well, I sincerely hope you don't expect a ground attack every night."

"I'll find something." That night he pulled his duffle bag out from under his bunk and dumped the contents onto his bed. He opened a box, and inside was a small purple transistor radio he'd gotten for Christmas when he was sixteen. He turned it on, but nothing happened. He removed the batteries from his flashlight, put them in the radio, and tried again. This time he got static. He slowly turned the dial until he got the armed forces radio channel. It wasn't clear and had more static than music—but he had noise to sleep by.

CHAPTER 10

Mac woke up, excited about having a new puzzle to solve. All the knowledge he'd been learning was going to be put to use—he was finally in charge. The entire night before had been spent in preparation of the coming day. Once he got to the aircraft 3-2-7, he noticed immediately that Rock had recruited Ensley to help. He laid the TM on the deck of the aircraft and began to explain how he wanted to proceed, "There are three ways of getting rid of the one-to-one vibration. First, using the trim tabs; second, using the weight balance; and third, make sure the blade spread is not off center or out of alignment. Let's start with the blade trim."

Ensley picked up a long pole with two rods at one end. They were about eighteen inches long and two feet apart. He began to wrap the ends of the rods with one-inch masking tape. At the same time, Rock pulled out two grease pencils, pulled down the main rotor, and, with the red grease pencil, covered the end of the tie-down tab. He did the same thing with a black grease pencil on the other blade, "Sir, we're ready for you to crank."

When Mac got the aircraft to full RPM, he pulled just enough power to get it light on the skids. Holding the controls steady, he nodded to Rock, who took the pole, stuck it in the ground, and then slowly pulled it up until the blade barely struck the tape. When he heard two strikes of the blade, he lowered the pole to the ground. McKay shut down the aircraft. When they inspected the blade strikes, the red mark was six inches above the black one. Rock adjusted the trim tab at the end of the rotor blade, and then Mac repeated the process. This time the red and black marks were only a quarter of an inch apart. Rock gave Mac a big grin and thumbs up, and Mac hovered out to the runway to make a test flight to confirm that was the problem. When he returned to the revetment and shut down, he said, "I couldn't tell any difference. Our next step is to figure out if one blade is heavier than the other. Let's put some weights in the retaining pins. Remove the bolt in the top of the pins, and I'll go get some double-O buckshot. We can use that to figure out if it needs weights."

When he returned, he dropped six of the pellets inside the pins and had Ensley replace the bolt. The check required him to take the aircraft high enough to be out-of-ground-effect hover. He decided his best bet was to fly north of the traffic pattern. Remembering what Woody had said about getting above fifteen hundred feet, he started to climb. As he did, he noticed several summer rain clouds in the sky. When he saw an opening between three of the clouds—or, as they called them, sucker holes—he climbed through it. He had to climb to a little more than four thousand feet to get above the clouds. He made a slow right-hand turn back toward Quan Loi. As he approached the airfield, he began to slow his airspeed to come to the out-of-ground-effect hover. Normally, he'd pull more power than needed to hover, but as he began the maneuver, he got a call from operations. Immediately he answered, and they told him, "A code wants to see you." He knew that mean it was an O-6 or above waiting. While talking, he allowed his airspeed to drop to zero, and with too little power, the aircraft began to drop. He was settling with power, which meant the air around the main rotor blades was just circling and not providing any lift. He looked down at the instrument panel and saw that he was falling at fifteen hundred feet per minute—which, according to his math, meant he had about two-and-a-half minutes to recover. Somewhere deep in his head he could hear his instructor's voice from flight school saying, *The only way to recover is to fly out of it and get fresh air.*

Mac immediately pushed the cyclic forward and held his breath as he watched the airspeed indicator. It only bounced from one to five knots. Suddenly he was enveloped by clouds. It was so white, he felt like he was inside a Ping-Pong ball. He took a deep breath to steady himself and pushed the cyclic as far forward as it would go. The airspeed didn't budge. He began talking to himself to calm down, *Push more.* But there was still no change in airspeed. Then it jumped to seventy knots and slowly climbed to ninety knots. Suddenly he popped out of the clouds at about twelve hundred feet and saw he was pointed nose first at the bright red clay dirt road below him. He was screaming inside, *Oh, my God! I'm going to die, and no one will even know what happened.* Again he heard that voice in his head telling him, *Don't panic, pull the cyclic back slowly, you don't want the main rotor blades to hit the tail boom from too big of a correction.* Slowly he regained control of the aircraft and saw he was only four hundred feet AGL, or above ground level, and already in Quan Loi's traffic pattern. He made a call to the tower. The man responded in a high-pitched voice, "3-2-7, where did you come from?" Then without waiting for a reply, he added, sounding much calmer, "3-2-7, you're clear to land."

Mac was still shaken from the ordeal and realized he wasn't going to be able to hover the aircraft into a revetment. He just landed it in the grass near the runway, shut down, and opened the door. Brigadier General Griffin Boyd was standing there, smiling as he looked up. Mac saluted, and the general responded, "Mac, do you think I come visit you a little too often?"

Mac grimaced, "Sir, if you come any more often, I think I'll put you on one of my PE teams."

"Ask a foolish question, and you get an honest answer. Captain, I heard Bravo Company now has fourteen flyable birds, and I wanted to personally congratulate you."

"Thank you, sir."

"Keep up the good work." Then he circled his hand in the air which was the signal for his pilot to crank. Mac just collapsed on the deck of the aircraft and tried to collect his thoughts.

Unaware of the near-death experience, Rock innocently asked, "Did the weights help?"

Mac tried to sound calm. "No, they made it worse. Guess we have to pull the rotor head blade off and scope the blades."

Rock shook his head in disgust. "That's an all-day job. Do you want to wait and start in the morning?"

Ensley interrupted, "Sir, I know how we can scope the blades." He cautiously looked to see Rock's reaction. "It's not by the books, but it'll work, sir."

Clearly disagreeing with Ensley, Rock said, "The blades droop too much. You'll never be able to see the rivet on the end of them."

Ensley rushed to explain, "If we put a block of wood on one side of the mask, and lift the other blade with a forklift, we can scope it. I've done it before and know it will work."

In less than an hour, they were looking down the scope for the rivet. When Mac couldn't find it, Rock held a ruler at the end of the blade until Mac could see the numbers on the ruler. He looked up and smiled in satisfaction, "Boys, we've found the problem. The rivet is four inches off center."

Excited, Rock yelled, "Ensley, what are you waiting for? Cut the safety wires and make the adjustment. Looks like you get to send a change back to Fort Eustis for our TM."

The other side was only two inches off. When Mac returned from the test flight, he had Rock and Ensley climb aboard so they could experience the results of their hard work. He put it back in the revetment and entered *one-to-one vibration* in the logbook and signed it off as test flight completed. He placed the logbook in the pilot's seat and turned to the men. "You know, this is one of the best days of my life."

As they watched him walk away, Ensley whispered to Rock, "I didn't know officers could be so human."

Rock chuckled. "You know, a lot of them put their pants on the same way as us."

CHAPTER 11

Dixon and a TI were the only people in the maintenance shed when Mac entered. Dixon looked up and asked, "Is 3-2-7 better?"

Pleased with himself, Mac grinned and said, "Yeah, it's a little better." As he said this, he realized he was exhausted and was done for the day. He looked around and asked, "Where's Palmer?"

"Probably in the bar."

"Oh, well, do you mind taking the list to Captain Green? I need a beer, and then I need to write some letters."

Dixon nodded and confirmed, "Just fourteen, right?"

"You got it, but put 3-2-7 on the top of the list, and I'll see you in the morning."

He passed a civilian tech supervising some Vietnamese laborers as he walked to the bar. They were working about fifteen feet in front of the main entrance. He could see they'd dug a hole about two feet deep and placed half of a metal culvert on one side of the hole. He watched as they filled it back in with gravel and sand and asked, "What are you building?"

The civilian answered, "A place we can take a piss. The nearest latrine is more than a hundred yards away."

Seeing the logic in that, Mac laughed. "Need is the mother of invention."

The civilian stuck out his hand and said, "A philosopher. I'm Quail."

Mac shook his hand and said, "They call me Mac."

"You must be the new maintenance officer."

"I am."

"Haven't seen you in the bar much. The old one almost lived there," Quail said, then put his hand under his chin and continued, "Mmm, maybe that's why they fired him. He was a big talker and not much of a doer. Do you play chess?"

"Used to."

"Good, I need some fresh meat. I'm getting rusty, playing losers."

They walked inside together. Palmer was sitting on one of the barstools and turned to comment, "I see you finally gave up on 3-2-7. If you'd just asked me I could have told you it was a waste of time. Me and Captain Chase spent two whole days working on her, with no luck. He thought about replacing the main rotor hub and blades but decided the old bird wasn't worth the cost or the effort. Is it still flyable?"

Mac had to restrain himself from acting like a kid and saying, "Nanny, nanny boo-boo, I showed you." He remembered his daddy always saying, "When people think you're a fool, don't open your mouth and remove all doubt." So he just replied, "I had Dixon put it at the top of the list of flyable aircraft."

Quail yelled over at him, "You playing or what?"

As Mac sat down, Quail held out his closed fists. Mac tapped his right hand, and when Quail opened it, there was a white pawn. Quail cautioned, "You move first, but let me warn you, I have no mercy."

"Okay, but before we start I have to know. How'd you get a name like that?"

Quail frowned. "My name is Bob White. You know, like the bob white quail?"

Playing chess was just what Mac needed. His mistake of trying to do two things at once had almost resulted in getting him killed. At least no one knew it had even happened. He liked the fact that Quail didn't just talk about the war. Quail was at least ten years older, but it felt like they were peers. The other civilian techs watched them play and played their own game of who could drink more beer than the other. The heaviest of the group stood and said, "It's time I recycled this beer. I'm going to christen Quail's new invention."

Everyone laughed as he stumbled out the door. Quail took the opportunity to announce, "Checkmate."

As they were resetting the board, Mac said, "Just one last game. I've got letters to write."

Everyone looked up in alarm as the civilian tech came busting through the door, shouting, "Cobra! Cobra!"

One of them yelled, "Yeah, Jack, you work on Cobras, so what?"

"No! No! A snake, a real snake! A cobra—I nearly pissed on him."

Everyone ran to the door to see. When they saw the cobra, they couldn't believe it. More unbelievable was that, being in a war zone, they couldn't find a single gun among them to dispatch the six-foot snake. All the noise and yelling drew the attention of the green line, and the sergeant from the nearest guard post came to their rescue. A burst from his M-16 did the job. Mac turned to Quail. "I think it's time for me to write those letters. I'll see you later."

The next day was uneventful until 3-2-7 returned from its mission. Mac had been to operations and was walking back to maintenance when the crew saw him. Everyone began to talk at once. They were trying to describe how wonderful the ride was. "It's like a Cadillac. No, it's like a Rolls Royce. No, a new Buick."

Mac smiled serenely. "So it's flying a little better now?"

Mr. Hewitt shouted, "Better? I bet it didn't fly that good when it was brand-new. How can we thank you?"

"Just take care of her. You might mention to Mr. Palmer that old 3-2-7 is going to be around for a long time."

CHAPTER 12

If someone looked at Quan Loi as a large clock, with the airstrip running up the middle from six o'clock to twelve, Bravo Company would occupy the area from six to ten o'clock. The Vietnamese Air Force helicopters, UH-34s, occupied from three o'clock to six o'clock. A Cobra Company from the 1st Cav Division occupied from one o'clock to three o'clock, and from ten o'clock to one o'clock would be the refueling area and ammo point. Bravo Company's maintenance shed backed up to the refueling area; the primary target for the VC. For more than a week after the latrine attack, there hadn't been any action from Charlie. The inactivity was lulling everyone into a false sense of security. Then one evening, about an hour before sunset, Charlie sent in two 122-mm rockets to liven up the party. Everyone ran for cover as the rockets exploded. If the fuel point was the target, they missed by one hundred yards; in fact, the destruction was minimal. For the next three evenings, after around sixteen hundred hours, everyone would gravitate to the nearest bunker. By seventeen hundred, all were inside. Once the rockets made their entrance and exploded, everybody just went back to work, preparing the aircraft for the next day's mission.

Mac looked at Rock and asked, "Is this how normal people react, or are we all crazy?"

"What is it the marines always say? Adapt, improvise?"

"There's one thing I won't do, and that's write my folks about this week."

Just as soon as they all got used to the rocket attacks, they stopped. The joke was, Charlie had to hike back up the Ho Chi Minh Trail and get more rounds. They even took bets on how long it would take. Even so, around sixteen hundred, many of the soldiers would move toward the bunkers.

A few days later, Rock came running into the shed. "Captain Mac, you've got to do something about the new replacement," he exclaimed.

"What's the problem?"

"The company got in four new 67N20 UH-1 helicopter repairmen. The first sergeant wants to put two in maintenance and two in the flight platoon."

"What's wrong with that?"

"All four should be assigned to maintenance."

"What about the flight platoon?"

"If they need a crew chief, we should send one of our mechanics who have earned the knowledge to crew chief a bird. One of our problems is that the chiefs don't know how to take care of their own aircrafts. Only the chiefs from 3-2-7 and three others came from maintenance."

"I see your point, but what can I do?"

"Talk to the commander and first sergeant and set up a new policy that crew chiefs must earn their position."

"Sounds like the right way to do things, but before I go see the commander, give me names of three mechanics who will make good ones. Let the PE team leaders suggest who should be promoted."

Rock smiled. "Promoted? I like that. With the PE team leaders saying who it should be, they can't complain when they use them." He stood there for just a minute, thinking, then added with a chuckle, "Sir, don't ever call me sneaky again."

In less than thirty minutes, Rock returned with the three names. "Hall, Parker, and Stewart," he announced.

Mac nodded and asked, "What about Ensley?"

"He was my first choice, too, but said he wanted to stay right where he was."

"That's okay with me. I like working with him."

"He likes working with you, too. I think that's the real reason he wants to stay."

When Mac went to see the commander and first sergeant, he was prepared for a fight; however, when he described the need to upgrade the crew chiefs and how he felt they should be promoted to the position, the first sergeant was sold and asked, "Captain Mac, do you have some men in mind? I'd like to put this in the NCO chain, if you don't care. I think we can solve a couple of problems. Sir, this is the best idea I've heard all year. Thank you."

"I'd like to take the credit, but it was Staff Sergeant Williams's idea."

"Hmmm, wonder why he didn't just come to me?"

"Don't tell him I told you, but he's had a lot of first sergeants tell him they didn't want to hear suggestions from an E-6," Mac told him.

"Sorry to hear that; maybe I can change it," the first sergeant replied.

"Great, I feel like it's in the right hands now." Mac turned to the commander and continued, "Sir, if there's nothing else, I'll get back to maintenance."

The commander said, "Hold on. I was going to handle this tonight, but guess I can take care of it now." Then he turned to the first sergeant and said, "Have the XO, Captain Green, and you join us in my office."

When everyone was present, the commander sat on the corner of his desk and began, "Gentlemen, we're moving to Bear Cat next month. I need for you all to determine what kind of logistical support we'll need—trucks, helicopters, and such. Mac, let me know how many aircraft we'll need to haul down to Bear Cat. When we start, the battalion commander expects us to move in no more than five days."

When Mac took his list to operations, Captain Green motioned him aside. "Mac, Mr. Palmer has asked if he could fly missions until he DEROSes next month. Is that okay with you?"

It was all Mac could do to keep from doing a happy dance. He tried his best to keep a straight face and drawled, "Sure it's okay with me. I think Mr. Dixon and I can handle the test flights. I just wonder why he really wants to fly."

Green stepped closer and whispered, "Between you and me, those mortar rounds have gotten a little too close for comfort. It's obvious he has a short-timer's attitude, and I understand, because I have it too. I only leave this bunker to use the latrine these days. When we get moved to Bear Cat, I'll only have four days and a wake-up."

The next morning all the men were surprised when Palmer was a no show. Mac just took Mr. Palmer's customary seat and began to ask questions of the NCOs, just like Captain Rogers had run his meetings in Bien Hoa. He could see the grin on Rock's face, and there was a cautious air of excitement amongst the group. When they had all finished giving their input, he just sat in his seat watching them, like a teacher waiting for the room to become totally silent. When he knew he had their complete attention, he slowly met the eyes of each of the men. He asked, "What is our mission?"

Someone yelled out, "Fix helicopters?"

"Okay, but what else?" Mac sat and waited, but no one answered. "Well, why do we fix aircraft?"

Another man yelled, "Cause they're broke?"

Everyone laughed nervously. Mac continued, "Guys, we fix them in order to meet Bravo Company's combat mission. If you check your history, you'll see that during the four years of fighting in WWII, grunts actually saw combat for an average of forty days. Here in Vietnam, the grunts average over two hundred days of combat in just one year. Why? Because of the helicopters we work on every day. There isn't a day that goes by that a flight of helicopters isn't inserting or removing troops from the field. In between, other helicopters are either resupplying troops in the bush or medevacing the wounded out of harm's way. Over the past couple of months, how many of those grunts do you think Bravo Company was able to help?" He held up his hand and touched his thumb and forefinger together. Maintaining eye contact with them, he said, "Zero. We have eighteen aircraft, which means we have eighteen crew chiefs and eighteen door gunners. Most of those door gunners were grunts taken out of the field. The next time you're drinking a beer with them, ask how they felt when a helicopter showed up with water, rations, and bullets after they'd been in the field for days. Ask how they felt when a bird came in, picked them up, and returned them to their firebases. Now, let me ask you; how do you feel knowing that because Bravo had no birds that were flyable, men didn't get picked up on time? Because our company wasn't pulling our load, maybe some of them didn't get water or had to stay in the field days longer than they'd expected. It's scary to think about, but men may have died because we gave Charlie a few extra days to locate them. I promised the battalion commander that Bravo Company would give him fourteen flyable birds a day. Forget about the last couple of months; let's make sure the rest of the time we're here, no 1st Cav grunts are let down by Bravo Company maintenance. Now that we're clear on that, I need to let you know that we'll be moving to Bear Cat. It's about a thirty-minute flight east of Saigon."

No one in the room moved a muscle. He continued, "The company commander asked me how many of our aircraft would have to be hauled down there. I want to be able to tell him none. My question to you guys is: can we fly all of our birds to Bear Cat?"

Mac could see Rock wanted to answer, so he made eye contact and shook his head slightly to signal him. Ensley held up his hand, "How long do we have, sir?"

"No more than two weeks. When we start the move, the battalion commander expects it to be complete in five days."

Tom spoke up, "We have two hangar queens. My team will take one of them, but I'll need help on getting some parts."

Webb chimed in, "My team will take the other."

Sheridan added, "We'll be finished with the PE on 3-1-8 tomorrow."

Mac looked over at the schedule board. "It looks like 3-2-7 is next."

Sheridan smiled. "Sir, we can have that one done in a day and a half."

"Okay, guys, but let's see how we do before I tell the commander."

When they broke from the meeting, Mac was pleased everyone seemed so motivated. Since the night of the snake incident at the bar, he'd tried to fit in a chess game or two with Quail whenever he wasn't needed for a test flight, so he headed in that direction. He'd just checkmated Quail when

Dixon approached him. "Captain Mac, I want you to meet Savage." Mac looked up at the man's name tag. Even though he couldn't make out the letters, he was pretty darn sure it didn't read "Savage."

He just nodded and said, "Nice to meet you, Savage. Do you play?"

"Not for a long time."

Dixon interrupted, "He wants to take Palmer's place in maintenance."

Mac asked, "Do you have any experience?"

"I was a crew chief before I went to flight school."

"Do you know how to test fly a Huey?"

"No, sir, but I can learn."

"Well, maybe later. Dixon and I can take care of things for a while."

"Until we move?"

Mac gave Dixon a glare. He got a shrug in response. "I didn't say a word, sir."

"Yeah, until we move." He decided to try to relieve the tension in the room, "Mr. Savage, how did you get your nickname?"

Savage pulled his holster around and handed Mac a pistol with "Savage" marked on the side. Mac was surprised. "How did you get a pistol over here?"

"It was a present from my uncle. He put it in the bottom of my duffle bag when I wasn't looking."

Dixon laughed. "Now tell him how you *really* got the name."

His face flushed, but Dixon couldn't hold back. "He shot a water tower at the south end of the runway."

Savage said, "We were talking about it, and I just stuck my pistol out the window and shot."

Dixon laughed. "We didn't have water for three days. Boy, was Captain Fitzgerald pissed off."

Mac laughed too. "In situations like that, my daddy would always ask if I learned anything."

"Yes, sir—your actions have consequences."

Dixon just couldn't let it go. "He also learned a little pistol makes a big hole in a water tank."

Laughing and dismissing them, Mac said, "Try me again in a couple of weeks."

Quail punched him. "Hey, it's your move."

Five days before the move, the VC got a new supply of ammunition. This time, they fired four rounds instead of their usual two. The second day, they changed their routine and fired three rounds, waited twenty minutes, and then fired three more. The surprise tactic worked. Three of the troops from the Cobra Company were caught in the open. None were killed, but all of them had to be medevaced out. One of the men had only been in-country for three weeks. The rocket and mortar attacks increased every night. The rumors started that the VC knew the unit was moving and wanted to catch the Americans with their pants down. When the first rounds hit the next evening, everyone was tucked away in the bunkers. After five minutes without a second round, they began to worry they were making a ground attack as well. There was total silence for the next fifteen minutes. Then it was broken by the sound of a Cobra making tight circles over the airfield. Dixon came running from operations. "They got 'em. One of the Cobras coming home from its mission saw them launch the first rocket. He dropped his nose and blew all three of them away." As the news spread, a steady roar of excitement enveloped Quan Loi.

Because the American soldiers were packing up to leave, most of them were near the airstrip when five CH-34s prepared to take off the next morning. A squadron of CH-34 Choctaw helicopters was located on the southeast side of Quan Loi. They were flown by the Vietnamese air force. The CH-34 is a reciprocating engine helicopter made famous by the US Marines. The loud noise of their taxi and takeoff each morning drew the attention of the American soldiers. The Americans always wondered why the Vietnamese pilots taxied instead of hovering. After much discussion, it was decided it was because it was easier to use the wheels on the aircraft and taxi rather than hovering which required more skill. It was as if time had regressed by ten years, because they had become accustomed to working on the new, modern version of helicopters. The crew chiefs almost felt sorry for the Vietnamese that they were flying those old dinosaurs. If more than one taxied out at a time, the sound always drew a crowd. The American soldiers just stood and watched the Vietnamese display as if they were receiving a farewell salute from their fellow allies. The pilots didn't seem to be in any rush to leave, and as their numbers increased, so did the noise and the excitement. The Americans began to wave and, from the smiling reactions of the Vietnamese pilots, you could tell they were enjoying every moment of it. As the fifth aircraft joined the formation, the lead aircraft began to taxi down the runway. By the time all were moving down the runway, everyone was shocked when, without warning, the lead aircraft stopped. The second aircraft's pilot was looking back at the Americans and didn't see what had happened until it was too late. It created a domino effect with the remaining helicopters. When the second bird's main rotor blades hit the first helicopter, everyone gasped in horror and began to run for cover. Rotor blades and pieces of aircraft began to fly in all directions. In less than two minutes, three aircraft had lost their main rotors. When the last engine was shut down, the spectators began running toward them to see how they could help the crews. Groups were running from one aircraft to another and couldn't believe what they'd found. Not one crew member was hurt—not even a skinned knee.

Mac just shook his head and turned to Dixon. "I saw it, but I still don't believe it. I guess I can add something to my old saying that God looks after fools and country boys—and Vietnamese pilots."

Dixon laughed in relief. "In a way, I wish we were staying. I'd like to see if they ever get them to fly again."

"Why don't you go find Rock, and let's fly down and see what the hippies call our new digs? Unless you've already been to Bear Cat."

After Dixon cleared the flight with operations, he ran back toward the aircraft. "Captain Fitzgerald and Top are on their way down to Bear Cat with a small convoy."

Mac asked, "Do you know where we'll be located there?"

"On the southwest corner, from what I understand."

As they passed east of Bien Hoa flying south, Rock came on the intercom, "My God, how big is Bear Cat? It looks like it's five times bigger than Quan Loi."

Mac said, "It's a good thing we know where to go, or we could be walking around all day."

When Dixon contacted Bear Cat Tower, they directed him to a helipad close to where they needed to be. They landed and began to walk toward the buildings. The perimeter around Bear Cat looked identical to every firebase in Nam; however, the buildings reminded him of a ghost town he'd seen in the movies located in Death Valley. The only difference was, at Bear Cat, it was paper and other trash blowing between the buildings instead of tumbleweeds. Dixon pointed and exclaimed, "Look, there's a stagecoach on the side of that building!"

As they got closer, they realized it was an old sign with a wagon painted with a tank gun mounted on it, called a war wagon. They could barely read "D Troop, 3rd Squadron, 5th Calvary, Aero Scout Platoon." Rock shook his head and asked, "Do you think John Wayne got the name *War Wagon* from them, or did they get it from the movie?"

Mac shrugged. "Does it really matter anymore? I wonder where they went."

Dixon said, "Think Quan Loi will look like this when we leave? Sure hope it doesn't look this deserted."

They just wandered around through the area for a while and had about given up and started back to the aircraft when Captain Fitzgerald and his three-vehicle convoy arrived. It was apparent he had been there before when the First Sergeant began to post signs on the buildings. Captain Mac was surprised that he would be located in the same building as the company commander. He opened the door that had his name on it and was surprised to realize it was only a two-man room. The building had been divided into five separate areas. He now knew where he'd be sleeping, but where would he be working? He found Fitzgerald and asked, "Sir, where's the maintenance area? There's no place large enough here that I can see."

"Hop in the jeep, and I'll take you." Rock and Dixon climbed in the backseat, and the commander started down a little dirt road that paralleled the green line. After about two hundred yards they saw a large sign that said "ROYAL THAI ARMY VOLUNTEER FORCE" with (Black Panthers) underneath. Mac looked around and commented casually, "I didn't realize they were in this war."

"Yeah, even the Royal Australian Navy is on the other side of Bear Cat," replied Fitzgerald.

When they'd gone another three hundred yards, they turned right, headed straight for the control tower. The commander stopped the jeep and announced, "This is it, guys. That's B Company, 228th Aviation Battalion, our Chinook unit, located straight ahead and behind the control tower."

Looking around, Mac only saw one shed in the vacant spot. Rock spoke up, "We can put our maintenance tents next to the 228th, and with the Conex containers lined up on the north side, we'll have plenty of room."

Fitzgerald said, "Oh, yeah, make room for another section. The 15th TC is sending down a direct support section to each company. It's something new they want to try. It consists of one captain, three NCOs, and fourteen enlisted men."

Mac didn't blink. "When do they arrive?"

"Same time we do."

On the return trip, Mac asked Dixon, "How long until you DEROS?"

"January. How about you?"

"Not until July. I've never asked before, but where's home for you? I don't see a ring on your finger, so I'm guessing you're still single?"

"I'm from a little town north of Phoenix. I'm not married yet, but plan on asking my girl, Joyce Pinson, when I get home. She's a teacher. I'm going to ask her on my R&R in October."

"Are you going to Hawaii?"

"Yes, sir. I've already made all the reservations."

"I was stationed there after flight school. Those folks at Fort DeRussy really take good care of the people there on R&R."

"How about you, sir?"

Mac just laughed and shook his head. "Unfortunately I'm still looking for my soul mate."

Rock leaned forward and chimed in, "Mr. Dixon, let me give you some advice, and I suggest you pay attention. It would be a lot easier and cheaper to just find a woman you hate and buy her a house. I speak from experience and have lots of friends who'll back me up."

The two pilots just looked at each other for a minute and then burst out laughing.

When they landed in Quan Loi, Mac suggested they all go to the maintenance area and do some scheduling magic. Rock asked, "Do you need me to get the PE team leaders?"

"No, let them keep working. I've got a couple of ideas I'd like to run by you first. We can get them later. But would you go get Pappy?"

When all four were standing in front of the scheduling board, Mac examined the aircraft closest to the hundred-hour inspection. He complimented the team, "You guys have done a great job of spreading out the schedule. There isn't a single area where they're all bunched up." He turned and looked at Pappy, Rock, and Dixon, purposely meeting each of their eyes. He continued, "That didn't 'just happen.' Each of you made it happen. Thank you. Now, let me tell you what I was thinking. It looks like 4-9-2 and 3-6-8 will be next up for PE. What if we flew them down to Bear Cat on Thursday morning, take any parts we might need to get the others flying, and then return here, put them on whatever aircraft needs them, and fly the last two to Bear Cat? Tell me why that won't work."

They all smiled, and Dixon was the first to respond, "The only problem I see is, who will fly 4-9-2 and 3-6-8 to Bear Cat?"

"Captain Fitzgerald and Green should jump at the chance to fly," Mac said. Then an evil grin spread across his face. "I'll bet even Mr. Palmer could be talked into it."

Dixon cackled. "Well, don't even think about having me ask him."

"Just kidding. There are plenty of straphangers eager for a flight to Bear Cat."

Pappy waved for attention. "Sir, I was thinking I could do my inspection of both of those aircraft on Wednesday. I don't need to wait until they get to Bear Cat."

Rock came alive and said, "By God, this just might work. We've come a long way from just one flyable bird. I knew those students of mine weren't losers."

Mac asked, "What's that old saying? 'When your image improves, your performance improves.' Rock, I think it's time for you to go get Gibbs, Sawyer, and Sheridan and let them in on our secret. We're flying everything to Bear Cat."

CHAPTER 13

In operations on Wednesday morning, Mac expected to see the mission board but was surprised to find everything had been packed. Captain Green turned and asked, "What's up, Mac?"

"I've got several things. First, how many missions are there for tomorrow, and who can fly 4-9-2 and 3-6-8 to Bear Cat first thing in the morning?"

Green picked up his clipboard. "Right now we're committed for twelve," he said. "I can fly 4-9-2 with Lieutenant Jewell and Captain Fitzgerald, and the XO can fly the other one. What else do you need?"

"It's pretty important that I have those two aircraft at Bear Cat by ohnine-thirty at the absolute latest. Can you make that happen?"

"If it's that important, I'm sure we can."

"We need to take parts off of them, so we can fly the last two down on Thursday afternoon."

"Are you kidding me? You're flying all of our aircraft to Bear Cat?" Green asked incredulously.

Mac smiled. "If you hold up your end of the mission, we are," he said.

"I can. Can I be the one to tell Fitzgerald? What a way for him to end his command and leave Nam! You do know his change of command is in two weeks? Anything else?"

"When you give out the mission this evening, tell the pilots, when they're through, to go to Bear Cat and not come here. No one will be left at Quan Loi by tomorrow night." Mac left operations and headed to the bar to find Quail. He was sitting in his usual spot and called out when Mac approached, "Got time for a game?"

"Not really. I just wanted to come by and tell you I'll miss our chess games."

"When are you leaving?" Quail asked.

"First thing in the morning."

"Well, then, you still have tonight."

"We've got two aircraft that need test flights sometime this evening."

"The rumor is you're flying all of the aircraft to Bear Cat. Is it true?"

Mac grinned. "Yep."

"You know, when I first met you, I just thought you were another skinny captain, but I guess I should have known that meant you were hungry." Quail stood and extended his hand in a show of respect. "I sure hope we meet again."

As Mac walked back to maintenance, he realized time really had no bearing on making friends. Woody, Nick, Sandy, and he had only been together a few months, but he felt closer to them than most of his high school buddies. Even though he didn't know how that could be, he knew it to be true.

He saw Dixon before he even got to the first revetment and called out, "Hey, is Savage still interested in helping us out?"

"Sure, I guess so. When did you want him?"

"See if he can fly one of the last aircraft to Bear Cat."

"Okay, I'll go check to see if he has another mission. If not, I know he'll do it. I'll let you know as soon as I can confirm."

The maintenance crew were loading the last of the two tents when Mac finally got to the maintenance area. They had a trailer at the entrance to the shed, and he just watched them load. When they picked up a little green field table, he noticed a box, covered in dust, about a foot square and six inches tall. He reached out and opened the top. It was filled with playing cards. Curiosity was driving him nuts, so he asked around. No one seemed to know how it had gotten there, so he just placed the box in the trailer himself and decided he'd try to find out why they were there later. Just as he started back inside, Sheridan approached with a huge grin and said, "Sir, 3-2-7 is ready for a test flight."

"Good, I'll get my helmet. Get yours, and you can ride left seat. Maybe you can get some stick time."

As they were strapping in, Sheridan asked, "Why do you always fly right seat? I thought aircraft commanders always fly in the left seat."

Mac looked over, trying to think of how to explain. "The simple answer is, all the gauges and controls are on this side.

Sheridan just looked at him for a moment. "Okay, but what's the more complex answer?"

"That's easy," Mac told him. "I went through flight school in the right seat, and I got my instrument ticket and went through test flight school in the right seat. I'm just comfortable on the right side in a way I'm not in the left seat. In fact, the story goes that Stanley Hiller had the same problem. He was one of the very first men to work with helicopters back in the early 1940s. He learned to fly his creation in the left seat, like all fixed-wing pilots do. When he started to teach others to fly it, he discovered he wasn't at all comfortable in the right seat. Bottom line, he stayed in the left seat and taught the first helicopter pilots to fly the right seat. How's that for an answer?"

"You sure know a lot about helicopters."

"Not really; I just had a lot of instructors who loved to talk about helicopter trivia. Now, let's stop all this talking and do some flying."

When he was doing the postflight ninety minutes later, Dixon came up with Savage. Mac could tell from the expressions on their faces that they had bad news. "Savage is flying with Captain Fitzgerald to Bear Cat tomorrow, so he won't be able to fly the last bird."

Mac smiled. "Oh, yes, he can. We were planning to take parts off of Fitzgerald's bird and bring them back up here to get these other two ready. Savage can just fly back with us."

Dixon slapped his leg and laughed. "Captain Mac, you always make everything seem so simple."

"That's because it is. Wish all of our problems could be fixed that easily. Why don't you go tell Mr. Hewitt he has 3-2-7 back, effective right now?"

"God, is he going to love hearing that."

Thursday had finally arrived. It was the last day of the move. A deuce and a half truck was parked in the middle of the company area. It looked like an anthill as each soldier walked by and tossed his duffle bag on the back. Mac made a final check of his hootch and smiled when he saw the picture in his mind of what the next occupant would see—a sandbag bunker in the middle of a well-built shelter. Only sandbags and dirt covered the floor, and he realized not even a rat lived there. When he got back to the maintenance area, Dixon greeted him, "Captains Fitzgerald and Green just took off."

Rock and Ensley were sitting in the gun wells, waiting to leave. Eagerly, Mac approached the bird and said, "Okay, boys, let's make this happen."

When they landed at Bear Cat, Mac was surprised and worried that 4-2-9 and 3-6-8 were nowhere to be seen. Rock was about to panic and started running from one revetment to the next yelling "They're not here!"

Mac had just crawled back in the helicopter to call the tower to see if they had called in, as two Hueys came from the south side of Bear Cat and landed. Savage stuck his head out of the pilot's window and yelled, "Captain Green said to tell you he still has fifteen minutes to spare. Where do you want them parked?"

Forty-five minutes later, Rock, Savage, Ensley, Dixon, and Mac were back on their way to Quan Loi with the parts needed to repair the remaining aircraft. In less than three hours, after two test flights, the last of the mechanics and tool boxes were loaded on the last remaining aircraft to leave Quan Loi for good. As the three pilots cranked their birds, they each called to Mac in sequence, "Maintenance One, this is Maintenance Two, ready."

"Maintenance One, this is Maintenance Three, ready."

Mac's chest filled with pride at the call sign Savage and Dixon had given him. He was about to give the go-ahead when Dixon called, "Hold up, everybody! We can't leave Hobo."

Mac figured it was some type of code he didn't know about and just shrugged. Five minutes later Dixon came back on, "Hobo's onboard. We're ready."

Mac keyed his mike and said, "Dixon, someday you'll have to explain what Hobo means. Boys, it looks like we've done it. This reminds me of what Gil Favor would say, 'Head 'em up, move 'em out. Rawhide.' Dixon, we'll follow you."

Dixon tuned into the tower's frequency and announced, "Quan Loi tower, this is Killer Spade, flight of three, requesting hover and departure clearance."

"Killer Spade, you're clear. Have a good day."

With only one pilot per aircraft, things were pretty quiet on the way down. They flew what most pilots call a *flight school formation* (three aircraft in the sky at the same time). As they weren't familiar with the area, for safety reasons it was easier to land one aircraft at a time, so Dixon had each

of them call the Bear Cat tower. Dixon landed first, then Savage, and then
Mac. When he finally found a revetment and shut down the aircraft, Dixon
got out and approached the others with a sheepish expression on his face
and pointed to a well-fed mutt, tagging along behind him and wagging his
tail. "This is Hobo."

Mac got out and patted the dog's head. "Okay, tell me his story."

"He's the company mascot. No one knows where he came from, but
everybody feeds him. On special mornings he'll come to the flight line,
pick a helicopter, and fly with it all day. He's a good-luck charm. Nothing
has ever happened to a bird if he's onboard. You know how superstitious
pilots are. You should see the things crew chiefs and pilots do to bribe him
to choose their bird, but Hobo only rides when he wants to."

"How come I've never seen him?"

"When he isn't flying, he hangs out with the flight platoon or at the
mess hall."

"Hmm, bet you felt safe riding with him this morning."

"Always—but more importantly, if we'd have left him, maintenance
would have been in deep shit again."

Mac smiled in satisfaction. "If I'm hearing you correctly, that implies
we're out of it."

When postflight inspections were completed, Mac pulled Rock aside
and said, "We need a meeting with the entire maintenance platoon. Don't
stop anyone who's working, but just make sure to grab someone to repre-
sent their section."

"When do you want them?"

"In fifteen minutes, in the maintenance shed."

Less than ten minutes later, the crowd was waiting. Mac just stepped
on top of a box and patiently waited until everyone stopped talking. "Men,
we did it. When the guys returned from their missions, every single aircraft flew from Quan Loi to Bear Cat. Congratulations." Cheers and hoots
followed this announcement. He allowed it to go on for a few minutes
and then continued, "That's the good news." There was immediate silence
as he went on, "The bad news is, we've got to have fourteen flyable birds

tomorrow and the next day. If we don't watch out, we could end up with egg on our faces. We're not set up to perform any kind of maintenance yet. The commander would understand if we did fail, because maintenance has let him down before." He paused and let that sink in for a while. He could tell they didn't like it. "We know what the problem is; so how do we fix it?"

Pappy stood. "Sir, we already have three birds ready in the revetments. Eleven more shouldn't be a problem."

Everyone laughed. Ensley stood and said, "Sir, we'll bet you a case of beer we'll have fourteen no later than twenty-two hundred hours."

That was just what Mac wanted to hear. "Well, then, you've got yourself a bet. Now when you don't make it, just put the beer in my hootch. It's right next to the commander."

Pappy challenged, "Sir, are you willing to make it two cases if we're done by twenty-one hundred hours?"

"Don't see why not. Now, get out there and earn your beer."

Mac couldn't believe how he felt. He'd never had such a feeling of pride and accomplishment. He'd realized he was leading one awesome team. If he had ever thought about getting out of the army, that desire was gone forever.

As the pilots returned from their missions, Pappy and one of the PE teams would assist with the post flight checks. As the afternoon passed, Rock would gloat as he updated him on the status of the bet. "Captain Mac, we've got six already." An hour later, he'd be back with an update of a couple more. After a couple of hours, he was getting on Mac's last nerve, so he decided to go check out Captain Green's new operation. He had expected it to be in the same building as the orderly room, but he hadn't anticipated it would be above ground like all of the other buildings. He stuck his head in and teased Green, "How're you liking your new home?"

"Hell, you know I don't like it. I feel naked out here in the middle of nowhere."

Mac laughed. "Boy, is that a picture I don't want rolling around inside my head."

Green then turned and introduced his turtle, James Willard. They exchanged greetings, and Green explained, "Mac is our maintenance guy. He keeps us flying. Don't piss him off, because you don't know what hell is until you're a flight operations officer with no birds to fly. I've been there, and trust me, you don't want to do it. When Mac got here, he promised me fourteen birds a day, and so far he hasn't let me down. In fact, you may not know it, but he flew all eighteen birds here during the move."

James smiled. "Guess I just met my new best friend."

"That's okay with me," Mac said. "I need a friend. I don't think I have more than five pilots who will give me the time of day."

Green asked, "Do you have a list for me yet?"

"It'll be a while. How many missions do you have?"

"Twelve so far, but we may need to cover Charlie Company. You heard they lost two ships on Saturday, didn't you?"

"No, what was it, a hot LZ?"

Green picked up the paper and started to read: "*On 26 September C Company 229th Aviation Battalion launched five UH-1 helicopters on a formation flight from Bien Hoa to Fire Support Base Green. The aircraft formed up in a "V" formation and climbed through an overcast to visual flight conditions on top. At 4,000 feet ASL, while in route, the flight leader directed a spread formation for the purpose of conducting aircraft DEER checks. UH-1H 608 was in the left echelon on the flight lead. During the checks, 608 accelerated forward and drifted right, impacting the lead aircraft's tail boom. Both aircraft departed controlled flight and disappeared into the clouds, impacting the ground about 250 meters apart. All eight crewmen died in the crash.* Here's the list of the people."

Mac reached out to take the report. As he read, two names jumped out at him: CW3 Woods and SP5 Sanders. "Oh, my God, Woody and Sandy! I still have Sandy's flight gloves."

Green turned in his chair and looked at him, concerned at the tone of his voice. "What are you talking about?"

"Woody was my roommate in Charlie Company before I got here. I can still see him on the bunk with his head propped up on his hand. He was sound asleep, and his eyes were always wide open. Sandy was our crew chief, and two days before I left, he loaned me a pair of his gloves. I was supposed to return them. God, it can't be true. There's no way. Not them." He just stumbled off in a daze and mumbled, "I'll bring back your list later."

CHAPTER 14

As Rock and Mac met at the flight line, Mac complained, "Rock, I'm not sure I'll ever get used to the walk from my hootch to here every morning at oh-four-hundred. It must be at least a quarter of a mile."

"You know it's alright. The army requires its soldiers to do PT every morning."

Mac shook his head in disgust. "Do they brainwash all the instructors at Fort Eustis?"

"Only the good ones. By the way, when do you plan on paying up on your bet?"

"Not sure yet; I've got to find the beer first."

"Hey, I can help you there."

The morning briefing was like a party. The men knew they'd won the bet and were anticipating a quick payoff. Mac began with, "I have good news, and I have bad news." They all knew the good news, so they groaned and waited to hear the bad.

"You won your two cases of beer, but the problem of maintaining fourteen flyable aircraft hasn't gone away. The bad news is, we'll need to postpone our celebration until next Saturday."

Ensley asked, "Are you sure we can celebrate then?"

"If you guys could get all of them flyable at one time, how hard is just fourteen? I'm looking forward to a hell of a party."

Later, as he was going for an early lunch, Mac watched two lowboy trucks drive up, carrying five Conex containers. A sergeant got out asking for the Bravo Company maintenance area. Mac confirmed it was and asked, "What's in the Conexes?"

"Not sure. The 15th TC sent them. Can you help us unload them?"

Pappy came driving up with a forklift. "Where do you want them, sir?"

"Check with Rock. I'm heading to the orderly room to find out what this is all about."

When he got there, twenty soldiers with duffle bags were standing around outside. As he opened the door, Green said, "Looks like you're getting some help."

"What do you mean?"

"Those guys are the detachment the old man said would be coming."

"I'd forgotten all about that."

"Well, they're here. Let's go see your maintenance twin."

"Twin? What on earth are you talking about?"

"They sent a captain with the detachment."

When they arrived at the orderly room, Mac couldn't believe his eyes at the sight he saw. "Barney? I can't believe it!"

"Hi, Mac. Guess I'm like a bad penny."

Stating the obvious, Fitzgerald said, "You guys know each other, huh?"

Barney confirmed, "Yes, sir. We were in the same AMOC class. If it weren't for this guy, I would have been first in the class."

Fitzgerald laughed. "Well then, Mac, meet your new roommate. I'll let you two nail out the details on how you'll work together. Just keep giving me fourteen birds a day. Captain Barnes, welcome to Bravo Company."

After leaving the commander's office, Barney introduced his two NCOs. "Mac, this is Sergeant First Class Walker and Staff Sergeant Hall. Hall is the best engine man in the country."

Mac reentered the orderly room and asked the commander's driver to go fetch Rock from the maintenance area. The remainder of the day was spent getting the new detachment settled. When Mac showed him their quarters, Barney said, "Hell, this is better than what I had at Phu Loi."

"It's definitely better than Quan Loi. Would you believe we have hootch mates here? They clean the room and do our laundry for about twenty dollars a week. Ours is named Mai."

"That's a lot cheaper than the one I had Phu Loi."

"You had a hootch mate? Boy, have you been living in the lap of luxury over here!"

"Where do you get their money? I'm guessing they don't take MPC."

"I've been exchanging MPC for Dong with the first sergeant," Mac said.

"I'll check it out with him later, but let's hit the bar for now."

Mac just stood there until Barney asked, "What's wrong?"

"You won't believe this, but we don't have a bar here."

Barney shook his head in disgust. "War really is hell. Well, then, show me where we're going to be working."

After the hike to the maintenance area, Barney complained, "I feel like a city rat visiting his country cousin. We've got to find us a ride."

"I'd forgotten how delicate you are. Before we go in, let me ask you, how old is Sergeant Walker? He looks as old as my daddy, and he's forty-five."

"He just might be older than that. All the men call him Papa-San. Until a year ago, he was a senior mechanic with Delta Airlines and a sergeant in the National Guard. When his son was killed last year, he volunteered for active duty. He treats us all like we're his kids and even runs a little school at night for the men who want an aircraft maintenance certificate."

"He and Sergeant Williams will be a powerful team. He was an instructor at Fort Eustis, and he's nicknamed Sergeant Rock," Mac told him.

Barney clapped him on the shoulder. "Then we'd better just stay out of their way and watch while they make us look good."

"I agree, but let's not tell them they have that much power over us. Let's go ask Papa-San and Rock what our plans are."

With the additional men helping, the maintenance area took shape almost overnight. Barney came with another benefit, too. He would play his tape deck constantly when they were in their hootch, even while they slept. The music was like a lullaby for Mac, and he slept like a baby.

Rock handed Mac a bill the next morning. "You'll find the beer under your desk. Where's Captain Barnes?"

"I thought about bringing him, but decided this oh-four-hundred ritual was ours. I didn't want to share."

Touched, Rock grinned. "You know, I agree."

Mac began to wonder if he'd shared a little too much information, because not another word was said until they got their first cup of coffee in the mess hall with Barney and Papa-San. It was nearly noon when Dixon came in the shed, shouting, "Heads up, guys, looks like we've got company. The battalion commander is here."

He picked up the landline to operations, and when they answered, he instructed them to tell Captain Fitzgerald the battalion commander's aircraft had just landed in the maintenance area. Barney asked, "How do you know it's his?"

"The butt number is 2-2-9. All the battalion commanders have Hueys with their battalion butt numbers on them. There's also 2-2-7 and 2-2-8. I bet some logistician got a medal for that one."

Everyone moved outside to see the special aircraft. When the pilot turned the nose toward them to hover closer, Dixon yelled, "See the stacked deck crest on the nose?"

Barney craned his neck to look and quizzed, "Stacked deck? What does that mean?"

"Four aces. Bravo Company is the ace of spades, and Delta Company is the ace of diamonds—but they go by the Smiling Tigers, since Walt Disney Studios designed the logo for them."

Barney shook his head in amazement. "Dixon, you're quite the historian."

"I'm a warrant officer. I'm supposed to know everything."

When the aircraft shut down, they were surprised to see Lieutenant Colonel Baxter open the cargo door in jungle fatigues, not Nomex. He was all smiles. "Captain Mac, I came down here to personally thank you for doing such an outstanding job."

"Thank you, sir."

"I remember asking you to just give me fourteen flyable birds, and in this morning's briefing, they told me Bravo Company flew all eighteen aircraft from Quan Loi to Bear Cat. Hell, that's not just good—that's a miracle. Where's that Sergeant Superman you wanted when I assigned you the task?"

"You mean Sergeant Rock?"

"Yeah, that's it."

Mac quickly turned to Dixon and said, "Find me Sergeant Williams."

When Rock came walking up to the colonel, Mac watched out of the corner of his eye, trying to see the colonel's reaction. The colonel seemed to have the same impression of the five-foot eight-inch, one-hundred-forty-pound man that Mac had upon meeting him. The colonel just turned and whispered to Mac, "Guess they're right about dynamite coming in small packages." Before the colonel could say anything to Rock, Captain Fitzgerald drove up. He greeted him and explained, "I had to come down and be part of this miracle. Almost two months ago, you had one flyable aircraft; and three days ago, all eighteen of them flew." Then he turned around and asked, "Sergeant Major, did you bring them with you?"

No one had noticed the sergeant major; they were all surprised as he replied, "Yes, sir, right here."

The colonel turned to one of his pilots and instructed, "Read the orders."

The captain read, "Captain Mac and Sergeant Williams are receiving an impact award of an Army Accommodation Medal for outstanding achievement in aircraft maintenance."

CHAPTER 15

When Mac took the evening list to Green, he asked, "Who can help me get medals for my men?"

"Well, hello to you, too. Thanks a lot for the sentimental goodbye. You do remember today's the last day I'm here to take the list."

"Are you serious?"

"Yep, I take a jeep ride to 90th replacement tomorrow, and the next day I get on a freedom bird. Okay, I forgive you if you didn't know. Now, you'll need to talk to Captain Miller; he's our awards and decorations officer."

"I really am sorry I forgot you're leaving. Where do you go from here?"

"I'm bound for Fort Benning and the advance course. I think I've decided to make the army a career."

"That's great. I've been thinking about that, too. Good luck to you. Where do you think I can find Miller?"

"Now, that's a good question, since we don't have a bar. I'd check the showers first. The pilots usually try to shower early, while the sun's still out, so they can stand the cold water."

Mac walked to the shower stalls and chuckled as he watched a number of feet jumping around trying to avoid the cold spray of the water. He called out, "Captain Miller? Are you in there?"

"Yeah, who wants to know?"

"Captain Mac."

"Captain Johnny Mac from Blue Ridge, Georgia? What can I do for you?"

Startled, he couldn't believe the man could know that much background information on him. "Can we talk?"

"Yeah, let me get the soap out of my hair." Seconds later he came out and slipped on a fatigue shirt and pair of trousers. "Now, if that doesn't get your blood moving, you must be dead," he complained. "Bet you wonder how I know so much about you. Well, let me tell you, buddy, Captain Fitzgerald said if I didn't get you and Sergeant Williams medals, he would make sure my next assignment was a lot colder than that water I just got out of. Now, what else can I do for you?"

"I need help on getting recognition for my TIs and PE team leaders."

"I heard Colonel Baxter gave you two green weenie awards. Tell you what, if you guys in maintenance can manage to get us some hot water, I'll write them up myself."

"You've got a deal. You'll have hot water if I have to heat it myself on Barney's hot plate. I have one more question, and I'm guessing you're just the guy to answer it. When we were moving from Quan Loi, I found a box full of playing cards, but they're all the ace of spades. You have any background on them?"

"I thought they were all gone. You know, we're the Killer Spades, and one of the guys wrote to the card company and told them that. They sent us ten or twenty boxes of them as a promotion. The Vietnamese are very superstitious, and they think the ace of spades is a bad omen. When we first got them, the pilots would throw out four or five of them at every LZ just to scare them and let them know the Killer Spades helicopters had been there. If you don't have any use for them, how about giving them to me, and I'll pass them out to the pilots?"

Mac was so excited, he could hardly wait for their mini breakfast meeting the next morning. He sipped his coffee until everyone was seated. Then he started, "I need you creative geniuses to come up with a way to heat water for the officer showers."

Rock just looked over at Papa-San with a guilty expression on his face. "Should we tell him?" Papa-San immediately got a guilty look on his face and just shrugged.

Curious, Mac asked, "Tell me what?"

"The NCOs and enlisted men already have hot showers."

"I didn't know that! Why didn't you tell me?"

"Sir, you didn't ask," and Papa-San flashed a fake smile.

"Well, tell me how Captain Miller can get a hot shower. He's agreed that when he does, our TIs and team leaders will get a medal. I feel bad that the battalion commander only recognized Rock and me because everybody knows who really did the work."

Papa-San spoke up, "If you can get us an immersion heater from the mess hall and a fifty-five-gallon drum, we can get them hot showers by this evening."

Mac beamed. "Papa-San, I just might start calling you Merlin, like the wizard." For the first time since he'd met him, he saw a genuine smile on the older man's face and realized that it doesn't matter who you are or why you do something—everybody needs a little praise once in a while. Everyone settled into eating their breakfast, and nothing was said until a man wearing a silver cross on his lapel approached the table.

"I'm Captain Dalton. Are you the maintenance officers from Bravo Company?"

Mac answered, "Yes, Chaplain. We're guilty as charged. What can we do for you?"

The chaplain looked over at the NCOs and said, "I don't mean to offend you guys, but I just need to talk to the captains—unless you are willing to help. When we moved down here, we got cut off from the other Americans by the Thai Army Headquarters. Bottom line is, there's no bar for the American officers. We found an old mess hall building next to the berm across the road from the Bravo Company commander's hootch, but here's the real problem. Because Bravo is flying a heavy load right now, there's no one left to fix it up. How are you two captains with hammers and nails?"

Mac said, "Okay, I guess, but I'm not sure I have the time."

Sergeant Rock coaxed, "Sir, just do it! We're getting really tired of the warrant officers coming over to our bar and drinking all of our beer."

Mac whirled around, shocked. "The NCOs have a bar?"

Rock just grinned, "That's the first thing we did. Why do you think Top made so many scouting trips down here?"

Mac just looked at Barney and shook his head in wonder. "Looks like we're working for the padre for a while. Chaplain, we'll be over to help you right after our meeting."

They finished quickly; all NCOs were anxious to get the captains on their way. Once Barney and Mac arrived, they were surprised to see two chaplains and two civilians carrying plywood into the building. Inside were several Vietnamese women, sweeping cobwebs and dust off the walls. Obviously, the chaplains had a plan and were just looking for people to do the work. Barney and Mac were perfect for the job; and after a full day's work, they were almost ready for business. Mac discovered the civilians were maintenance techs for the Smiling Tigers, and while on break, he asked them, "Do you guys happen to know Quail?"

Right away, one said, "Bob White? Hell, yes. He's why I'm here. We go way back. We're both from a little town near Fort Worth. My name is Jim Mayfield, but they call me Tex."

"Call me Mac. Quail and I played a lot of chess together at Quan Loi."

"He loves his chess. Did you know he's going back to Texas to take care of his folks?"

"Nah, I didn't, but it sounds like him," Mac replied. "You don't play chess, do you?"

"Hell, no, it's too complicated for me. Bob used to laugh when we'd play and say 'I've got you on a fools mate again.' I didn't know what he meant, but I learned pretty damn quickly it wasn't my game."

"He meant he got checkmate on you with only two pieces—the pawn and the queen, or in only two of his moves."

"That's okay; I'll just stick with checkers."

Two days later the bar was open. With the pilots from Smiling Tigers and Bravo Company, it was almost a full house. There wasn't anything on the walls or tables, but they had both liquor and beer. Mac wondered how they'd stocked the entire bar, when he couldn't even manage to buy beer for the men. He asked the bartender and was told to see Captain Miller.

The next maintenance meeting had good news and bad. The good news was, Papa-San had the immersion heater welded into a fifty-five-gallon drum and installed in the officers' showers. The bad news was, one of the aircraft scheduled for maintenance was dead-lined because of worn stack bearings on the tail rotor—the one replacement part that was almost impossible to find, because the demand in-country was so high. Mac began to worry that this one might become his first hangar queen.

CHAPTER 16

The battalion commander flew down the next week for Captain Fitzgerald's change of command. The new company commander was Major Reese from division headquarters. The colonel took the opportunity to pin on medals for the pilots and crew chiefs. Mac couldn't believe nobody else in the company received anything. When he expressed his frustration to Rock, the response was, "We can always hope for next time." Then Rock walked back to the maintenance area.

After the ceremony, Barney teased Mac, "You should be happy. Major Reese is from Tennessee."

"I don't think we'll be beer-drinking buddies. I noticed he's a ring knocker."

Barney laughed. "West Pointer, huh? Guess I better start polishing my boots."

Sheridan reported to the group at the next meeting that they couldn't do anything else with 4-7-4 until the stack bearings came. Dixon asked, "Mac, do you think you can get us some from your friend, Nick?"

"Not sure, but I can try. How about letting operations know we're going on a maintenance run?"

"Which aircraft?"

"Which is the next one scheduled for PE?"

"That would be 5-0-6."

When they got to Bien Hoa, they landed near Charlie Company's maintenance area. Mechanics all stood and looked at the aircraft, and when Mac crawled out, Nick was the first to recognize him. "Well, has the prodigal son returned?"

"Nah, more like the brat looking for a handout. I need some stack bearings."

"Guess you'll just have to get in line like the rest of us. I'm not sure what's worse on bearings—the dust or the monsoon season," Nick complained. "We have two down ourselves. With the two losses and two more in PE, we can't even meet our load."

Mac nodded, stepped closer, and lowered his voice, "Tell me about Woody and Sandy."

Nick's eyes welled with tears. "It was such a stupid accident. They were on a five-ship insertion mission. Woody was the mission commander. It was cloudy, and they had to climb to four thousand feet to fly VFR. "Woody ordered them to break out and do a DEER check. Richard was flying left and to Woody's rear. He had a new captain with him. It was his very first mission. It's kind of obvious now that Richard must have been explaining to him what they were doing, and they were both looking down at the instruments. Richard must have sped up to maintain altitude, and his main rotor hit Woody's tail boom. Woody immediately realized they were in trouble and called, 'Richard, you've killed us.'" Both men were overcome with emotion as Nick continued, "They talked all the way down, but nobody remembers what they said. Richard lost his main rotor blade, and he hit the ground first. Woody lost tail rotor control and spiraled all the way down. Sandy must have been thrown, because they found him about five hundred yards from the impact area. The recovery team said he'd crawled about a hundred feet before he died."

Mac tentatively held out a pair of gloves as tears streamed down his face. "Sandy loaned me these two days before I went to Quan Loi."

Nick didn't have an answer; he just repeated, "It was just a stupid accident."

When Mac looked up, Dixon was also wiping his eyes and asked, "Boss, what are we going to do about those stack bearings?"

Trying to shake off the mood, Nick reasoned, "If that's the only thing keeping it on deadline, you could fly down to Hotel 3 and see the quartermaster colonel, and maybe he'll give your request a higher priority. He's a real asshole to work with, but if you need it, you need it."

Mac turned to leave and then stopped. "Thanks. Nick, you take care of yourself," he said.

"You do the same."

On the flight back to Bear Cat, Mac instructed Dixon, "If you fill out the requisition form for the bearings, we'll fly on down and see that colonel."

Later, they landed at Hotel 3 and got directions to the colonel's office. Mac couldn't believe his eyes when they entered. It looked like a general's office back in the States; he even had a secretary sitting out front. Dixon whispered, "We look like tramps. Do you think he'll let us in? Remember what Nick said? He's a real A-hole."

"All we can do is try," Mac replied. When they approached Colonel Douglas, he just waved back a salute. "What can I do for you?"

"Sir, I'm the maintenance officer from Bravo Company, 229th. I have an aircraft dead lined for stack bearings. I was told you had to sign off on the requisition to order it at 0-3 priority."

He looked down at the paperwork they handed him. "Is that all that's needed? Have you cannibalized any parts on 4-7-4?"

"No, sir; when we get the stack bearings, it will come out of PE."

The colonel quickly signed the back of the requisition card. "You should get them in a couple of days," he said. "Tell the men in the field we're here to help. Captain Mac, Mr. Dixon, thank you for letting me assist you."

As they walked back to the aircraft, Dixon punched Mac's arm. "That guy couldn't have been any nicer. Nick must have really pissed him off!"

"I bet he cannibalized some parts," Mac said. "What do you want to bet?"

Later, he told the team to expect the bearings and to make part runs twice a day until they arrived. Gabby raised his hand, "We have another aircraft that's gone down with stack bearings."

Mac grimaced. "Well, work off all the gigs on it, and when we only need the bearings, I'll go see Douglas again."

Three days later the stack bearings arrived. Mac's enthusiasm increased, as he had dodged another hangar queen. His mood affected the entire team; however, it was short-lived. Around fourteen hundred hours, six aircraft returned from an insertion mission, with three of them shot up from enemy fire. Fortunately, only one crew member had been hurt, but his right trigger finger had been shot off at the second joint. Two of the three aircraft had just taken hits in the sheet metal, and Pappy suggested using hundred-mile-an-hour tape (army green duct tape) until the scheduled maintenance, when the sheet metal guys from the DS detachment could take the time to do it right. Pappy finished by saying, "4-7-4 is down for the count. The engine took a lot of damage, and Sergeant Hall said it's too bad to be fixed and will need a new one."

Mac shook his head in frustration. "We just got it out of PE. That's going to screw with our maintenance flow chart."

For the next couple of weeks, Mac felt he was on a downward spiral. Every time he got one flying, he'd lose two more the next day. His daily operations list only had fourteen aircraft, and for the first time since his arrival there, he didn't have any in reserve. What was worse was that he was being forced to fly two birds that would require major maintenance when they reached their one-hundred-hour mark. To add to his problems, when he needed them to fly only a few hours a day, most were logging eight to ten hours. He only shared his concerns with Dixon and Rock, as they feared talking about it would make their nightmare come true.

Sitting in maintenance, wallowing in self-pity, he looked up when Barney entered and said, "The old man wants all of his RLOs in his office ASAP."

Mac continued to just sit there, looking puzzled, "RLOs?"

"Yeah, real live officers, no warrants. Do you live under a rock or something?"

When everyone entered Major Reese's office, he had them close the door, so he couldn't be overheard. "Gentlemen, I hate to have to have a meeting like this, but unfortunately it's been brought to my attention that we have a drug problem." His words couldn't have shocked the group any more than if he'd announced they had a spy among them. He took advantage of their silence and explained, "It seems the Thai Army has four whorehouses within five hundred feet of our troops. I can live with that, but evidently drugs are easier to find there than women. We've got a problem with both marijuana and heroin. I've got you here for two reasons: first, to let you know we have the problem, and second, to let you know I'm going to do something about it and need your support."

Captain Wright spoke up, "Sir, just how bad is it? We didn't seem to have a problem at Quan Loi."

"There, the troops didn't have easy access like here. If you walk around the enlisted hootches at night, like I have, you can smell marijuana around almost every single one of them. I'm afraid they'll move on to heroin next. We can't have our troops high when they're flying. I am installing a chain-link fence around the Bravo and Delta Company areas." They all looked at each other in amazement and left.

As soon as they got back, Mac approached Rock and Papa-San and asked them to walk with him and Barney out to the revetment area. Once there was no risk of being overheard, he asked, "Major Reese says we have a drug problem. Are our guys using?"

Papa-San didn't hesitate. "No doubt in my mind there's a problem in the flight platoon, but I'm not sure about our guys. There are two of them I've had my eye on."

Mac nodded, "The commander is taking steps to stop it, and I want to help, so let me know what you find out. I'm going to increase the number of times I just happen to drop by their hootch, and I suggest you both do the same. We have an awesome team, and drugs could destroy everything we've accomplished if we let them."

Barney suggested, "Let's take turns, so they know we're constantly checking on them."

As he and Barney walked back to the company area, Mac said, "Stack bearings grounding all my aircraft, and now drugs. What's next?"

Barney laughed. "Don't ask—you might not like the answer."

The commander's intensity on the drug problem quickly brought things to a head. Just after dark one evening, Mac strolled over toward the enlisted men's hootch, and when he came around the sandbag bunkers between them, he came across four men beating up one man. As they stumbled toward the light, he could make out it was Captain Wright, the flight platoon leader. It was apparent the four men had underestimated him, because by the time Mac got close enough to help, Wright already had two of them on the ground. Mac couldn't believe it; Wright actually seemed to be enjoying himself, but he eagerly joined in anyway. After taking a few well-placed blows, he helped Wright move all four to the company commander's office. "Thanks, Mac. These four didn't think I had any business taking their drugs away."

Since there wasn't a place to hold them, Major Reese locked them in a CONEX container the first sergeant used for storage. The next morning, right at morning formation, three MPs arrived in a three-quarter-ton truck. Everyone could see them as they got out and opened the container. One stood about six foot six inches tall and weighed about two hundred sixty pounds. He held the door open and turned and asked Captain Wright, "Which of these was the ring leader?"

Wright pointed to SP5 Andrei. The entire crowd's eyes widened with respect as the MP reached in, grabbed him by his shirt collar and belt, and hefted him across the top of the truck into the bed. Before he could turn back around, the remaining three dove into the back of the truck. No one said a word as they watched the truck go out of sight on its way to Long Bien jail.

When Rock got to the maintenance area, he looked at Mac, "Nice shiner you've got there, sir. You do know we've got to give the flight crew two new crew chiefs to replace the ones you and Captain Wright sent off to LBJ."

Mac rubbed his eye. "Just doing my part to control the drug problem. What about the other two?"

"They were door gunners. The grunts will have to replace them. Bottom line is, there are four users gone."

After the meeting, Barney teased, "Guess you got your answer as to what could happen next."

"I've got another question for you. What in the hell does our hootch maid put on our flight suits? It stinks to high heaven. The Nomex I put on this morning smells worse than the one I took off last night."

"That wonderful aroma is rice starch. It does two things: first, it lets you know she actually washed it, and second, it keeps the mosquitoes away."

"Leave it to you to find a silver lining," Mac said. "Barney, I think you and my mother must have gone to the same personality school. Like you, she always looks for the best in people."

"Hmm, I'm not sure I want to be compared to a woman."

"Yeah, but she's a strong one. Let me tell you a story about her. When my younger brother was a baby, mother had all of his diapers hung on a line to dry. A big dog from the area decided it was his mission in life to jump up and pull them off the line and then rip them to shreds. Mother threw rocks at him, trying to run him off, and he turned on her and ran her back into the house. You know what she did then?"

"No, but I'm guessing you're going to tell me."

"She went in the house, loaded Daddy's shotgun, came back outside, and when he came at her again, she shot him. When Daddy came home from work, she told him the dog was under the clothesline and needed to be buried."

Barney couldn't believe it. "What did your daddy do?"

"He buried the dog, what do you think?"

"Yep, sounds like she's a strong woman."

Now that Mac had begun telling stories on his family, he couldn't stop. "One day, a few days later, she got a call telling her one of her neighbors had been approved to adopt a baby. That neighbor didn't have a phone, and Daddy had our only car at work. Mother was so excited for them, she just put on her jacket, told us kids to behave, and took off walking. It was more than a couple of miles on an old dirt road, but that didn't slow her down. She was determined to let the neighbor know, and so she did."

Barney laughed. "I'm beginning to like being compared to your mother."

"I could tell you stories about her all day long."

"What about your daddy?"

"Daddy didn't respect his own father, and for as long as I can remember, he tried in vain to be absolutely nothing like him. Daddy was always quick to say no or see the negative in anything. Mother and Daddy were a match made in heaven. He was raised on a farm and was forced to learn how to build or repair just about anything. He expected the same thing from me, but Daddy did things at his own pace. Mother was the only person who could ever motivate him to do the stuff around the house that only he could do; and believe me, he got worse as he got older."

"Which one of them do you take after the most?"

"I'd like to think both of them."

"Sounds like you had a good set of parents," Barney said.

"Yeah, I think so. They were stern, but they were loving."

CHAPTER 17

For the next ten days, it was all Mac and his crew could do to squeeze out fourteen aircraft a day. He feared his system was fragile and like a house of cards and it was just a matter of time until it would collapse. At breakfast he looked across the table at Barney and commented, "My daddy would have said this slump is all Colonel Baxter's fault."

Barney chuckled. "Okay I'm beginning to agree, your daddy is a pessimist. How on earth is it Baxter's fault?"

"Daddy always said, 'As soon as you start bragging on someone, that's when they let you down.' Colonel Baxter was bragging on Rock and me, and now we're going to let him down."

"It won't be because we haven't tried," Rock said, in an effort to make him feel better.

"I know, but that doesn't take away the hurt when you do fail."

Trying to cheer him up, Barney argued, "Well, we haven't failed yet. Let's just take it a day at a time."

"We have been; this makes the thirteenth day."

"Well, that's good then, we have it made. Haven't you heard? That's our lucky number!"

Everyone laughed, and Mac stood and said, "Well, that settles that. Let's go hear some of Barney's good news."

The meetings had become pretty depressing of late, as everyone sat with their heads down, praying not to be called upon for any explanations.

Mac started with, "Okay, let's start with the status of 6-8-5. When will it be ready for a test flight?"

Pappy glanced over at Rock, who just shrugged as if to say, "Is he kidding?"

When no one spoke up, Mac began to get a little pissed. "Gibbs, isn't your team doing the PE?"

Gibbs just looked at Pappy for support, who said, "Sir, you signed off on 6-8-5 last night."

Mac just stood there, speechless and confused, for a full minute before asking, "What time last night?"

"Sometime after midnight." Gibbs handed Mac the logbook, and there was the signature.

Mac looked up with a sheepish grin. "And which one of you woke me up last night?"

Barney howled with laughter. "I thought I did, but after this, I think we'd better get out there and do another preflight."

Mac said, "I agree. Does anyone else have a surprise for me this morning?"

A sergeant he didn't recognize walked up toward him and announced, "Sir, here are two sets of stack bearings."

Speechless, Mac just sat there with his mouth open, embarrassed because he didn't recognize the man, who wasn't wearing a name tag. Mac stammered, "I'm sorry. Do you work here—and where on earth did you get those bearings?"

"I'm Staff Sergeant Sheppard, and I just got in-country. I'm your new maintenance supply sergeant. I noticed you always needed these things, so I figured I should get some for our PLL."

"How did you get them without Colonel Douglas's signature?"

"I just ordered four sets on a 13 priority. They go through another route, without so many people being involved."

Mac was so excited, he almost grabbed the guy and kissed him. "Can you get more?"

"Sure, how many do you want?"

"Let's go with five sets. You're a godsend, Sergeant, ah…"

Rock stepped in to prevent his boss from being embarrassed yet again, before it became obvious he'd already forgotten the name. "Sergeant Sheppard's nickname is Buddha, sir."

Mac smiled. "Well, Buddha, welcome to our family."

For the rest of the morning, Mac walked on air. Just before noon, Ensley came running toward him, calling out, "Sir, the commander wants you and Captain Wright in the orderly room ASAP."

Mac took off at a fast pace, and when he arrived, the first thing he saw was the huge MP who had taken the prisoners to jail. The MP yelled out an order that Mac didn't quite understand, but he watched the prisoners stand in the back of the truck, form a line, jump down and march into the commander's office. He could hardly believe it was the same men who had left almost two weeks ago. They had all lost weight and had empty eyes as they stared coldly ahead. When the commander gave them at ease, all four went to a parade rest that would have made a West Point Plebe proud. Their rigid positions reminded Mac of mannequins in a department store window. That big old MP had put a steel rod up their butts. When Major Reese saw Mac, he asked, "Which of these men hit you?"

Mac could only identify the one who had hit him in the eye. When the same question was asked of Captain Wright, Mac realized the rumor that he had been a Georgia State Patrolman must be true. Wright pulled out a little green notebook and recited the details of the incident in exact order. When he finished, Reese just smiled and said, "I couldn't have said it better myself. I'm recommending all four of you for court martial." He looked up at the huge MP and winked. "They're all yours, Sarge. Get them out of my sight."

Following the MP's instructions, the four double-timed it to the truck. Major Reese said, "I bet it'll be a long time before they forget about picking on my two little captains. Guys, I'll let you know when we need you for the court martial."

Later, Papa-San and Sergeant Hall approached Mac and said, "Captain Mac, we've been talking, and with the exception of three, all of our aircraft are weak."

"Define weak."

"When loaded, they won't pull fifty pounds of torque. In fact, some of them start to bleed off RPM at about forty-seven pounds. Sergeant Hall would like to pull the engines when they come in for PE, open them up, and clean the inside."

"I thought running pecan shells through the engine while it was running is the way we cleaned them."

"That's the procedure for company-level maintenance, but we're direct support maintenance. Pecan shells are just a temporary fix, anyway."

"Sounds good, but won't that add to the time it takes to do a PE?"

Barney had slipped in while they had been talking and suggested, "It wouldn't if we had an extra engine. They could trade it out when the aircraft first came in."

Hall loved that idea. "With an extra, my guys could change one out in about two hours."

Mac still needed reassurance. "Are you sure you can do it in two hours?"

"It's really easy, sir. It's just a few connections," Hall said with confidence.

Looking at Barney, Mac asked, "Okay, where do we get an extra engine?"

"If you don't mind parting with some of those stack bearings, I bet you could use them to make some awesome trades," Barney said slyly.

"Who should we call first?"

"Thought you'd never ask." Barney pulled out a list he just happened to have in his pocket and went on, "You probably don't even know half of our AMOC class is here in Nam. We should start with Captain Don Gray at Phu Loi."

Picking up the field telephone, Mac rang the switchboard and asked for a line to Phu Loi, and once he got it, he asked to be connected with Gray. He looked up at the group and smiled. "Hell, boys, this might actually work."

Once Gray was on the line and they'd caught up, Mac said, "Barney and I are with B Company, 229th. We are in need of a Huey engine. Can you help me?"

Hesitant, Gray asked, "Yeah, I've got one, but what have you got to trade?"

"Stack bearings."

Gray couldn't believe his ears, "Did you say stack bearings? Tail rotor stack bearings?"

"I did; how many do you need?"

"Two sets. For three sets, I'll even deliver the engine."

"You're not on your way yet?" Mac teased.

"You really have three sets? You're not pulling my leg, are you?"

Mac said, "Well, I don't lie, so we'll expect that engine soon."

When they hung up, he confirmed to Sergeant Hall that he'd gotten the extra engine. Papa-San and Hall left the shed and went straight to one of their five CONEXs, opened it, and began to set up an engine shop under a large tarp. Barney looked over and said, "Thanks, Mac. You've just made us a critical part of your team. My guys thought this experiment was a waste of time, but now they're going to get to do what they do best—fix engines."

"They couldn't fix them before?"

"Nah, all they'd done before was prepared them to send back to the States or the Corpus Christi Bay repair ship."

"Barney, you never cease to amaze me. Sometimes you and Dixon can be so deep. I'll be glad when he gets back from R&R. I miss that little pain in the butt."

"Yeah, he's like a little brother I never had. He grows on you."

Over the next few days Mac watched with satisfaction as Sergeant Hall fulfilled his promise of changing engines in two hours. The grapevine had spread the news across the maintenance sections in Nam that he had stack bearings. Officers who hadn't even spoken to him in AMOC were calling him up trying to make a deal. The best thing offered was a new transmission for just one set of them. The funniest was when a Huey came flying in with a tail boom sticking out of both sides of the cargo compartment, wanting to trade. Buddha had solved Bravo Company's parts problem.

CHAPTER 18

Dixon came back from R&R a happy man. He'd asked Joyce to marry him, and she had said yes. Over the next few days, he would tell his story to anyone he could corner to listen. Unfortunately, Barney and Mac were a captive audience; and after one of their sessions, Barney turned to Mac and complained, "You know, he was cocky before, but he's been really hard to live with now. He acts like he's the only person who's ever been in love."

"Give him a break, he's just a kid. Haven't you ever been in love before?"

"You know he works for you; why don't you just tell him to shut up?"

"He's a friend, just like you. I just can't understand why all my friends seem so sarcastic."

"You just have no idea what an easy target you are."

A couple of days later, Dixon approached Mac and Rock and teased, "Boy, you two won't miss this maintenance meeting for anything, will you?"

Confused, Mac said, "We have these meeting every single morning; what on earth are you talking about?"

"I thought you'd have been there to send Palmer off this morning. He went to the 90th replacement center, and tomorrow he'll be on the freedom bird to Fort Rucker to honor those guys with his presence. I really can't believe you missed the opportunity to say good riddance."

"Dixon, I just don't think we keep you busy enough."

It was Barney's turn to do test flights, so Mac and Dixon met in the bar. Mac sipped his beer while he looked over the improvements. Someone had installed lights around the wall about twelve feet apart. Each was a cluster of three candles with small white bulbs. They didn't put off much light, but they went a long way toward adding some ambiance to a bar in the middle of Vietnam. The small stage that had been constructed out of ammunition boxes was impressive. It was raised about a foot high, and the tops, which served as the floor, still had the lettering visible. That seemed okay, because with all the red clay their boots would track in, it wouldn't take long for the letters to disappear. Mac smiled when he looked up and noticed all of the camouflage print parachutes hanging from the ceiling. They were the one thing that was characteristic of every bar he'd been in since he arrived in Vietnam. Obviously, each facility just decided to mirror the bar at the 90th replacement unit that everyone visited when they arrived in-country. Behind the bar they had added a large mirror, and he could only imagine what they'd had to trade for that prize. All kinds of liquor bottles were stacked around it, and if people didn't know better, they could think they were in any bar in the world. Mac looked up as a group of Smiling Tigers pilots came bursting through the door in extremely high spirits. In fact, most of them were having a little trouble navigating. They all lived up to the drunk's creed—when you're drunk, everyone else is deaf, so speak as loudly as you can. He didn't know what they were celebrating, but was surprised their commander was in the middle of the group. The more they drank, the louder they got. Suddenly, an argument broke out over who was buying the next round. Then someone issued a challenge—the person who could shoot out the candle lights with their .38 would be the one to buy. That was bad enough, but all at once they produced a couple of .45s. After a few minutes of wild shots and ducking, Mac decided it was time for him to check the enlisted men's hootch.

He used the shortcut behind the mess hall. As he moved out into the light, he noticed three men approaching, one on each side of what appeared to be a severely inebriated man. He wondered how one of the Cobra pilots had gotten over there. Spying him, the drunk in the middle stood up straight and yelled out, "There's one of them now!" Without saying another word, he pushed forward and hit Mac with a vicious uppercut just below his cheekbone. The sucker punch caught Mac completely off guard. He thought he'd been hit by lightning because of the bright lights and stars he saw. By the time he figured out what had happened, the other two had grabbed the drunk and gotten him under control. Mac just took deep breaths, trying not only to stay conscious but to calm down. One of the men rushed to explain, "Sir, he just got a dear john letter. She ran away and married a warrant officer just out of flight school."

Still dazed, Mac explained, "But…I'm not a warrant officer."

"You're a pilot, sir, and that's all he saw. Are you going to put him in LBJ like the other guys?"

"I don't know yet. Put him to bed, and have him and his platoon sergeant report to me in maintenance at ten-hundred in the morning." He stumbled back to the bar for some ice and then went straight to bed.

The next morning at breakfast, Barney just sat there and looked at Mac's battered face. "You know, this is becoming a habit. What happened this time? And more importantly, what on earth would your daddy have to say in this case?"

"That's easy, I've heard it before," Mac replied. "My daddy is a simple farmer with simple solutions. He'd say, 'You should watch where you're going, boy.'"

"There doesn't seem to be much pity with your old man. I assume he always speaks his mind."

"Seemed like it to me."

"I'm guessing the guy that hit you is in the CONEX container, right?"

"Nah, he and his sergeant are coming to see me after the meeting this morning. I'll decide what to do with him then."

He looked around and changed the subject. "What are all these Vietnamese guys doing to the mess hall?"

"They're replacing the screening and patching the roof," Rock explained. "The mess sergeant said there are five of them and to expect them to be here for a couple of weeks. Do you need any work done on your hootch?"

"Nah, Mai keeps it shipshape in spite of Barney. Let's go to work."

When SP4 Porter and his platoon sergeant reported, the sergeant just stood to the side and let Porter do all the talking. His body language conveyed he knew he was in a heap of trouble. "Sir, I don't know what came over me. All I can say is that I'm really sorry."

Mac just glared at him sternly. "Did it make you feel better to hit me?"

"No, sir, not really."

"Do you have plans to hit any other pilots?"

"No, sir!"

"Then let me ask you this. Do you think I should send you to LBJ for a while so you can learn a lesson?"

"I've learned my lesson, sir."

"Specialist, when do you DEROS?"

"July, sir."

"That's the same month as me. Do you think until then you could try to be the type of soldier your parents would be proud of?"

"I know I can," Porter said, as he gulped for air. "You're not going to put me in a CONEX container?"

"Not yet, but I will be watching you." Mac looked over at the sergeant and warned, "If he even throws trash in the company area, you let me know."

The sergeant quickly agreed, so Mac said, "Okay, Porter. I'm holding you to your word. Go back to work."

CHAPTER 19

Just after noon, Mac wandered over to see Dancing Bear, the nickname for the new operations officer. Instead of going back by the roadway, he decided to take a shortcut through the Thai housing area. Just as he passed one of the prostitute quarters, he saw an American soldier pop out. Obviously a member of Bravo or Delta Companies, he was standing in an area that was off limits to Americans. As the soldier tried to duck around the corner of the building, Mac called out, "Soldier, stop where you are and come here."

He froze in his tracks and ducked his head in shame. He knew he was busted. Mac looked at his name tag and recognized Weaver as being one of Barney's men. "Where are you supposed to be?"

"Papa-San sent me to the orderly room to pick up some paperwork."

"Did he tell you to stop by a Thai fun house on the way?" Mac asked. "Do you know this area is off limits?"

"Yes, sir."

"Yes, Papa-San said you could stop, or yes, you know it's off limits?"

"I know it's off limits, sir."

"How long have you been a SP4?"

He stood straighter and braced. "Four months, sir."

"Don't you like being one?"

"Yes sir, I do."

"Well, tell me what I should do with you."

"Sir, if you'll let me go, I promise I won't do it again."

Mac stared him down. "Have you picked up Papa-San's paperwork yet?"

"No."

"Well, if I were you, I'd run all the way to the orderly room and back. If you make it there before me, we'll keep it just between us." He watched the soldier take off at a run and smiled, knowing he had no plans to return to maintenance area for at least an hour. He reasoned the punishment fit the crime.

He continued on to operations and pulled Dancing Bear aside to discuss his problem. "Can you tell me how much longer you plan to schedule these longer missions? Our aircraft are coming into their hundred-hour inspections every twenty-five days. I'm not sure how we're going to keep up."

"Mac, I don't have an answer for you," was the reply. "I just take the missions from the S3 and farm them out to the flight platoon."

"Would you mind checking with them to see what they say?"

"I'll do it, but I can't promise you any answers."

On his way back to the maintenance area, Mac noticed the chain-link fence installation was in progress. The workers had started on the east side of the company area and were moving toward the western limits. The major must really have some connections to make it happen so fast.

Pappy approached him when he returned and said, "Sir, 7-8-1 is ready for a test flight."

Mac said, "Good, I'll get my helmet. Where's the crew chief?"

"Waiting at the aircraft."

They did a thorough preflight inspection. Mac moved around to the side to check the engine deck for leaks. He pushed the cargo door forward and pressed down the step door and peeked inside. Everything looked okay, so he released the step door and pushed the cargo door back against its stop. He did his normal thirty-minute hover check and then departed toward the semi-safe territory of Saigon. The last thing he always did in a test flight was to cut the engine and go into an auto rotation. This was the final check to make sure if the engine quit, the rotor blades would maintain their speed, so a pilot could still safely land. As always, he gave the crew chief an opportunity to fly some in 7-8-1, one of the best birds he had. The chief turned toward a small village, but he was more interested in sightseeing than flying, so Mac took back the controls. This gave the chief an opportunity to look at the picturesque village below. The aircraft was flying so smoothly, Mac was reminded of his first solo flight, and he began to just enjoy the freedom of being in the air. He turned toward the river leading to Saigon. The crew chief kept pointing out the sights below, but Mac was in another world, just enjoying the feel of the controls. For a short period of time, he forgot everything—he didn't worry about how they'd meet their daily quotas or that he was in a war zone. For over an hour, he just let instinct take over, like he had in Hawaii, and soared like an eagle over the landscape below. He hadn't felt this joy of flying since arriving in Nam. When the twenty-minute fuel light came on, he was jerked back to reality.

He landed, refueled, and began the post flight inspection. When he reached the engine deck, he popped the step door down and peeked inside. There didn't appear to be any leaks, but he had a nagging suspicion something was off. Slowly he scanned the engine and deck one more time, and when he didn't find anything, he stood back from the aircraft and just looked it over, wondering what was wrong. Then he saw it: the cargo door was missing. Immediately he panicked. What on earth if it had fallen on the village? The force of that door falling from two thousand feet would decimate whatever was below, especially one of those grass houses. He yelled, "Chief, untie the rotor blade! We've got to go back. We lost one of the cargo doors, and we've got to go find it."

Mac flew the same route he'd taken before, praying he wouldn't find it in the village. He could only imagine the headlines: *Careless maintenance officer destroys a peaceful Vietnamese home. Investigation pending.*

When he reached the location where he had done the auto-rotation, he turned toward the village. The chief yelled, "There it is! See it lying in the top of those trees?"

It stuck out like a neon sign, facing up in the center of a small rubber plantation. He sighed with relief when he realized it was at least five hundred feet from the village. "I see it, but there's no way we can get it. Doesn't looks like it did any damage, so let's go home."

After filling out the logbook for 7-8-1, he went back to the shed and placed the tag number at the bottom of the flow chart. He sat down in his chair and just stared at the group of aircraft clustered at the top of the chart. He mumbled to himself, "How on earth are we going to keep up?"

Rock had come in behind him and overheard. "You know it's a bad sign when you start talking to yourself."

Barney countered, "Nah, it's only bad when you start answering yourself. What's eating you, big guy?"

"The way I figure it, the aircraft come into PE about every twenty-eight days. It takes them three to four days to complete one. Right now we're making it, but if any aircraft goes down for a maintenance problem, we won't make good on our fourteen-a-day promise."

Barney said, "Mac, I understand worrying is what gives you grey hair."

"I'll quit worrying if you give me a solution," Mac retorted.

"That's easy. Do PEs faster."

Disgusted, Mac asked, "And just how do we do that?"

"Give them an incentive. Remember the two cases of beer?"

"I need a long-term solution. Beer might work for a short project, but we're looking at a minimum of two months."

As always, Rock was the voice of reason. "Why don't we just ask them?"

All of the PE teams stayed after the morning meeting the next day. "Guys, we have a problem that is going to hit you more than anyone else. Operations is flying more aircraft and for longer periods. That means you'll see it back in here sooner. How do we fix that? I don't want you guys to work harder, just smarter. Any ideas?"

The men looked around at each other and remained silent. After a pregnant pause, Mac said, "Right now it takes three to four days to complete a PE. Is there any way we can speed that up?"

Ensley suggested, "A case of beer seems to work."

Mac laughed. "I know you're looking for free beer, but I can't afford it for the next two months. What's another idea good enough to motivate you guys to make it happen in two days?"

Ensley came back with, "How about a trip to Hotel 3?"

Everyone yelled, "Yeah, that's it!"

Mac just looked confused. "What's at Hotel 3?"

Ensley quipped back, "What's *not* there? They have a fantastic PX, and it's in Saigon. They've got everything."

"Tell you what, if you can do a PE in less than forty-eight hours, after the test flight, I'll put the whole team on that aircraft and take you there for a couple of hours. What do you think?"

The leaders looked at each other and agreed to the deal.

"Good; the forty-eight hours will start when the TI finishes the initial inspection. We'll see how it goes."

That evening Dixon volunteered to take the test flight, so Mac and Barney went to the bar. Mac pointed at a sign and noted, "Looks like the commander has taken away the kids' toys."

Barney read out loud, "No weapons of any kind in the bar, by order of the Alpha and Bravo Commanders." He looked confused, "Wonder what brought that on?"

Mac remembered Barney had been in maintenance the evening of the event, so he just shook his head and said, "You wouldn't believe me if I told you. The Smiling Tigers were using the light fixtures on the wall for target practice."

"That's not good."

"It's obvious the commanders agree."

CHAPTER 20

Their eyes had just adjusted to the dark bar, when Mac thought he recognized someone sitting at the other end. He stood and walked over, "Kawania, is that you? When'd you get here?"

"Couple of weeks ago; how about you?"

"Almost four months. You with Bravo Company?"

"Nah, Delta. I'm flying a LOH with a scout platoon. Are you still in maintenance?"

"I'm Bravo Company's maintenance officer. Barney, come over here and meet Tom Kawania. He was a crew chief in my company in Hawaii. He left last year for flight school."

Barney greeted him, "Looks like you made it through."

The rest of the night, they talked about flying OH-23Gs. Kawania explained, "After you guys taught me how to fly on that old aircraft, flight school was a breeze. I soloed in ten hours."

Barney complained, "It took me almost thirty hours before I did it."

Mac asked, "Didn't you have about a hundred hours in that old 23?"

Kawania nodded. "Probably."

The rest of the night was fun for Mac; seeing Kawania was just like visiting with family.

Rock came rushing up at oh-four-hundred the next morning, exclaiming, "You won't believe what I just saw! There's a pilot asleep in the backseat of that Cobra." He pointed toward the last revetment located near the maintenance tent. "He's got his helmet hanging above his head."

"After that target practice they had in the bar the other night, nothing they do would surprise me now," Mac replied.

They all laughed about it at breakfast, and Papa-San came in and announced, "Major Reese wants everyone at the morning formation."

Mac asked, "Officers too?"

"I don't think so; the first sergeant just wanted all the NCOs and enlisted men there."

Barney and Mac decided to head over to see what was so important. After the company had been called to attention, Reese came out of the orderly room. He placed three Coke cans to the right on the bunker, walked to the center, and saluted the first sergeant, who moved to the rear of the formation. "At ease, listen up. I understand some of you don't like my fence. Well, I had it put in for your welfare. It's only there to keep out the drug dealers, but that's not why I wanted you here. I heard that some guys have threatened to frag me." Pulling out his .45 pistol, he turned to the Coke cans. He fired three times, and each can exploded. "This is a warning. If I hear any noise around my hootch at night, I'll shoot first and check later. Company dismissed." Then he returned to the orderly room.

Barney looked at Mac with concern. "You do realize we live right next door to him, don't you?"

"Well, guess you'd better do something about your snoring," Mac replied. They both laughed and headed to the morning maintenance meeting.

Pappy came in, holding the clipboard, "Captain Mac, here's the first PE in the forty-eight-hour challenge."

"Which team gets it?" Mac asked.

"Sawyer's."

"Did Ensley have anything to do with this?"

Pappy shrugged. "Maybe just a little."

"Pappy, I didn't think you'd take a bribe."

"Sir, you know I wouldn't do that," Pappy protested. "Ensley had the rest of his team work straight through on 4-9-2 so they could get this one."

"You know, I'm thinking he might make a good team leader one day."

Rock overheard. "He's on our list, if he doesn't become a crew chief."

"He'd be a good one. Oh well, let's see if they get it done on time."

Mac took his list to Dancing Bear later that evening and asked, "How's it looking? Are the missions slowing down?"

"Just the opposite. Charlie Company is still snake-bit. One of their maintenance officers crashed one of the aircraft at the fueling point and killed one of the mechanics onboard."

Worried that it might be Nick, Mac asked, "Do you know the pilot's name?"

Bear picked up a piece of paper and said, "CW2 McIntyre. Know him?"

"Not really, but I've met him. He took me on the scariest test flight I ever had. Looks like that boldness finally caught up with him."

Captain Miller walked in. "Thought I heard you, Mac. I've got something for you."

Mac followed Miller to the orderly room. Miller opened one of the drawers in his desk and pulled out a small box. "Here's the award Fitzgerald wanted you to get. You want it presented in front of the company, or do you just want to take it?"

"Just give it to me. What is it?"

Miller opened the box and smiled as he looked up. "A bronze star. Captain Fitzgerald kept saying you and Sergeant Williams saved his butt. Here's the write up. Thanks, Mac."

Caught totally off guard, Mac stammered, "Uh, thanks. How about the one for Williams?"

"He's got one, too, but I'm saving that one for the next awards ceremony."

"That's good. I like that. He really deserves it."

He and Rock were waiting for the next aircraft to leave the next morning, when he noticed there were lights on in the maintenance tent. Curious, he walked over to see if they'd been left on overnight by accident. When he came around the side and started inside, he couldn't believe what he was seeing. Sawyer and his entire team were crawling all over 3-4-0. Rock whispered, "Do you still think they won't make it?"

Mac put his finger to his lips. "Shhh, let's go." They backed quietly out of the tent without the team seeing them. On the way to breakfast, Mac suggested, "Why don't you tell Tom and his team they don't need to attend the meeting?"

"Sir, are you getting soft?" Rock asked, incredulously.

"No way, I just don't want to waste their time."

At the meeting Pappy released 4-7-4 for a test flight. Mac volunteered. When he asked about the crew chief, he was told he was busy with another mission. Mac looked around and said, "Okay, Gibbs. You get the honor of flying the left seat."

Mac began his preflight. He turned the screws to release the tail rotor drive shaft cover, flipped the cover back to look at the drive shaft, and saw something he couldn't believe. Someone had left a knife next to the number two hanger bearing. He held it up and barked, "Gibbs, who does this belong to?"

"I don't know, but I'll find out." Gibbs hollered for the team to report. While they were at attention, he said, "While we're on the flight, I want you to inventory your toolboxes. Have them ready for inspection when I get back."

Mac liked how Gibbs had taken charge; and as a reward, after the test flight, he let him fly until the twenty-minute fuel light came on. When they landed, he instructed, "Gibbs, I'll do the post flight. You go see how the inventory went."

Before he finished, Gibbs escorted one of his team to the aircraft. "SP4 Weaver is missing his knife from his toolbox, sir."

Weaver just stood there expecting trouble. Mac stared him down and said, "Weaver, I thought we had an agreement. If I didn't say anything about your other mistake, you wouldn't let anything happen again."

Gibbs grinned. "Sir, that's a promise I don't think he should ever have made to you."

"Why is that?"

"Sir, Weaver's nickname is Murphy."

Mac couldn't help but laugh. "Like Murphy's law?"

"You got it. If it can go wrong, it'll go wrong with Weaver."

"Weaver, I know you're smart, or you wouldn't be a 67N. You understand that by leaving your knife where it was, you could have gotten us killed?"

"Yes, sir. I'm really sorry." Weaver just ducked his head.

"I'm not sure what to do about you."

Gibbs asked, "Can I make a suggestion, sir? Make him leave his toolbox in the CONEX container and only take out the tools he needs to work. He can give me his inventory sheet every night."

"Weaver, can you manage that?"

"Yes, sir, I promise."

Mac shook his head. "Murphy, huh?"

Gibbs laughed. "That's it sir."

As Gibbs turned to walk away, Mac said, "A deal's a deal. You guys get ready to go to Saigon at thirteen hundred hours. I just need to find a copilot."

"We'll be here, sir." Gibbs said with a smile.

Mac walked to operations. "Bear, how would you like to fly to Saigon? I need a copilot."

Bear was caught off guard; the request was special and meant a lot to him. Like Mac, he had a position that often forced him to tell pilots news they didn't want to hear, so he was seldom asked to socialize or interact with them. Not about to give Mac a chance to change his mind, he jumped up and said, "Let me go get my helmet and put on my Nomax. When are we leaving?"

"Thirteen hundred hours. I'll wait, and we'll walk down together."

When they walked up to the revetment, Gibbs jumped out and untied the main rotor. As Mac climbed in, he did a silent headcount. Realizing someone was missing, he looked at Gibbs. "Who's not here?"

Gibbs quickly said, "Oh that would be Evans. He doesn't want to go."

Murphy chimed in, "He hates to fly."

Mac shook his head incredulously. "An aircraft mechanic who hates to fly? What's wrong with this picture? Okay, then, climb aboard, and let's go."

All the time he was in Saigon, Mac thought about Evans. There had to be more to the story. He decided Pappy was the one who could clear up the mystery. He was the one NCO who'd been here long before he and Rock had arrived.

When they returned and sat the aircraft down in the revetment, Gibbs and his men jumped out and headed toward maintenance. Once they were out of earshot, Bear thanked Mac again for allowing him to ride along.

Mac looked over at him. "Bear, you did me a favor. It wasn't the other way around. If you thank me one more time, I'm going to be pissed off."

"Okay, I hear you. I had fun today and wanted to let you know."

"Bear, I believe they must need you in operations."

Bear laughed. "Okay, you've made your point."

Mac quickly began to search for Pappy and found him on the flight line, checking out a bird. He quickly looked around to ensure it was just the two of them before saying, "Pappy, I need your help."

"How's that, sir?"

"I need information. Why is Evans afraid to fly?"

Pappy climbed down and moved closer, "Almost ten months ago, he was a crew chief on a bird that got shot up. The pilot and gunner were killed, and the co-pilot had to be Medevaced back to the states. When they found Evans, he was unconscious. He woke up on the flight back to Quan Loi and went crazy. It was all they could do to keep him from jumping out. He's never gotten on a helicopter since. It's a real shame, too, because he's one of the best mechanics and crew chiefs in the company."

"One more question. Why is he so afraid of me? At first I thought it was my imagination, but now I realize he's purposely keeping his distance. What's up with that?"

"I don't think it's you, sir, but that you're the maintenance officer. Captain Chase constantly made fun of him for not flying. He kept calling him a sissy or a little girl. It was embarrassing for the rest of us to hear, but we couldn't say anything without being disrespectful."

Mac laughed at that one. "Pappy, you can't believe how many captains have been put in their place by a strong NCO."

Curious, Pappy asked, "How is that?"

"Well, you start by saying: with all due respect, sir, you're an asshole, sir."

Pappy laughed. "Well, with all due respect, sir, Captain Chase was a real asshole, sir."

Mac asked, "Do you feel better now? The truth will set you free. Thanks, Pappy, I just needed to know the back story. I will never embarrass him."

The next morning was exceptionally hot. There was absolutely no wind, which made it almost unbearable. Mac felt sorry for Tom's team, because they were working on an aircraft in the revetment with no cover. He could only imagine how miserable they were. He walked up and suggested, "I'm buying if someone will fly and get us some cold drinks."

SP4 Whitehorse quickly volunteered, "Sir, I'll fly. What do you want?"

"Cokes or anything cold. No beer, though."

"Roger that." He left at a dead run.

Mac just shook his head. "I can't believe he's running, as hot as it is."

Tom said, "He's a full-blooded Indian. That boy loves to run."

When Whitehorse returned and passed out the cold drinks, Mac asked, "What's an Indian doing over here? I didn't think they drafted you guys."

"I volunteered. My father is a chief in the Cherokee tribe, and I'd like to be one someday. But before a warrior can become a chief, he must prove himself in battle. I couldn't let this war pass me by."

"Wouldn't you be better off as a grunt?"

"That was my plan, but when I took the test to enlist, my recruiter told me the test scores told him I'd be perfect as a helicopter crew chief. So here I am."

Jonesy teased, "Sir, maybe he'll tell you the secret of the Indian rain dance."

Noticing the teasing had embarrassed Whitehouse, Mac reasoned, "If he told us, then it wouldn't be a secret anymore."

Whitehorse grinned. "Maybe someday."

The team finished and went back to work. Mac had enjoyed the afternoon and quickly decided he needed to do more to learn about his men's backgrounds. Their stories seemed a lot more interesting than those of a farm boy from North Georgia.

Later that week, Mac decided to spend some time with the men in Barney's maintenance detachment. He finally found Papa-San and the team behind the row of Conex containers. One had been offloaded behind the rest of them, so it had been overlooked. When they cut the lock, they discovered a complete machine shop. It was like Christmas all over again for Papa-San, and he was thrilled. He began to talk incessantly about all the projects they could do now. The enlisted men enjoyed watching his delight and excitement. They'd never seen him so animated. Mac decided to just stand back out of the way and let them have their moment.

When Papa-San looked up and saw him, he immediately launched into all the things they could do with the new equipment. Mac just shook his head and let him talk.

One of the team members called out, "This calls for a celebration. Sir, I'll fly if you'll buy."

The phrase sounded familiar, and Mac realized somebody had blabbed to the entire team about his buying Cokes earlier. He grinned. "Okay, but just Cokes, no beer."

"Roger that, sir."

Mac looked the man in the face and was caught off guard when he realized the soldier didn't have any teeth. He looked at his name tag; it read Morgan. When the man returned and passed out the Cokes, he handed Mac back his change. Mac thanked him and asked where he was from. Morgan grinned from ear-to-ear and said, "West-by-God Virginia!"

"That's up in Yankee land, isn't it?" Mac teased. "Now, tell me, is it true that Yankees eat their own kids?"

Morgan didn't hesitate. "Only the runt, sir."

Everyone laughed, and Mac was pleased. They were letting him into their world without even realizing it. Even though he was their captain, today he was just their friend. For the next few hours, they opened up and told each other their stories. At first they were all about Morgan, but he soon came back with his own stories about each of them. Mac watched as they bonded and simply enjoyed each other's company in the middle of a war zone.

CHAPTER 21

Days later, Mac was in high spirits. The PE teams had put out five aircraft in the allotted forty-eight-hour targeted time period. Once again he was able to tell operations which aircraft they had. It felt good not to be at the mercy of the mission gods on which aircraft flew and how long.

Dancing Bear was talking to Captain Wright when Mac entered operations with a skip in his step. Looking up, Wright said, "Well, if it isn't my old fighting buddy. You're just the man I wanted to see. I've got a couple of pilots on R&R, and I need a man for the right seat. How about you fly a mission with me tomorrow? It should be a fun day. We'll be flying a bunch of mountain yard."

Mac rubbed his chin for a second. "I've heard about them, but haven't ever seen them. You've got your copilot. What time do we leave?"

"It's a late one, and we won't leave until oh-eight-hundred."

Turning to Dancing Bear, Mac asked, "Which aircraft?"

The bear smiled. "How about 4-7-4? It's just out of PE."

As they departed Bear Cat, Mac asked, "Can you tell me more about the Yards?"

"I love working with them. You don't have to worry that one of them might turn on you, like you do when you're hauling the Vietnamese. *Montagnard* is a French word that means *mountain people*. *Yard* is the American slang for the French term. Wait until you see them. They don't look anything like Orientals. I guess you could say they look and sound

135

more Polynesian. Most of them don't even speak Vietnamese. They are the locals; the Vietnamese are actually the new kids on the block. It's like they're our Native Americans, and the white men came in and took over. Trust me, there's no love lost between them. When the Special Forces approached the Yards about fighting the Vietnamese, they jumped at the chance. The only real problem is keeping them focused on just shooting VC. To the Yards, the only good Vietnamese are dead Vietnamese."

When they landed in a small field next to a village, Mac immediately noticed a big difference in the appearance of these people versus the Vietnamese. They seemed happier and quicker to laugh. None of the men had pants, and it reminded him of what Wright had said about the Indians. He felt like he'd gone through a time warp. Some of the older men were carrying crossbows. A Special Forces sergeant came forward to meet them as they shut down the aircraft. The mission was to fly replacements to Yards who had been guarding some of the bridges in the area. There were multiple locations requiring several sorties, so it was going to be a long day. As a group gathered to climb onto the aircraft, Mac was reminded of a high school baseball team, waiting to board a bus. They didn't look like soldiers. They moved as a mob, and there didn't appear to be anyone in charge. The first sign that they were a unit was when one of the older ones yelled something in a language Mac didn't understand. The younger ones immediately gave him their complete attention. He'd always thought the Vietnamese soldiers were small, but the Yards looked like adolescents. He felt kind of sad that men so small were being asked to defend their country. Mac looked at the sergeant and said quietly, "They look so young and innocent."

The sergeant smiled. "They may look like that, but I'd take this one platoon over an entire battalion of Vietnamese any day. If I were a betting man, I'd say these guys have taken out more than fifty VC with no casualties."

Mac was surprised. "They're that good?"

"Better. They've been hunters all their lives. These mountains and jungles are their home. They can move through them just like cats and make the VC look like city boys in this environment."

As the Yards climbed in, Mac watched in disbelief when he saw how many were able to cram onboard. It was double the amount of American soldiers the aircraft could transport. Wright turned to Mac and instructed, "Take the controls. I've got to check something out first." He swiftly climbed into the back with the Yards and began to check their web gear. It took him a few minutes to make the adjustments, and then he climbed back into the left seat.

Mac couldn't help himself; he was curious and had to ask, "What on earth was that all about?"

"Trust me, it was for our own protection. Anytime you fly the Yards or Vietnamese soldiers, always check their weapons—especially the grenades. Some of them aren't strong enough to pull the pins, so what they do is tie the lever down and get someone else to pull the pin out for them. All we'd need is for one of those grenades to slip loose while that guy is onboard, and we'd be toast. I always carry extra pins with me on every mission I fly. I only found two of them this time, but one would be all it would take."

Mac couldn't believe what he was hearing. "You know, if you don't watch out over here, you could get hurt."

"Yeah, it's the little things you've got to watch out for." As Wright pulled pitch, he was pleased at the power the aircraft had. "What did your boys do to this bird? I can't ever remember it being so powerful."

Mac smiled at the compliment. "We've got an engine shop now. They guarantee you can pull fifty pounds of torque on every one of our birds."

"Can I tell my pilots that?"

"Sure; they need to know how good our maintenance team is."

After a short flight, Wright shot an approach to a dirt road fifty yards short of a wooden bridge. Mac looked around and didn't see anyone. He began to wonder if they were in the wrong location, but as soon as the skids hit the ground, Yards appeared out of the jungle. A Special Forces sergeant came forward and directed the replacements to their new assignment. Watching them swap positions, Mac felt like they still didn't look like they were in the middle of a war. They were all so relaxed; it was like they were switching positions in a baseball game.

It was a much longer day than Mac had expected, as they fueled for the fourth time. Dark slipped up on them. It was Mac's turn to fly when Wright instructed, "Let's go home. Climb to four thousand feet, so Charlie can't take a shot at us."

They'd been flying about twenty minutes when Mac noticed what looked like fireworks ahead. He asked Wright, "What's that?"

Excited, Wright replied, "It looks a mad minute. God, isn't it great to be a pilot and see stuff like this?"

Mac agreed. "Look how the machine gun tracers form two perfect capital W's with their overlaying fire. What're those little balls of fire in between them?"

"My guess would be M-79 rounds exploding. I bet Charlie is down there in his spider hole, laughing at the Americans wasting all of that ammunition."

"Are you saying the VC actually caused this? I remember hearing mad minutes at Quan Loi, but I didn't know how beautiful they were from up here."

"Yeah, they're the one time the perimeter guys get to fire all of their weapons. The only thing they'll find out there will probably be a dead pig, but it sure does relieve the boredom for the guards."

Then the area went dark. Wright said, "Looks like the fireworks are over. Wish I'd had my camera. The people back home wouldn't believe how beautiful it is."

"You're right. They'll never know how wonderful it is to be in a helicopter flying above all that action," Mac agreed.

Not much was said the remainder of the way home. As they walked from the airfield to operations, Mac thought about how different it must be to just fly and not have to worry about keeping the bird maintained and in the air. When they got close to the new fence, they noticed a four-by-five-foot, white sign. Mac asked, "What language is that? I don't understand what it says."

Wright said, "I think it's Thai. The bottom line is English and says *American personnel only*. Guess Reese is still trying to stop the dealers. Hope he succeeds. I've got a couple of door gunners that always smell like burning leaves."

"I thought you got rid of them when you sent the others to LBJ."

"Mostly, but I still worry about a few."

When the debriefing was completed at operations, Wright asked, "How about another mission tomorrow, Mac?"

"Let me check on how the day went with my guys. If I can't make it, I'll cut Barney or Dixon loose. Either way, I promise you'll get a copilot from maintenance."

"That's cool; I prefer Barney if you can. Dixon is too short. He has less than thirty days until he DEROSes."

Mac laughed. "Are you telling me you're superstitious?"

"Nah, but I don't believe in pushing my luck, either."

After eating, Mac went back to maintenance. He wasn't surprised to discover everything was running as efficiently as a Swiss watch. Dixon was completing his post flight on an aircraft just out of PE. Mac asked, "How'd it go?"

"Great! I can't get over how much more power they have now. I guess we'd just gotten use to their being so weak. Sir, do you think we could get Captain Miller to get Sergeant Hall and his men some recognition?"

"Dixon, that's a hell of an idea. I'll get on it tomorrow. By the way, what's scheduled for tomorrow?"

"I've got to fly Tom and his team to Hotel 3 in the morning, and we should have another one ready for a test flight late tomorrow."

"Where's Barney?"

"Bar, I'd guess. I saw him heading that way when I took off in this one."

"Okay, I'll see you in the morning." Mac headed to the bar to let Barney know about the mission with Wright.

The next morning, the mess sergeant came out to talk as they were eating breakfast. His enthusiasm was contagious as he exclaimed, "Did you hear all the action in the perimeter night before last?"

Rock couldn't help himself; he just had to poke fun at Mac. "I know someone who probably didn't. Last fall, a M122 rocket destroyed the latrine fifty feet from his hootch, and he slept through it just like a baby."

"I can't help it that I like noise when I sleep," Mac explained.

The mess sergeant couldn't wait to continue his story. "But you haven't heard the best part! There was a ground attack, and some of the VC were caught in the concertina wire. Yesterday when I got back from my ration run at Long Bein, their bodies were laid out. I recognized them right away—they were four of the men who'd been fixing the screen in the mess hall. The fifth one didn't show up for work the next day."

The information sobered them all, and Rock tentatively asked, "Have you checked the mess hall for booby traps?"

"Yeah, the first sergeant had the MPs bring in the dogs and do a search, but they didn't find anything."

Papa-San asked, "Think there are more of them?"

"Heaven only knows. I can tell you this, though; I'm not letting any Vietnamese near here until I DEROS."

Rock just nodded his agreement. "I like the way you think."

CHAPTER 22

Everything fell in place over the next couple of weeks. The mission loads were still heavy, but enemy activity had been low. There was speculation that they were preparing for another Tet offensive, like the one in January 1968. Tet, which means the first morning of the first day of the New Year, is the Vietnamese New Year. The celebration typically lasts for seven days; and like the Chinese custom, the Lunar New Year is one of their most celebrated holidays. Preparation for Tet starts weeks before the actual day. Families even paint their houses to give it a new look, and everyone gets new clothes and shoes. The Vietnamese people are very careful about what they do on that day, as they believe the events on that day determine their luck for the coming year. That was the reasoning behind the Tet offensive in 1968. On the thirtieth of the month, six provincial capitals and many US bases came under attack. Later it was learned that this had been a mistake, due to the use of different calendars by the NLF (National Liberation Front, or Viet Cong) and the PAVN (People's Army of Vietnam). The next night, on 31 of January, 1968, the real blow was dealt as hundreds of targets were attacked throughout South Vietnam. NLF fighters attacked key points in Saigon and even invaded the US Embassy.

The current fear was that the calendar problem would have been resolved for the coming Tet, and many more targets might be hit. Bravo Company missions were in support of the impending battle. It was Barney's turn to fly as co-pilot on the day's mission. As he and Dixon walked toward the maintenance area, Mac asked, "How does it feel to be so short?"

"I'm a little scared, but excited knowing I'll be home soon."

"When's the wedding?"

"We decided just before Christmas next year would be perfect, so we can spend it as a married couple."

Mac teased, "How romantic."

"Not me, it's her idea."

"You scared?" Mac asked.

"Not really."

"That's good. I believe if a person is nervous about getting married, it's their subconscious telling them *don't do it*."

"That why you're not married?"

Mac smiled. "Maybe."

"Are you afraid of anything else—or I guess a better question would be, what's your biggest fear?"

"You know, on the plane coming over here, a young private asked me if I was afraid. I told him no, and that if he'd just do his job, he'd be okay. My biggest fear is that I won't be able to do mine. I get a sick feeling in my stomach every time we get down to just fourteen flyable birds. I'm so scared I'll let the battalion commander down. I gave him my word."

Dixon burst out laughing, "So that's why you get as nervous as a cat in a room full of rocking chairs sometimes?"

"Okay, now I'm not sure why I was dumb enough to tell you about that."

"Could it be because I'm leaving in two weeks? Want me to say hello to Palmer for you? I'll be in Rucker by January."

Mac shot him a wicked grin. "Nah, just casually mention how we flew all eighteen birds from Quan Loi to here. You can also remind him he was the maintenance officer of a company that only had one flyable bird."

Dixon chuckled. "Captain Mac, you do have an evil side, don't you?"

When Rock and Papa-San came in for the meeting, they passed out little cloth bags the size of a lunch sack. Puzzled, Mac held his up. "What's this?"

Rock explained, "Christmas is next week, and these are gift bags sent to the soldiers by churches back home. The Red Cross delivered them yesterday, and the first sergeant said everybody gets one—even officers."

Mac untied the pull cord at the top and peeked inside. Everyone else began to do the same. It was like Christmas morning. But when he saw what was inside, he felt guilty that it hadn't been passed on to a grunt out in the field. He knew he was depriving them of a gift that would mean much more to them. The bag contained a toothbrush, tooth paste, toilet paper, paper and pen, chewing gum, Tootsie rolls, a Butterfinger bar, and a Christmas card. He squirmed in shame, because items such as these were easily accessible at the PX located within five hundred yards of where he currently sat. The men in the field would really appreciate these goodies. He closed the bag and handed it back to Rock, saying, "This bag was meant for guys in the bush, not me."

Even hard-hearted Rock's eyes teared up, and he stood there for a moment, thinking. "Mine too, sir. Think you could drop them off on your next mission?"

"I can do that." Before he even looked up, his desk was covered in Christmas bags. He asked, "Guys, are you sure?"

Ensley answered, "It's our gift to the real fighting men."

"Okay, on one condition. Each of you take a bag back, eat one of the candy bars, copy down the name and address on the card, and send them a note thanking them and telling them how much you enjoyed it. Everybody agree?"

No one said a thing. They just retrieved a bag and did as instructed. After the meeting, everyone found a quiet place and scratched out a note to a new friend. Mac realized it had been one of the best days of his life.

That evening, when he took the list to Dancing Bear, he was excited about the pillowcase full of Christmas gifts he had to surprise the grunts with. He was disappointed that Wright wasn't there and asked, "Bear, who's with Wright tomorrow?"

"I think he was planning on you. Need me to find a replacement?"

"Absolutely not. What's his mission?"

"He hasn't broken them down yet, because he's running late. He should be here in a while."

Mac paced back and forth. He was excited about playing Santa Claus and didn't want to fly some VIP or ash and trash mission. Tomorrow his goal was to surprise twenty-five men with bags. When Wright finally came in, Mac explained what he wanted to do, and Wright said, "Bear, I'll take the mission to Nancy." He smiled and turned to Mac. "Guess you owe me a drink."

"Fair enough."

Mac ate breakfast before heading to the airfield. He felt almost giddy, knowing what he had planned. Because he beat Wright to the aircraft, he handled the preflight. Wright walked up and said, "Looks like we've got company today." He sat on the deck of the aircraft and began to rub Hobo's head, "Nice boy. You want to fly with us, huh? Welcome aboard."

Mac remembered Dixon had told him Hobo always chose which flight to take, and obviously, today it was theirs. He'd never admit it, but having Hobo onboard made him feel safer. When they landed on the short airstrip at the base of the hill where Firebase Nancy was located, two buck sergeants ran to the helicopter. They were all grins until they saw Captain Wright get out of the left seat. The taller of the two asked, "Where's Mr. Dant? He said he'd be here today."

"He's on an insertion mission. I'll tell him you said hi."

They turned and slowly walked back up the hill. Mac asked, "What was all that about?"

"I think I know, but I'll need some more proof."

Mac shook his head. "You never make any sense at all. I'm going to find the first sergeant." He picked up his pillowcase and headed off. After getting directions, he finally found him heating some coffee. He handed him the case and said, "Top Sergeant, here are some gift bags from a church in Missouri. I figure you'll know who needs them the most."

"I sure do. Some of the boys here have never been away from home on Christmas. You know, sir, you're the first skinny Santa Claus I've ever seen."

Mac smiled. "Skinny or not, it feels good."

Rock and Papa-San couldn't wait to hear all about it at breakfast the next morning. Mac could see how disappointed they were when they heard he hadn't been able to hand them out personally. Rock sounded dejected when he said, "It was the right thing to do."

He hadn't realized how much they had anticipated hearing about their simple act of kindness. Every single day, he learned being a soldier was like being part of an extended family. They really did strive to take care of each other.

The sound of a helicopter landing in the middle of the company area interrupted their meal. The rotor wash sent dust and dirt rushing into the mess hall, making the mess sergeant cuss about how inconsiderate the pilot was, and how they all felt they were God's gift to the army and the United States of America. It was obvious he knew the pilot couldn't hear him, but the ones present surely could, and maybe they'd get the message and be more careful the next time they landed. The ranting and raving stopped abruptly when they heard someone call out, "That's the 1st Cav's commanding general's aircraft."

Everyone rushed forward to see what was happening. When they saw him exit the aircraft, they stopped just outside the door. None of them wanted to draw the attention of a general. Lieutenant Colonel Baxter, the battalion commander, got off the aircraft, and Mac whispered to Rock, "Something must be really wrong." A major followed him off the aircraft, and Rock asked, "Do you recognize him?"

"Never seen him before."

All of a sudden, Major Reese and the first sergeant came running out of the orderly room. Before he could report, the CG picked up an empty Coke can next to a bunker and said, "Major Reese, you can't even keep your company area policed. There's trash everywhere. You're relieved of your command." Then he turned to the unknown major and announced, "Major West, you're the new Bravo Company Commander. Get this area cleaned up, and get that sign on the fence removed and destroyed." He turned to the company first sergeant and said, "Pack up Major Reese's personal gear and have it sent to battalion headquarters. Major Reese, get on the aircraft."

Reese didn't say a word. He just climbed aboard. After Lieutenant Colonel Baxter and the CG climbed aboard, they came to a hover and departed. Everyone just stood there with their mouths hanging open. They couldn't believe what had just happened. Mac was the first to speak, "Guys, let's get back to maintenance, where we belong."

That night in the bar everyone was talking about it. Wright hadn't been present, so he was really curious about the incident. Mac just repeated what the general had said when he picked up the empty Coke can. "It must have been something about that sign, because the CG told the new commander to get it down and destroy it."

Tex was sitting at the bar, listening to the conversation. "Don't you know what it said?"

Mac shook his head. "How could we? It was written in Thai."

"It said, 'Thieves, murderers or any lowlifes can come on base except for the Thais.' I'm betting that sign pissed off the Thai general."

Mac asked, "Why would the major put up a sign like that?"

"I'm guessing that's not what he thought the sign said. It looks like he asked the wrong person to do the job."

"Tex, why didn't you tell Reese what it really said?"

"I thought that was the message he wanted to send. Especially after the .45 rounds he put in the Coke cans that morning."

Wright raised an eyebrow. "Let's hope Major West is a little more subtle in his approach."

Mac held up his glass, clicked it against Wright's and said, "Amen to that."

Only two missions had been scheduled for Christmas Day. Wright invited Mac to play poker on Christmas Eve. He hadn't played in years, so he jumped at the opportunity. Poker was only second to chess in his mind. Seeing Major West shuffling the cards for the game was a surprise. He looked up in welcome as Mac entered. "Come on in, maintenance man; we need some new money. Draw poker is the name of the game, no limit and a dollar ante."

It was a fun night, and everyone was in high spirits, trading jabs and stories. It turned out to be a profitable night for Mac. When he counted his winnings at the end of the evening, he'd made eighty-seven dollars. Major West laughed and said, "Most of that money is mine—I mean, was mine. Damn, I see you play poker as well as you fix aircraft. Boys, next game is in my hootch Friday night."

Wright turned to Mac and said, "Treat you to a night cap?"

"Okay, but make mine just a 7-Up."

"Do they even have that?"

"Just came in today. They only got five cases, though, so I'm hoping some are left. You know being over here makes you appreciate the little things you took for granted, like fresh bread. Can you tell me how bread can smell so good in the mess hall and taste two weeks old, just two hours later? When I get home, I'm buying two loaves of fresh bread, a jar of peanut butter, 7-Up, Vodka, and music that isn't the Carpenters."

"What's wrong with the Carpenters?"

"Nothing the first hundred times I heard them. But apparently, Barney can't sleep without playing their song. I was tickled when he first got here with his tape recorder, because I need noise at night in order to sleep. I'm afraid to complain, because he might just shut it off."

Wright laughed and agreed, "Yep, war is hell."

The next couple of poker games went well for Mac. His winnings were smaller, but the camaraderie was much higher. Major West was always telling stories about his adventures as a company commander. They couldn't believe some of the things soldiers would do or say in order to get sent back home earlier. The best story of the night was about a SP4 climbing on the roof of his hootch, yelling that he was going to jump to his death. After three hours, West had lost his patience and advised him to go ahead and jump, because he had more important stuff to do. The soldier's bluff had been called, so he slid down to the lowest point of the roof and jumped. He landed in a ditch and messed up his ankle. The medics carried him to the orderly room first, where West gave him an Article Fifteen for destruction of government property. He reduced his rank to PFC and restricted him to the barracks or his work area. Wright couldn't stop laughing. "What did he say?"

Major West just grinned. "Thank you, sir."

Wright howled. "What a man will do to get attention."

Major West just said, "Now you sound like my wife."

The morning of Dixon's departure finally arrived. Instead of taking a jeep ride, Mac had arranged to fly him to the 90th replacement. The gesture wasn't wasted on Dixon, and he protested, "Only VIPs get a ride on the helicopter."

Mac could see Dixon was emotional at the sign of respect. "Who said you're getting a ride? You're flying the darn thing. I expect everybody to pull their weight until they leave."

"But I'm in khakis."

"I won't tell if you don't. Look who's your crew chief. Rock is on one side, and Ensley is in the other gun well."

Dixon took advantage of the surprise, and for the next two hours, they toured South Vietnam. For once, they were flying for the pure joy of it. When it was time to let him off, Mac didn't even shut down the engine. Not a word was said as Dixon unstrapped, and Rock moved up and took his seat. Dixon grabbed his duffle bag, bent over, and ran out a safe distance from the rotor blades. Like most military men, he never said goodbye; he just gave a till-we-meet-at-our-next-assignment wave.

CHAPTER 23

Mac was staying so busy, keeping helicopters in the air and playing poker at night, that time began to fly. It was already the second week in January, and the fear of the Tet offensive continued to grow. While picking up his distribution in the orderly room, Mac noticed a long envelope with his name on it, so he opened it and found the most recent copy of his OER. He'd heard that when someone was relieved of command for cause, the next man in the chain of command had to write the OERs for the men. The man who was fired was not allowed to evaluate the men beneath him, to prevent him from maliciously destroying careers. With Reese gone, the task went to Lieutenant Colonel Baxter and Colonel Roberts. Baxter had been true to his word; not only did he give Mac a maximum on his OER, he rated him first among all the captains he supervised. Mac read the report with pure joy, and his first thought was, *Wait until daddy sees this!* Then reality set in; if he could get his father to read it, he knew just what he'd say—*boy, looks like you're bragging.* That was if his father even understood what it really meant to his career. He decided to write a simple letter, telling his parents that things were going great and that he loved them.

After eating, Mac walked back to maintenance. Gibbs' team was working hard to get 3-2-7 out of PE. While he waited, Mac pulled out some paper and began writing the letter home. Just after twenty-one hundred hours, Gibbs came in to get him. "Sir, 3-2-7 is ready, and we still have four hours left," he announced.

"Forty-four hours for a PE—almost a record."

Gibbs beamed with pride as Mac suggested he take his men and get something to eat. "Thanks, sir. You sure you don't want me to ride in the left seat?"

"Not tonight. You deserve a break."

After Mac did his preflight and hover check, he called the tower, "Bear Cat tower, this is Killer Spade maintenance for test flight."

"Killer Spade, you're clear. You're the only one up tonight."

"Bear tower, roger that."

Mac departed Bear Cat, climbed to two thousand feet, and headed southeast toward Vung Tau. He loved flying at night; the air was so smooth, it was like driving a brand-new car on freshly laid asphalt. Tonight it felt like he had wings of his own. He climbed to four thousand feet, rolled the throttle off, lowered the collective, and began his auto rotation to some-place in the dark below him. He checked the rotor needle, and it was right where it should be, so he smiled in satisfaction. He rolled the power back on and pulled enough pitch to climb to three thousand feet. The test flight was complete; now he could fly just for fun.

"Killer Spade Maintenance, this is Bear Cat Tower. Where are you?"

"I'm about ten clicks south of you."

"This is Bear Cat Tower. Be advised there will be an arc light at your location at twenty-two hundred hours. Recommend you get out of there."

"Roger that."

Mac immediately made a steep right turn, picking up a heading of three hundred degrees northeast. Looking at the little clock in the console, he saw he only had three minutes to get out of the way. He began to pull more power and push the nose of the aircraft over so he'd pick up speed, but it was liked being trapped in a nightmare. There was total darkness, so he couldn't perceive any movement by the aircraft. It was like a dream when you were desperately trying to run from something and seemed to be going nowhere. According to the airspeed indicator, he was moving, but his mind kept telling him it wasn't true. He began talking to himself to calm down. His thoughts quickly went back to his settling with power at Quan Loi.

There, he had just known he was going to crash, and no one would have even known why. Here, at least, Bear Cat Tower would know why he'd been lost. He began to imagine what the notice to his parents would say:

Dear Mr. and Mrs. McKay,

Your son, Johnny, tried to fly his helicopter through an arc light, a B52 strike. They drop at least eighty-four 500-pound bombs and four 750-pound bombs. Each bomb creates a crater thirty feet wide and fifteen feet deep, leaving an area of 1100 X 2200 yards devastated; it will blasts a furrow through twenty-story-tall trees for a mile and a half. Needless to say, there's nothing left of your boy or the aircraft. Was he always this foolish? Sorry for your loss.

Mac decided to quit thinking and focus on the clock. He was flying well above a hundred and ten knots, and time was almost up. As the second hand swept past twelve, a flash of light, similar to the sun coming up, appeared just to his rear. He mumbled, "Leave it to the Air Force to be on time." The smooth, calm night air was gone with a strong force like he'd never felt before. Cold sweat popped out on his forehead, and he wondered if this was it. Then, as if in a dream, he saw the lights of Bear Cat Tower. "Bear Cat Tower, this is Killer Spade Maintenance. Requesting clearance to land in maintenance area."

"Killer Spade, you're clear."

He breathed a sigh of relief and replied, "Roger that. Bear Cat Tower, when you're old and your grandchildren ask you what you did in the war, you tell them you saved a dumb maintenance pilot's life."

"Killer Spade, this is Tower. Can I quote you on that?"

"Roger that. As Gomer Pyle would say, *thank you, thank you, thank you.*"

Mac spoke to Gibbs after the morning meeting the following day. "Are you guys ready to ride to Hotel 3?"

Gibbs looked embarrassed. "Sir, if it's okay with you, we're skipping this trip. We spent all of our money last week. Most of us need to wait until payday."

"That's fine with me. Just wanted to live up to my side of the challenge."

"We know that. You know, it's fun competing with the other teams."

Barney teased, "And I was so looking forward to spending the day in Saigon."

Mac looked at him. "Well, if you're feeling generous and willing to pay their way, we can still go."

"Nope, don't want to go that bad."

Later when Mac took the list to operations, he asked, "Bear, did you know they were going to put in an arc light last night southeast of here?"

"Nah, that's the Australians' area of operations. I guess they requested one in preparation for the Tet threat. But boy, you ought to see what one of those things does. It cleans a path a half-mile wide and a mile long. How did you hear about it?"

"Oh, some guy told me about it last night."

"On your next test flight, you should check out what it did to the countryside."

"I'm not really that interested."

Bear looked over and said, "Well, I do have some info you might be interested in. They gave Major Reese another company command—with the 101st. I guess the big show of the CG relieving him was for the benefit of the Thai general."

Mac nodded and agreed, "Yeah, probably so. He had to do something."

The next morning, as he and Rock did their normal oh-four-hundred watch, Mac noticed Hobo. He patted him a couple of times, but Hobo was on a mission to find which aircraft he was gracing with a ride that day. They just watched and wondered which he'd choose. Rock looked over and said, "We have a new problem. Today makes the third aircraft this week Mr. Bennett has grounded. If you ask me, he's just afraid to fly."

Mac asked, "Were they good calls on dead lining the aircraft?"

"Not really; he wrote things like connecting rod worn out of tolerance. How can he tell that by shaking the connecting rod?" Rock seemed disgusted. "When the TI checked them, they were loose, but well within the limits. He's just looking for a reason not to fly."

"I guess maybe all this talk about the Tet thing is getting to everybody."

"Not everybody. Just a few of the weak ones; however, fixing that problem is well above my pay grade," Rock said, then ducked his head. He knew just how to get Mac steamed up enough to solve the problem. He continued slyly, "But I'll tell you what, something needs to be done quickly. His games have dropped us down to just fourteen birds."

That evening, Mac pulled Wright aside. "I need to talk to you about Bennett," he said. "I think he's losing his nerve. He's grounding my aircraft for bullshit reasons—anything to keep from flying. Is he short?"

"Nah, he's got at least five more months," Wright said, puzzled.

"Well, do you think all this talk about the Tet thing is getting to him?"

"Could just be his real character is just coming out."

"Well, whatever. Something's got to be done, because he's destroying my scheduled maintenance plan. Every time he grounds one on a whim, I have to pull a mechanic and TI off of a scheduled bird. Do you think I should talk to Major West?"

"I would; if maintenance fails, so does his command."

When Mac talked to the major, he was surprised at the response. "Mac, they're just little kids, playing war games. It's not real at first, then all of a sudden they figure out what war really is about. Most of them adjust, but a small few never do. They don't want to play anymore but don't know how to make it stop. You and I know they don't have that option. It's our job to keep them on the straight and narrow. I'm telling you; don't take any crap from any of the weak ones. If you need my help, just let me know, and thanks for keeping me in the loop."

Three mornings later, Rock walked up, laughing. "That pilot is sleeping in his Cobra again."

"Yeah, a strong drunk front came through the bar for the Smiling Tiger pilots last night," Mac replied.

Rock shook his head. "Pilots are a strange breed."

Pretending to be offended, Mac said, "Hey! I resent that remark."

"Sir, you're not a pilot, you're a maintenance officer."

"Well, glad you cleared that up for me."

A short time later, Rock got Mac's attention. "Sir, you're not going to like hearing this, but Bennett wants to ground 7-8-1. He says the magnetic compass is out of tolerance."

"Bullshit! No one uses them anyway. That's what a RMI is for. Where is he?"

"In the last revetment."

The closer Mac got, the more pissed he got. Bennett saw him coming and defensively called out, "There's no way I can fly this aircraft with the mag compass like it is!"

That plucked Mac's last nerve. All the pent-up anger and frustration he'd held in for months boiled over. He saw a two-foot reinforcing steel bar holding the sandbags together. He pulled it out and snatched Bennett by the front of his flight suit, pulled him to the front of the aircraft, and whispered just loud enough for Bennett to hear him, "I know you're afraid to fly. You're a coward, scared you might get hurt. Well, I'm going to help you. If this aircraft doesn't crank and leave within the next ten minutes, I'm going to break so many bones, they'll have to medevac you back to the States. I'll tell everybody you fell off the top of the aircraft. They all know how methodical you are in a preflight. Besides, nobody cares what happens to a coward. Now get out of here."

In less than five minutes, 7-8-1 was airborne. Mac walked straight to operations. Bear was listening to the radio calls as each pilot left. Major West was standing in the doorway. Mac said, "Sir, 7-8-1 will be calling in soon with some maintenance problem."

West smiled in delight. "I guess I need to let him jump off the building."

Mac remembered the story at the poker game and grinned, "Destroying government property, sir?"

"Something like that."

Sure enough, several minutes later Bennett called 7-8-1 in with a fluctuating transmission temperature gauge. West picked up the mike and said, "This is Killer Spade Six. What's your location?"

Bennett gave his coordinates. West looked at the map and noticed a firebase nearby and directed him to land and wait until the Killer Spade maintenance officer came to relieve him. There was complete silence for a moment. Then Bennett came back on the air, "Looks like the problem is clearing up. Will finish mission. Out."

West came back, "Good work. Come see me when your mission is complete."

He turned to Mac and said, "That will give him something to worry about instead of being scared."

Mac laughed. "Thanks for the help, sir."

"My pleasure. Coming to the game tonight?"

"Yes, sir, I'll be there."

CHAPTER 24

There was a new face at the nightly poker game: Major Wynne, the new company XO. At first Mac liked him; however, he didn't particularly care for how he approached the game. He was very aggressive, and it messed with the usual friendly vibe. Experienced players realized quickly that he liked to buy the pot, if given the chance, so he could control the game. He would raise large amounts, and almost everyone would immediately fold. Mac didn't enjoy playing anymore, since the game had changed.

Later that evening, Mac asked Major West how his conversation with Bennett had gone. West laughed and said, "I mentioned he had a reputation as a problem identifier for aircraft, and I wanted to put his expertise to use. I suggested that because Dixon was gone, he could take his place and work for you until he DEROSes."

Startled, Mac asked, "What did he say to that?"

"After he was finally able to speak, he begged me to let him stay in the flight platoon. He insisted he'd be a much better asset flying missions. I asked if he meant finding gigs on our aircraft, and his answer to that was he would only teach the new pilots how Killer Spades fly on missions. I let him go with the threat that I would check in with you to see how he was progressing. I don't think he'll be dead lining any more aircraft."

Wright interjected, "That's a relief. We're short on pilots now, and losing him would have really hurt."

Mac reassured Wright, "Barney and I are there if you need us."

The next evening, when Mac took the list to Bear, there appeared to be a little excitement in operations. Bear explained, "A Cobra pilot was playing gun runs on a sand pan in the river between here and Saigon. Apparently he got too close to the water and let his skid hit the river. The impact flipped them end over end. It sank and killed both pilots. A unit on the shore saw the accident and reported it up the chain of command. It seemed the Smiling Tigers operations officer had reported all of their Cobras were accounted for. Our battalion S3 reported the information to division. When they pulled the Cobra out, it was a Smiling Tiger bird. Smitty and a new guy were in the aircraft. I've heard rumors Smitty had a habit of getting drunk and sleeping in his aircraft."

Mac asked, "What's going to happen?"

"It already has. The battalion commander was relieved of his command. It's sad, because he only had a couple of months left before DEROS."

The news hit Mac hard. "He was a straight-up fellow with me, but I guess that's the end of his career."

"Yeah, guess so. The Smiling Tigers commander is on pins and needles. I sure would hate to be his operations officer."

"How could he miss an aircraft?" Mac asked.

Bear shook his head. "They're trying to figure that one out now."

Getting a new battalion commander was the biggest event of Tet. There were a few skirmishes, but nothing like the one in 1968. As soon as the powers that be realized their fears were unfounded, the offensive operations in Cambodia and Laos picked up. With the return of heavy recon platoons needing insertions in the 1st Cav's AO, there was a major increase in flight missions for Bravo Company. Luckily, with the competition between PE teams, Mac and Barney's maintenance platoons maintained a constant fourteen birds a day.

Barney and Mac were getting more flight time than ever and averaged three missions a week. During the second week of February, an aircraft landed in Bravo Company's maintenance area. A major got out and introduced himself as Major Underwood from the maintenance school at Fort Eustis, Virginia. He was pleasant initially and told Mac,

"You've got quite an operation going on here. The average flight time for a UH-1 in Vietnam is eighty-five hours per month. Your company is averaging one hundred thirty hours per month per bird. I'm here to find out how you get it done."

Mac couldn't believe the school at Eustis wanted to know how his guys were keeping their birds in the air. He gave Underwood a tour through the maintenance area and let him watch several of his teams at work. When they finished, Pappy came up and released one of the aircraft for a test flight. Mac was disappointed when Underwood refused to go on the flight with him. Underwood suggested, "While you're gone, I can check your logbooks and 2404s."

When he got back, Mac found Underwood sitting at his desk, writing something in a notebook. Rock and the TIs were patiently watching. Mac handed Pappy the logbook, and Underwood looked up and said, "It's obvious to me your people are doing paper maintenance."

Mac was puzzled and asked him to clarify. Underwood replied, "Just what it sounds like—signing off write-ups without actually fixing them."

Once again, Mac lost his temper and was reminded of his altercation with Bennett. This time was different, though; the man outranked him. He paused for a moment and quietly asked, "Sir, can I see you outside?"

"We can talk in front of your men. They should be aware of what I'm writing in my report to take back to Eustis."

Mac glanced over at Rock and realized he was even more pissed than he was. Rock saw the look on Mac's face, and his experience told him the best thing to do when the captain was that mad was to clear the room. He pushed everybody outside quickly. Mac said, "Major Underwood, I cannot believe you have just insulted my entire team. You haven't learned a thing since you came here. It's clear you came here with a preconceived notion that we were doing what you call paper maintenance. If you're so smart, how do you explain how none of our aircraft have gone down due to poor maintenance, and that we have all eighteen birds that can pull fifty pounds of torque? Major, how long have you been in Vietnam?"

Caught off guard, he stammered, "Two weeks, why?"

"You may not know it, but the enlisted men over here know how to get rid of a stupid officer. They call it fragging. I really don't need to clean up a mess like that, so I would suggest that you leave and never come back."

Underwood could hear the anger in Mac's voice, and he decided not to push it. He picked up his notebook and departed in his aircraft to the north.

The major was the topic of conversation the next morning. Ensley was the most outspoken, "What kind of men does he think we are? Doesn't he realize if you just sign off gigs, you can get somebody killed? Sergeant Rock, do you know him? Was he one of your bosses back at Eustis?"

"No, I've never seen him before. I believe the problem was that he just couldn't figure out how we did it."

Mac interjected, "To tell you the truth, I'm not sure I know, either."

With that, everyone laughed and settled down. Barney was flying for the day, so Mac just wandered around, checking on each team's progress. The routine of the day was interrupted by a helicopter landing on the far side of the revetments. When it began to hover toward the maintenance area, Ensley yelled out, "That's Colonel Roberts's helicopter."

There was instant silence, and the men just looked at Mac with pity. Everyone knew you didn't tell a major to buzz off and get away with it. Mac looked at Rock and Papa-San apologetically and said, "Guys, it looks like I really screwed up this time. Working with you has been an honor and one of the best times of my life." With that, he walked to the landing aircraft and reported to the Colonel.

The pilot landed in the clearing next to the maintenance shed. Because it wasn't a normal landing site, dust, dirt, and paper flew everywhere. Colonel Roberts caught a piece of paper as it flew by him. Mac had a flashback of the general picking up an empty Coke can just before he had fired Major Reese. He gritted his teeth and prepared for the worst.

"Captain Mac, I understand you threw Major Underwood out of your maintenance area."

"No, sir, I just requested he leave after he told me we were doing paper maintenance."

Colonel Roberts gave him a huge grin and replied, "Yep, that's what I heard. I came down here just to shake your hand and tell you I wish I'd been here." He handed Mac the piece of paper he'd picked up and said, "You've got a little FOD problem here. Think you can take care of that?"

Mac smiled in return. "Right away, sir."

"You do that, and I'll make sure you're not bothered by any more stupid majors. That is what you called him, right?"

Mac blushed. "Yes, sir."

Colonel Roberts put up his right hand and made a circle with his thumb and index finger, which indicated to his pilot to crank the aircraft. As he left, the men ran out eagerly, asking, "What did he say?"

Mac held up the paper and said, "I have a FOD problem. Rock, I think we need a police call."

Rock grinned in relief. "Looks like you might still be our boss."

"Yeah, I don't think the colonel cared much for Underwood, either."

CHAPTER 25

The next morning, as they were walking toward the maintenance area, Mac and Rock heard a vehicle approaching from their rear. They automatically moved to the side to let it pass, but it stopped next to them. Ensley's voice called out playfully, "Want a ride?"

The vehicle had a four-foot-by-eight-foot platform mounted on two axles; it was an army mule. Mac asked, "Where'd you get that?"

"From the motor pool. One of the pilots slung it in from a firebase. They couldn't fix it, but Sergeant Pepper did." Ensley was grinning with pride.

Mac shook his head dubiously. "But I don't think we're authorized one."

"Sir, I think you're asking too many questions," Rock said, as he looked over at Ensley and grinned.

"Okay, I hear you." Mac just sat down on the rear of the vehicle. Because it was mounted directly to the axles and had no suspension system, the four tires were the only cushion they had. They could feel every single pothole in the area. When they finally arrived, Mac immediately hopped off, complaining, "My God, how can you stand to ride on that thing?"

Ensley ignored the question as he continued to grin. "Can we keep it, sir?"

Rock looked over at Mac and winked. Knowing he was outnumbered, Mac said, "I guess, but make sure you don't crash it—and please, try to keep Major West from spotting it."

"Roger that, sir."

Mac whispered to Rock in astonishment, "A mule in an aviation company? What will we do next?"

Rock cautioned, "Don't ask in case you don't want to know."

That made Mac really nervous, "Oh, my God, they've already done something, haven't they? Rock, I swear we're going to jail yet."

Rock laughed. "Yeah, probably, but think of all the fun we've had. Let's get to that meeting, sir."

Mac was flying as copilot with Wright the next morning. They had an early departure, and it was still dark as they came to a hover. After getting clearance from the tower, Wright said, "Let's go to the top of the rock."

Mac reminded him, "Remember, I just fix these things. I don't know anything about the landscape. What are you talking about?"

"Now, did I steer you wrong when I took you to see the Yards? Well, this is an adventure you won't forget anytime soon." Wright just grinned and departed to the west with a slow turn toward the northwest. All of a sudden, the crew chief yelled out, "We're taking fire! Can I shoot back?"

"No way! That's an orphanage down there," Wright warned. He made a steeper turn to the right and climbed to four thousand feet. "It's my fault. I shouldn't have gotten as close as I did. I know better." He flipped the radio switch to the VHF channel and called out, "Any Killer Spade aircraft, steer clear of the orphanage north of Long Thanh. There's a machine gunner down there, and he's trying his luck out today."

About five separate aircraft gave him a "Roger that."

Mac was immediately curious. "I didn't know we had a company freq on VHF."

Wright grimaced. "We don't. It's unauthorized, but someone figured out we'd never use VHF over here, so some enterprising pilot adopted the frequency 123.45 as Killer Spades special freq. They were using it long before I got here. It works great when we're flying, but not so good when we're on the ground." He made a slow circle to the left. Before Mac could ask, he said, "Let's make sure no one gets hit by that machine gun." As soon as he turned, Mac could see tracer rounds coming up toward one of the birds behind them. Wright pointed out, "He's not too good with it. Look how far his shots are behind that aircraft. How's that for a little excitement this morning?"

The crew chief immediately complained, "Yeah, well, it would have been a lot more exciting if you'd let me shoot back."

"Chief, relax—maybe next time. We were lucky today; remember, there are three solid rounds between every two tracer rounds."

When Wright turned the aircraft back to their original heading, Mac asked, "Bear said we were going to Nui Ba Den. Is that a big rock?"

"Close; it's an extinct volcano rising from the Mekong Delta. It's called the Black Virgin Mountain. Wait until you see it. It's almost a perfect cinder cone. It's located just a few kilometers from the end of the Ho Chi Minh Trail, across the Cambodian border. We'll land at the top. They built a large platform out of these huge wooden beams. The only way they get supplies is by air."

Mac was surprised. "They don't have any roads?"

"It's too steep, but that's not the real problem. The top of the mountain is under American control, and the bottom belongs to the VC. That's why we'll make a steep approach when we get there. I don't want to tempt Charlie to take a shot at us."

Mac was absolutely amazed. "You sure know how to make missions exciting. Did you work as a tour guide at Disneyland before you came into the army?"

"Would you believe I was a Georgia State Trooper?"

"That's what I heard. I guess the draft must be an equal opportunity employer after all," Mac teased.

Black Virgin Mountain, translation—Nui Ba Den (Vietnamese)

All conversation ceased as they approached the mountain. Now that he knew the VC held the bottom of the mountain, Mac craned his neck trying to see if he could see any movement. The crew chief yelled, "See that guy in the black pajamas down there?"

Mac whirled around, "Where? I don't see anything."

"See those dead trees at nine o'clock?" he pointed below.

"I can't see on that side of the aircraft," Mac complained.

Wright keyed his mike and cautioned, "If he's not shooting, don't worry about him. Chief, make sure we're clear of all those wires."

"Roger that, we're clear."

When they landed, the captain they had come to transport approached with a sergeant. He stepped on the skid and stuck his head in the pilot's window, "This guy needs a ride to the 90th replacement. Can you drop him off before you take me to Phu Loi with the classified information? He should have DEROSed two days ago. This is the first day the weather has been good enough for you guys to fly him out."

Wright grinned and replied, "Sure, we're here to serve."

While the captain was waving the sergeant onboard, Mac teased, "You left out 'protect.' Isn't that what you cops do? Serve and protect?"

Wright retorted, "You know, I could just leave your butt up here."

"If you did that, who'd have your back in your next fight?"

As they flew toward Long Bien, they listened as a pilot on the Killer Spade frequency called, "Panther, get over here. You won't believe your eyes. There's a pink elephant next to this village."

"Claxton, I told you not to drink so much."

"Honest! It's as pink as a pig."

Wright laughed. "It's like having your own radio show up here. I can't wait to see the pictures. One of those guys will have a camera on him, and what do you want to bet there'll be a lot of beers bought with those shots?"

Mac was skeptical. "So they really do have pink elephants over here?" he asked.

"Nah, they just wallow in all that red clay, and it makes them look that way. But hey, makes for a good story anyway!"

The captain yelled up, "Thanks, Sergeant Colwell thought he'd never get off that mountain. He's been in one of the bunkers for the last two days. Two years ago, this mountain was overrun, and everyone got killed. He was sweating blood during Tet. Thanks again."

When the sergeant jumped off at 90th replacement, he dropped down and kissed the ground. Everyone onboard laughed. Their next stop was for the captain to drop off his material, and then they were on to the most important part of their mission—a resupply of soft drinks and beer. The captain couldn't believe it when Wright volunteered to make a second beer run for them and asked, "Are you sure?"

Wright smiled and said, "We're here all day. Why not?"

Mac had liked Wright before, but now he had an even deeper respect for him. As promised, this was an adventure he wouldn't soon forget.

After breakfast the next morning, Ensley met Mac and Rock and offered, "Need a ride?"

Mac laughed. "No thanks, I need my kidneys too much to get on that thing again."

Ensley's toy had everyone in high spirits, but leave it to Rock to spoil the mood: "Sir, we have a damaged aircraft coming in. Operations called, and they need our help."

Mac went straight to the landline and called Bear, "What's up?"

"Mr. Johnson has ripped the skids off his aircraft and can't land. What can you do?"

"I don't know yet, but have him fly straight to maintenance, and we'll figure something out." Mac turned to Rock and asked, "Any ideas?"

Rock went to the doorway and yelled out, "Ensley, get your butt over here."

Ensley recognized the authority in the voice of his old instructor and responded accordingly, "Yes, sergeant?"

"Get the mule, take someone with you, and bring back six mattresses off your bunks. And for God's sake, hurry it up!"

Ensley did as instructed, and they stacked the mattresses three high, side by side. Everyone in maintenance stood and watched for the aircraft to come in. Someone yelled out, "Here he comes! Look! He doesn't have any skids. His underside is as slick as a baby's bottom."

Rock stepped out and began to direct the pilot to the mattresses. He had him come to a hover, and then he ran up next to him and yelled something to the pilot. The pilot nodded, and Rock immediately returned to the other side of the mattresses and guided him forward. The pilot stopped the aircraft just above them, and Rock stretched out his hands and cautiously guided him slowly down. Everything was going great until he was about a foot off the mattresses. Then it seemed the pilot couldn't get it to go down anymore. After a few anxious moments, Johnson slapped down the collective and pulled it back up just as quickly. It was an awesome move; it broke the ground effect and allowed the bird to move downward again. When he hit the mattresses, he didn't just cut the power, but kept it under control until Rock gave him the sign to cut the engine. Everyone was screaming and yelling as the rotor blades began to slow. When Johnson got out of the aircraft, Barney stepped forward and asked, "What happened?"

"We were at Firebase Sam when they started taking incoming fire. I pulled a lot of power and nosed way over so I could get out of there quickly. My skids caught the top rung of the perimeter's concertina wire. When I hit, I thought it would just pull loose, but those artillery guys really had it anchored. When it wouldn't stretch anymore, I felt a big bang, and the crew chief told me our skids were gone."

Barney asked, "What did Sergeant Rock yell at you a while ago?"

Rock blushed as Johnson answered, "He told me to pretend I was an old setting hen going to nest, and that I better not break any of the eggs or he'd kick my butt." He turned to Rock, "How'd I do, Sarge?"

"Okay for a pilot. At least you listened."

Johnson walked over to him and stuck out his hand. "Thanks, Sergeant, you saved my butt."

Speechless, Rock stood there for a moment and then began to bark out orders, "What's holding up those new skids? This aircraft is in the way. Let's get moving."

In less than an hour, Papa-San's men had a new set of skids put together, along with the bolts and brackets to put them back on the aircraft. For almost thirty minutes, they debated whether they should lift the aircraft with a wrecker or just have it hover. The answer was forced when Bear called to say the aviation safety officer from Pho Loi had heard there had been an accident and was on the way to investigate. Mac grabbed his helmet and said, "Rock, guide me. I'll hover long enough to get the skids on."

When he came to a hover, guys came from both sides. The first thing they had to do was to remove the broken bolts. They were attached in four places; three were easy to clean up, but the fourth was too damaged to fix at a hover. After about ten minutes, Mac directed them to attach the skids at three points, and they would work on the fourth one once they had the aircraft on the ground. Everyone was pleased at how smoothly it went. When the skids were attached, Mac hovered to an open revetment and sat it down. The fourth bolt was replaced in less than five minutes.

Ensley and his mule were on the way back to the company area when the safety officer arrived. A young captain got out with his clipboard in hand, looking very official. He announced, "I'm Captain Massey, the group safety officer. I'm here to check out the damaged aircraft."

Mac met him and innocently advised, "We don't have a damaged aircraft."

"I got a report from a Firebase that 4-7-4 had been hit by artillery fire."

Mac led him over to the aircraft and pointed. "Look for yourself. Does it look damaged?"

"I guess not," replied the captain. "I'm glad, because the old man has a theory. When a company has a couple of minor accidents, they always get a big one. He really rides my butt about any accident, no matter how small."

Barney joined them and said, "Well, since you're here, why not check out our bar and have a drink with us?"

When Mac picked up his mail, there was a letter from the Department of the Army. He immediately realized it would be his orders, and he wondered where he would be going next. Ripping it open, he scanned it quickly to find his new post, but it wasn't there. He sat down on a bench nearby and read the letter. It said:

Captain McKay, you have an outstanding record so far. If you should put in for a regular army commission, there is a high probability you would be selected. If you should decide to apply, please complete the attached form and return it in the enclosed envelope.
Good luck,
Captain Robert Cobb, Artillery Branch

Mac immediately filled out the form and handed the envelope to the mail clerk. He was excited but was afraid to tell anyone. His father's warning about bragging kept ringing in his ears. As he returned to the maintenance area, Rock smiled in welcome. "Hey there. We've got a bird that needs a test flight. The pilot dead-lined it last night when he came in."

"What's the problem?"

"A whole lot of little things, but the biggest one is the flight idle stop is sticking," Rock explained. "When we checked it out, we discovered it was missing a bolt. That put the button in a bind, and it wouldn't stop the throttle when the pilot rolled off the power. I personally replaced the bolt."

Mac teased, "I didn't realize a wrench would still fit in your hand."

"Whoa, wait a minute here. I taught half of these mechanics how to turn a wrench. It's like riding a bike; it comes right back to you."

"Okay, let me do the preflight. You want to fly with me?"

"Not this time. You know, this is Jonesy's aircraft. Remember he just took over as crew chief this week? Let him go."

"This should be fun. It's neat he's finally a crew chief."

Rock shook his head. "I didn't know captains said 'neat'."

"Oh, shut up and untie that rotor blade for me."

Mac couldn't believe how excited Jonesy was to be in the left seat. He came to a hover and moved out to the lane between the revetments, so he could check out the range of the cyclic control. The process was to quickly push the cyclic as far forward as possible and come back to the center before the aircraft could respond. Then the rear and each side were checked. This made sure the servos controlled the flight system. The worst thing that could happen was that they would have a hard-over, which was where the servo would expand to its maximum position and lock down. This would cause the aircraft to flip in that direction, and the only way to recover would be to turn off the hydraulic switch. When Mac explained this to Jonesy, the boy just looked at him like he'd grown a second head. Nervous and wide-eyed, Jonesy just asked, "Are you going to tell me when to turn the switch off?"

Mac said, "According to the emergency procedure, I'm supposed to say 'Turn off the hydraulic switch.' However, if we have a hard-over, by the time I say that, we'll have already crashed. So, if I grunt, scream, yell, or do anything, you just flip that switch. The worst thing that can happen is you'll turn off the hydraulics, and I can fly without them."

"Sir, I used to think you had the easy job," Jonesy gulped.

"It is if everything goes right. Are you ready?"

"I think so." Jonesy sat with a death grip on his seat.

After four sharp moves of the cyclic and the return to the center, Mac smiled and said, "Perfect." He let the aircraft settle down toward the earth, and when he was firmly on the ground, he told Jonesy, "Flip the hydraulic switch off."

Jonesy did as directed. Mac started talking out loud, "Hydraulic caution light on, feeling slight feedback in the flight controls. Jonesy, turn the switch back on. Hydraulic control light is out, controls are now normal. You can turn loose of that switch now. Let's go flying." He looked over and burst out laughing when he saw the beads of sweat on Jonesy's forehead. They flew south and then turned toward Saigon.

Jonesy asked, "Can you show me an auto-rotation? I've heard about them, but I've never seen one."

"No problem; that's usually the last thing I do on my test flights."

He flew up the river between Bear Cat and Saigon, and a while later he turned east back toward Bear Cat. He began to climb to four thousand feet. As he leveled out, he noticed an old, abandoned fire base straight ahead. He was always looking for a place to land in case of an emergency—it was second nature to him, and the firebase was just what he needed. He explained to Jonesy, "Here we go. We lower the collective, roll the throttle back to the flight idle stop, and maintain the speed and heading. Feel this? You're in auto-rotation. See how the engine and rotary RPM needles split? We need the rotor RPM needle to remain in the red arc. You see it does?" Then Mac noticed the engine RPM didn't stop at flight idle. The engine had quit. He said, "Jonesy, you're getting ready to see a real auto-rotation." With his left hand, he turned the radio to the guard frequency and said, "On guard, this is maintenance 4-7-4 going down, six kilos west of Bear Cat."

Jonesy laughed nervously, "You're just kidding me, right? We're not really going down. You're not on guard frequency."

Mac quickly looked down, and Jonesy was right; he'd missed the correct frequency. He quickly corrected his mistake and made the call again. Another aircraft called, "4-7-4, we see you and will follow you down. Good luck."

Mac responded, "Thanks, we might need it."

Jonesy finally realized it wasn't a drill. He turned as white as a sheet and began to point out places for Mac to set down. Mac realized the reason the engine quit was because the flight idle stop didn't work. He decided to try and crank it in midair as they went down. He quickly went through the startup procedure, but when he realized he was only a few hundred feet above the ground, he knew that option was out of the question. While concentrating on trying to crank it, he fell short of the abandoned fire base. He scanned for another place to land and turned toward a dirt road leading to the fire base. For the last hundred feet, he just concentrated on landing. At fifty feet he put the bird in a steep flair and was relieved to see the rotor

RPMs increase. He held the flair until forward airspeed had almost stopped and then leveled the aircraft. When he started to drop, he pulled the collective up. The aircraft wanted to fly, but he only succeeded in slowing down his fall. When the skids hit the red clay road, the aircraft rocked forward enough to raise the rear skids about six inches off the ground. He began to fear the road was coming up to meet them, and they would flip head first. Then it gently rocked backward and sat down. They were safe.

Mac looked over to his right and saw the other aircraft had landed as well. The pilot came on the radio, "Great job! Couldn't have done that better with power. Who are you with?"

"Bravo Company, 229th."

"Hang on and I'll climb up enough to notify your operations."

Two hours later a Chinook from 228th lifted 4-7-4 off the road and took it to the Bravo maintenance area. When Mac and Jonesy returned, Rock was fit to be tied. He kept apologizing for failing to fix the flight idle stop. Mac could see it was tearing him apart to know the aircraft went down because of something he'd done, so he finally said, "Rock, forget it. It was my own fault. I should have tried the flight idle stop three or four times while I was still on the ground. I guess I caught a little of Jonesy's excitement and didn't keep my mind on my business. We all learned a good lesson today. See you in the morning; I owe a couple of 228th pilots a drink."

CHAPTER 26

Unfortunately, Captain Massey had to make another visit the next morning and smiled as he approached Mac. "Heard you had to land sooner than you'd planned."

"Guess you could say that. You want to see the aircraft, right?"

"That's why I'm here. I understand you landed with no additional damage."

"That's right. We were really lucky."

After examining the aircraft, Massey went to his aircraft and then returned with a large beer mug. Mac was puzzled. "You planning on buying me a beer?"

"No, that would be later. You've officially earned the group's 'I Saved One' mug. Congratulations, Captain."

"So you can't help me fill it with beer, huh?"

"Not this time. I've got another unit to check out. Again, congratulations and good job. You should really be proud."

When Mac carried the list to Bear, the commander said, "Mac, you know you have to take a check ride before you fly again. That's a requirement of the Cav SOP. If you go down, you've got to do it."

Mac grinned. "Yeah, I knew that, but was hoping you'd forgotten," he replied.

Bear added, "Mr. Martin will give you your check ride tomorrow morning at ten hundred hours. How does that sound?"

"Okay, I guess. Do I have a choice?"

Major West asked, "What about 4-7-4?"

"There's no real damage on her, and we've got the flight idle stop working like brand-new. Barney will test fly it in the morning. We don't want to push our luck anymore today."

West laughed. "Mac, you'll do. I've missed you at the poker games. What's the story?"

"Sir, I play poker for fun. Some of those guys are too serious about the game."

West grinned. "And they try to buy the pot?"

"Sir, you said it."

The next morning CW3 Martin took Mac to a long, empty runway. He cut some of the requirements out of the check ride and began to give him force landings. It was frustrating for both of them. Mac always wanted his horizontal and vertical speeds to be zero when he hit the ground. Martin wanted to have at least twenty knots vertical speed so the aircraft would make a running landing, like back in flight school. After three tries, Martin gave up. "This is getting us nowhere. You can control the aircraft as well as I do, and apparently, you're not going to change."

Mac just patiently asked, "Do I pass?"

"Hell, yeah; I don't have the balls to ground our maintenance officer."

Mac laughed. "And I thought I had the only thankless job in the company."

"Sir, I can't believe you understand. I really appreciate that."

When they returned to Bear Cat and shut down, Martin said, "I'm releasing you to fly. I'll give the paperwork to operations. There's no real need for you to come with me."

"Thanks, then. I'll just hang around here and do a little work. Thanks for the check ride."

"Believe it or not, it was fun for a change," Martin responded.

Mac looked at him skeptically. "I'll just bet it was."

They both laughed as they went their separate ways. Barney saw him approach the shed and asked, "Did he say you're good to go?"

"Yeah, but he's worried about a Captain Barnes."

Barney put his hands on his hips and said, "Now, was that nice?"

Ignoring him, Mac asked, "Is 4-7-4 good to go?"

"Has been since noon. Oh yeah, I almost forgot. I'm sorry to hear about your friend."

Puzzled, Mac asked, "What friend?"

"Wasn't it Kawania or something like that? You know, the crew chief from Hawaii. He was killed by enemy fire last week. The bird was hit two times, and both shots hit him in the head. He never knew what hit him."

Mac just sat down on the ground for a moment. He had a sick feeling in his stomach. *Another friend lost.* "Barney, he was just a kid playing war." He felt so depressed, he just got up and walked off to check his mail. He'd just gotten letters the day before, so he knew his chances of success were slim for today. Each time he got mail, he had mixed emotions. In the beginning he was happy he had mail, but then the reality would hit that it would be days before he got any again. On the days there was no mail, he convinced himself to begin to look forward to his next haul. Today was one of those days—when he checked, there was nothing for him.

He didn't want to be alone that evening, so he decided to visit the maintenance enlisted men at their hootch. When he came around the corner, he could see they were having a party. Morgan staggered over to him and handed him a beer, "Here you go, sir. We're celebrating Jonesy's escape from death."

Mac took the beer and asked, "What escape from death?"

Morgan slurred, "Your test flight, sir."

"Oh, I'll drink to that." He tapped Morgan's beer with his, "Here's to a better day."

Everyone had been listening to their conversation and joined in with, "Hear, hear to Captain Mac."

Like most drunks, Morgan wanted to talk. Mac learned he'd joined up after graduating from high school. The more he listened, the more personal the information got. When the subject came around to his teeth, Mac quickly realized that Morgan's self-deprecating humor about the problem was really a defense mechanism. He asked, "Did the army pull them?"

"Yeah, some in basic and the rest when I got to AIT. They told me I needed to let my gums heal before they could fit me with false ones, but before they healed, they sent me here." He began to sob as he continued, "When I went home on leave before shipping out, all my friends made fun of me. My old girlfriends wouldn't even talk to me. It was like I was covered with mud or something—they didn't even want to touch me."

Mac asked, "Have you gone to the dentist over here?"

"No, sir, there isn't one. Believe me, I asked."

Mac didn't feel sorry for himself anymore—he had a new mission. He was going to get this soldier some teeth if it killed him.

At breakfast Mac shared what he'd learned about Morgan with Rock, Papa-San, and Barney. He wasn't surprised that the group didn't seem bothered by the fact that the soldier had no teeth. In an effort to gain some sympathy for Morgan, Mac told them the story of how he'd gone home and been treated so badly by his friends. It seemed to work—everyone began to brainstorm on how to fix the problem immediately. Mac suggested, "When I talked to the company commander and first sergeant about having the crew chiefs come from maintenance, the first sergeant seemed disappointed about Rock not coming to him first. So, Papa-San, why don't you approach him first? If he can't do anything, I'll go through the officer's channel."

Barney jumped in, "If that doesn't work, by God, I'll go to the IG. I'm planning on getting out of the army soon, anyway."

Mac could see the group was motivated and determined to help a soldier who wasn't even asking for their help. Once Papa-San met with the first sergeant, their project took on a life of its own. Anyone who heard about the problem wanted to be part of the solution. All day it seemed Papa-San received updates from his contact. Shortly after noon the company commander's driver drove up next to the maintenance shed and yelled, "Captain McKay, you're needed in operations. An aircraft is in trouble."

As Mac slipped out the door he just muttered, "When it rains, it pours. Hope it's not anything major." He jumped out of the jeep before it even stopped and hurried into operations. "Bear, what's the problem?"

"Mr. Saunders was hit by machine gun fire. One round hit the hydraulic reservoir, and he needs to know where he should land. Would you believe today is his first day as aircraft commander?"

Mac snorted, "Don't think he'll forget this mission anytime soon. What's his aircraft number?"

"3-1-8."

"Did you say 3-1-8?"

"Yeah, why?"

"Because it's always flown great with no hydraulics. Get him on the horn."

"3-1-8, this is operations. Over."

"Operations, this is 3-1-8."

It was clear to everyone that he was stressed to the max. His voice had risen by several octaves and he was breathing very erratically.

"3-1-8, this is maintenance one. How do you know you've lost hydraulics?"

"We took rounds near the engine. Cherry juice is running down the aircraft on the gunner's side. The hydraulic caution light is on, too."

"Do you have any feedback in your controls?"

"Not yet, that's why I'm calling. Should I land ASAP?"

Mac calmly replied, "I have good news for you. That particular aircraft flies just great without hydraulics. Bring her home, but don't try to hover. Make a running landing."

"Captain Mac, are you sure?" He evidently felt reassured because his voice was quickly returning to normal.

"Absolutely. I could never tell the difference when I'd turn the hydraulic switch to the off position on my test flights. Bring her on home, and we'll celebrate your becoming an AC."

A much deeper voice responded, "I just might go back to being a peter pilot."

Bear whispered, "Is that the truth? No difference in the way it flies?"

"Yeah, 3-1-8 and 7-8-1 both. You really can't tell the difference on those two, but I can't say that about the rest—3-4-0 is the worst."

The first sergeant heard Mac talking and approached, "Sir! Tell Papa-San we have a dental appointment for Morgan tomorrow at thirteen hundred at Long Bein."

"I will, Top. Good work."

He smiled in return. "Taking care of the men is my job, sir. Glad to do it."

CHAPTER 27

About midmorning Mac got a call from Captain Wright on the landline, asking if he had any reason to fly to Saigon.

Mac responded immediately, "Yes, I owe my PE team a visit. Unfortunately, I lost a bet. What do you need?"

"I may need a pilot to fly back an aircraft later."

"Are you talking about the new one we're getting?" Mac asked.

"No, didn't even know about that one. That would bring us up to nineteen. Why do we need a new one, since we don't have enough pilots to fly the ones we have now?"

"Beggars can't be choosers," Mac said, laughing. "Are you going to explain what this is about or not?"

"Can't; it's a secret. It's one of those need-to-know things."

"Okay, James Bond, when and where do you need us to be?"

"Hotel 3, ready to leave after sixteen hundred hours."

"That'll be good and give the men time to visit the PX and sightsee."

Pleased with the favor, Wright signed off with, "Thanks, Mac. I've got to go."

Later, in Saigon, Mac and Barney landed next to an aircraft that looked familiar. Puzzled, Mac observed, "6-8-5? Isn't that one of ours?"

Ensley said, "Yep, that's the aircraft Warrant Officer Dant and SP4 Blame fly. They won't let anybody else touch it."

There wasn't anyone else around, so Mac instructed his men to be back at sixteen hundred hours, or they'd walk home. They scattered in all directions and quickly vanished. Mac looked over at Barney and said, "They're like a bunch of kids at a county fair."

"Wouldn't know, as I've never had the pleasure of going to one." Barney said.

"So you're the one?"

"The one what?" Barney quizzed.

"The only person on earth who's never been to a county fair. Sorry you've led such a sheltered life. Come on, I'll buy you an ice cream and explain exactly what you've missed."

They returned to the aircraft about fifteen hundred. They were anxious to discover what Wright was up to. As they approached, Mac noticed an MP jeep parked next to it. In the back seat sat Murphy in handcuffs. Mac mumbled to Barney in disgust, "What on earth has Murphy done now?"

The MP saluted, "Sir, is SP4 Weaver one of yours?"

"Yes, sergeant, he is. What did he do?"

"A couple of things. We found him in an off-limits bar and were going to give him a warning, until we noticed he was carrying a .45. Weapons aren't allowed in that part of town. I can release him to you, and we'll forward the charges to his company commander."

Mac just shook his head, "Thank you, sergeant. I'll take good care of him."

After the MP left, Mac turned to Murphy and warned, "If you say one word, I'll take this .45 and shoot you myself."

Always the thinker, Barney asked, "Where'd he get a .45? I can only check out a .38."

Mac whispered back, "Don't ask him now, for goodness sakes."

They were so busy talking about Murphy they failed to notice Wright approach. He pulled Mac and Barney aside next to a wall where no one could overhear and said, "Thanks for meeting me here. I'm going to need your help."

Mac laughed. "You make it sound so serious. What's the joke?"

"Remember that day we flew the mission to Nancy, and the sergeants came up disappointed it was us instead of Dant? Well, they had good reason. Dant and crew chief Blame are dealers. CID just caught them making a buy in downtown Saigon. SP4 Holmes, their door gunner, is CID. He's been working undercover for a couple of months. Me and Barkley were the only ones who knew."

Mac asked, "What about Major West?"

"Believe it or not, at first he was a suspect, too. Remember when we converted our MPC to new money? The major had won big at poker and had converted the maximum amount he could. At first Holmes thought he might be getting a kickback."

Barney chuckled. "And I can't believe I was feeling guilty about trading stack bearings for an engine."

That surprised Wright. "You guys did that? You're having all the fun. How can I get into this maintenance business?"

Mac replied with a grin, "I'm not sure a cop would fit in with our group. What do you think, Barney?" He looked around and noticed for the first time that 6-8-5 was no longer there. He asked, "Where's Dant's helicopter?"

"He and Rogers had a load of people who were planning on going to a movie at Long Bein. Barkley and Rogers took them on up at thirteen-thirty. The Sunday matinee begins at fourteen hundred."

Barney looked at Mac and complained, "How come you and I don't know the movie schedule?"

When Mac entered operations that evening, Bear asked, "Hey, did you hear they caught Mr. Dant and his crew chief with drugs? He's a great pilot, but boy is he an ass otherwise."

"Sounds to me like he upset your schedule."

"Not mine; Wright's the guy that puts them in the seat. Oh, I got a call; they want you to pick up that new aircraft tomorrow."

"I can do that," Mac confirmed. "You want to go with me?"

The question caught Bear off guard for a moment, and then he grinned. "What time are you leaving?"

"We can leave right after the morning meeting. Why don't you meet me there?"

Bear was waiting for Mac when he entered the mess hall for breakfast. He was so excited about the trip, Mac took pity on him and cut the meeting short. When he got to the aircraft, Bear had already done the preflight and was just sitting there, waiting on him. Bear had no idea how short the flight to Saigon would be. When they landed, Mac grabbed his helmet bag and turned to Barney. "I'll see you back at the barn."

Barney continued to shut down the aircraft. "I'm going to the PX first. I saw something there yesterday I can't live without."

Mac nodded, and he and Bear walked to the building where the quartermaster colonel worked. Mac had never signed for an aircraft before, so he had no idea what it entailed. He was totally surprised that all he had to do was sign a little card for an NCO. It was like he was just picking up another part at Phu Loi. He looked over at Bear and shrugged. "That was easy," he said. "Now let's go see if it flies."

As they looked over 6-2-8, Bear observed, "You know, it even has that new car smell."

Mac sniffed the air. "You're right. Untie the rotor blade, and let's see what a new aircraft feels like."

It may have been his imagination, but when he came to a hover it seemed to be a lot quieter than normal. As soon as they crossed the river leaving Saigon, they cut loose, like kids with a new toy. They took turns flying up and down the river, buzzing sand pans and huts along the banks. When the twenty-minute fuel light came on, Mac snapped back to reality. He wasn't exactly sure where they were, and immediately thoughts began to run through his mind of their running out of fuel and crashing. He held his breath until he managed to land at the refueling point. It was a hot refueling, which meant the aircraft wasn't being shut down, so Bear was stuck with the job of pumping the gas, and he didn't like it. Mac couldn't resist teasing, "What? Are you afraid of getting your hands a little dirty?"

Bear glared at him and cautioned, "I'll remind you of this the next time you come in asking for a favor."

"Now, Bear, tell me. Have you ever had a better day in Nam?"

Bear grinned. "Can't say that I have. Thanks, Mac, for taking me along."

That evening when Mac was reviewing the aircraft list, Major West came in and told him, "I got a nasty report on a SP4 Weaver. The first sergeant brought me up to speed on your award system for your men. Weaver has forced my hand. The battalion commander suggests we stay out of Saigon except for business. Do I need to say anything else?"

"No, sir. I'll take care of it in the morning's meeting."

When West left, Bear turned and asked, "What was that about?"

"Murphy struck again. He got picked up in Saigon with a weapon in an off-limits bar."

Bear burst out laughing. "Every unit needs a Murphy. We'd be so bored if you didn't have him."

At breakfast, Mac informed Barney, Papa-San, and Rock about Major West's instructions. He suggested, "Let's just do this once. Have everyone at the meeting this morning."

Papa-San asked, "What do you want done with Weaver?"

Mac snorted. "Nothing. I'm guessing when the men find out that Saigon is now off-limits to them, that will be punishment enough."

Rock laughed. "You know, if it were anybody but him, I'd worry for his life."

Papa-San added, "Yeah, everybody just waits for him to screw up. They'll all be pissed off, but they'll get over it."

When everyone was there for the meeting, Mac announced, "I've got some bad news, guys. There will be no further trips to Saigon until further notice. Captain Barnes and I agree, but I just want you to know it's my decision. Any questions?"

Ensley asked, "Is this because one of us took a weapon to Saigon?"

Mac grinned and replied, "It had a big influence on my decision. Any other questions?" When no one responded, he continued, "Good. Pappy, I need for you to give 6-2-8 a once-over, before I release it to operations."

The company commander's jeep drove up as they exited the maintenance shed. Mac looked over to see if Major West was inside and was surprised to see four soldiers. Two were in khakis, and two were in fatigues. After thinking about it for a moment, he decided they must be on their way to the 90th replacement. He immediately recognized one of the men and called out, "SP4 Morgan! Where are you headed?"

He grinned. "Sir, I'm going to get me some teeth."

Thrilled to hear it, Mac said, "That's great news, and it's about time." He recognized the other specialists in khakis from their aid station. Evans came around the corner of the building just as he started to ask what they were doing there.

"Good morning, sir. I forgot I left my camera with Gibbs," Evans said. Then said, "Oh, yeah," came to attention and saluted, adding, "*Sir*, all due respect, Captain Chase was a real asshole, *sir*."

Mac's mouth flew open, and he turned to look at Pappy, who flushed and got real busy when he realized Mac now knew where it came from. Mac responded, "Didn't know the man, but I'll take your word for it." Everyone laughed as Mac continued, "Evans, are you staying in the army?"

"No, sir; I'm going to help my brother with his contracting business."

"Well, good luck to you. The army is losing a good man."

Evans again came to attention and saluted him. "Thank you, sir."

Mac returned and held the salute as he looked Evans squarely in the eyes; he knew this was one of the moments in his life he'd like to remember. Here was a man who had gone through hell as a crew chief on a helicopter, but he didn't let that stop him from being the best man to fix them in the company. The remainder of the team gave him a resounding cheer as the group drove away.

CHAPTER 28

Startling news was welcomed in the month of March: the 1st Cav would be standing down at the end of the month. Everyone had questions about what would happen to their company and their battalion. Most weren't really interested in the facts; they just wanted to be told their dream was coming true—they could go home. Days later that dream was killed. B Company would be assigned to the 222nd Battalion, 12th Group, effective April 1, 1971, and they would remain in Vietnam. As far as they were concerned, standing down only meant that the CG and division staff, with the colors, would fly back to Fort Hood, Texas. Mac quickly figured out that meant business as usual for himself and his maintenance team. If there were any thoughts of the war being over, they were squashed when the flight of five ships returned. They had landed in a hot LZ, and the new aircraft, 6-2-8, had taken the most damage. They were lucky only one person had been hit. He had taken a round through his right wrist. The crew chief said, "My gunner got a golden ticket. He's going home."

Pappy and all the other PE team members crawled all over the aircraft, counting the bullet holes. Pappy looked over at Mac in disgust and said, "I've found twenty-eight so far, sir. She's got six holes in her belly that go into the gas tank. The self-sealing tanks work; there aren't any leaks, but I don't think we can fix it."

Mac walked to the front. He noticed that the avionics cover in the center of the nose was pushed in on the left side. It looked like something about the size of a baseball had hit it. He pushed the two release buttons and opened the cover. Whatever had hit it had put a dent into the side of the FM radio and continued on into the console between the two pilot's seats. He climbed into the right seat and began to remove the control heads with a screwdriver. As he took out the third one, he froze. Just three inches away was a live RPG, lodged against the side of the console. Apparently it had been fired so close to the aircraft it hadn't had time to arm. He turned and yelled, "Get away from the aircraft! There's a live RPG round next to the pilot's seat!"

Rock ran to the maintenance shed and called operations to get an EOD team as soon as possible. A few minutes later, a three-man team in a jeep arrived, pulling a trailer containing a mounted heavy box. When the senior NCO saw the RPG's location, he suggested, "Best thing we can do is blow it in place."

Mac protested. "You mean the easiest thing you can do. I could have done that myself. I called you to remove it."

The sergeant laughed and replied, "Well, I tried. I need for you to keep your men at a safe distance until we take care of it."

When the EOD team drove away with the RPG safely secured, everyone breathed a sigh of relief. Later that evening, Bear asked, "How long will it take you to fix 6-2-8?"

Mac shook his head. "Bad news; her damage is way above our echelon. Even Papa-San's guys can't fix her. It's been less than a week since we picked her up, and now 15th TC battalion will haul her out to the bone yard. You know, her loss reminds me of a captain I served with in Hawaii. He came here and got hit with shrapnel from a mortar while he was still at 90th replacement. He got a purple heart and never even reported to his unit. Poor old 6-2-8 doesn't even get a purple heart."

Bear shook his head in disbelief, "Mac, you do know they're just machines, right? They can't feel anything."

Embarrassed, Mac looked over at him and protested, "Are you sure about that? They sure feel alive when you're up there flying by yourself. It's too bad Hobo didn't ride with them today."

"He probably didn't like that new car smell 6-2-8 had. I guess we're back down to eighteen aircraft again, huh?" Bear complained.

"We will be tomorrow, when they haul her off."

Changing the subject, Bear asked, "Did you hear about Mr. Sasin? He was the new copilot on 6-2-8 today. His Nomax pants took three rounds; not one of them touched his skin. He's been in the bar drinking, ever since he got back. The guys have a pool going on how many he'll get down before he passes out."

Mac looked at him skeptically. "You're pulling my leg, right?"

"No! I've got fourteen and twenty drinks."

"I was going to the bar, but I don't want to see that," Mac replied. "Guess I'll head over and see about my mail. Good luck on your pool."

He had two letters waiting for him. The first was his monthly letter from his paternal grandmother. Ever since her younger son had died, they had a special bond. He had been only a year older than Mac, and his grandmother had transferred all of her attention to Mac. He loved getting her letters because they came straight from the heart. He could feel her loneliness, and he knew she could feel his as well. The other letter was from the Department of the Army, Artillery Branch. He quickly opened it and read that to be nominated as a regular army officer, he had to be airborne or ranger qualified. It said he needed to submit paperwork to volunteer for one of them before they could continue to process his application. He knew airborne school was three weeks long, but he wasn't sure about ranger school. He seemed to remember it lasted six or eight weeks. He didn't even know anyone he could ask. Bear was a West Pointer, so he was already a RA officer. The others were just like him; they had a reserve commission. He decided to use simple math to make his decision—three weeks or six weeks? Three weeks won, and he filled out the paperwork for airborne school, licked the envelope, and returned it to the mail clerk.

The morning meeting had an air of excitement. Guys were whispering and laughing when Rock and Mac came in. Unfortunately, since losing 6-2-8, Mac wasn't in such a good mood. He headed straight to the schedule board and pulled the tag for that aircraft. It only had sixteen hours on it.

He heard a low voice in the back mumble something and then another respond with, "Not yet!" Mac just ignored them and began the meeting. He was pleased to see that even though the PE teams couldn't go to Saigon anymore, they were still trying to make their forty-eight-hour goals. No team wanted to be the first to fail and exceed the time frame. Finally, the men couldn't stand it anymore and insisted on revealing the surprise. Papa-San stood and said, "Captain Mac and Captain Barney, we have a surprise for you in the third revetment." The men ran outside, eager to see their reaction. When Mac and Barney finally got there, they looked around; not seeing what the surprise was. There was a Huey sitting in the revetment, but there certainly wasn't anything unusual about that. Puzzled, Mac asked, "What's the surprise?"

Rock said, "Look at the tail number."

Mac read it out loud, "4-4-3. We don't have that number."

Papa-San said, "We do now! When the Thai gave up on fixing it, they pushed it over the berm. We went and got it and fixed it. We now have our own maintenance bird, and it's ready for your test flight."

Barney looked over at Mac. "I'm game if you are."

"Let's go get our helmets," Mac replied. Once again the team had surprised him with their efforts. When they did the preflight, the only thing missing was a VHF radio and the clock.

Barney asked, "Wonder where they found all the parts?"

Mac laughed, beaming with pride for his men. "I'm guessing Rock and Buddha had a lot to do with that."

The test flight was much rougher than usual. The aircraft had a major one-to-one vibration, but Mac told Barney how they had fixed 3-2-7. When they finished the flight and pulled out the logbook to sign off, they discovered a real problem. The logbook was incomplete. Not all of the major components had been entered. Any new component that the men had to replace had an entry, but those still on the hull when it was pushed over were missing. Mac shook his head, "We can't let anybody else fly this until we get the paperwork straight."

192

"Then it'll be our little secret. What do you say, partner?" Barney winked.

When they walked away from the aircraft to the maintenance shed, all the men gave a loud cheer; like little kids who had just given their parents their most prized possession. Mac whispered to Rock and Papa-San, "You two know we have to keep this under our hat. Do you think the men can keep a secret?"

Rock laughed, "It's taken them almost six weeks to fix it, sir. How was that for keeping a secret?"

Mac couldn't believe it. "I guess this aircraft is what you were hinting about a couple of months ago."

"Could be. You do have to admit, it's a better gift than getting socks for Christmas."

"I'm not sure we'll be allowed to keep it, but we'll play it by ear for now."

Tom approached and said, "Captain Mac, 3-4-0 needs a test flight. The crew chief is out on another mission. If it's okay with you, Ensley would like to take the left seat."

Mac nodded his approval. "That's fine with me. Tell him to grab a helmet."

Tom grinned and ducked his head, "He's already in the aircraft, sir."

Mac looked over at Rock. "Am I really that predictable?" he asked.

"Didn't you know? We think that's one of your strong points, sir."

After a thorough preflight, Mac and Ensley departed to the east to complete the customary ninety-minute test flight. They began to climb to four thousand feet to make the auto-rotation check. It was a beautiful, clear day, and Ensley commented on how far he could see. As they got higher, Ensley asked, "Is that the ocean out there?"

Mac was too busy watching his instruments to look up. He just answered, "It could be; I'll check it out in a minute. For now, I need to do this test flight."

As he was turning into the wind, a "Mayday" call came over on guard. An aircraft had taken enemy fire and was going down east of Bear Cat.

Mac immediately focused and said, "Ensley, help me look for that aircraft. We've got to be close to them."

Ensley scanned the area. "There he is at two o'clock, below us," he exclaimed. "He's going for that open area."

Mac switched the frequency to guard. "Aircraft on guard, have you in sight and will follow you down." His thoughts went back to the pilot who had followed him down when he had the flight idle stop failure. He remembered how that radio call had immediately reassured him.

The pilot called back, "Appreciate you flying cover for me. The engine is gone."

Mac advised, "I'm on your left side, about fifty feet behind you."

The pilot clicked and said, "Roger that."

As the aircraft hit the ground, it tilted forward. Mac could see air between the rear of the skid and the ground and clearly remembered the sensation he'd had when he landed. As it dropped back down, Mac admired the pilot's perfect landing. He quickly landed to the left rear of the downed aircraft, and before the rotors on the other helicopter had stopped turning, the crew chief and door gunner came running with their machine guns to his helicopter. Surprised to see the gun mounts empty, they quickly attached their weapons to Mac's bird and took up defensive positions, ready to fire. When the pilot, CW3 Wilson, got out of his helicopter, Mac told Ensley to move to the back and give the pilot the left seat. The copilot climbed into the back next to Ensley. Wilson mumbled, "A stupid rookie mistake. I dropped down to five hundred feet to find the location of the patrol. A rookie mistake...I flew right into the dead man zone. Ah, hell, I'll never live this down. Get us some altitude so, I can call operations and get somebody out here." Mac quickly climbed to three thousand feet and made slow circles around the downed aircraft.

About twenty minutes later, two Cobras arrived and took up a protective circle, clearing Mac to drop off the crew at their home station in Bien Hoa. When he got back to Bear Cat, Ensley looked over at Mac and grinned. "Man that was fun!"

Mac grinned back. "It was, wasn't it? I'm just glad it wasn't one of ours. We finally have a smooth maintenance flow, and I don't want that to change."

Ensley cautioned him, "Sir! You're going to jinx us."

Mac shuddered, and then laughed, remembering his grandmother always called these feelings "all-overs." He signed off the test flight in the logbook, walked to the maintenance shed, and moved 3-4-0's tag from the top of the board down to two hours on the maintenance flow chart. Later that evening, when Mac took the list to operations, Wright was grinning at him when he opened the door. "They sent Dant to Leavenworth for a very long time. Became Blame testified, he got a shorter sentence, but the end result is, they're both going to jail. It's a real pity, as they were both good at their jobs, but they let greed screw them up. What is it they say? If you can't do the time, don't do the crime."

Mac laughed. "Yeah, that must be what all you cops say."

"Wise guy, are you ready to fly tomorrow? We've got a five-ship lift mission at Nancy, and I need a copilot."

"I'm your man. When?"

"Skids up at five-thirty. Barkley is the mission commander, so it should be fun."

"Sounds good. I'll get Barney to do the test flights tonight."

Out of habit, Mac still met Rock on the flight line at oh-four-hundred the next morning. The only difference was that they were joined by Hobo. Mac caught himself patting Hobo's head as they stood there. When Wright arrived, his crew chief helped the dog onboard, and he scrambled to his customary place on deck between the pilots' seats. Mac could see the little smiles on the faces of all of the crew. Wright was chattering about Dant being on his way to prison, trying to hide the fact he was thrilled Hobo had chosen his flight for the day—but he wasn't fooling anyone, so Mac just asked, "So what's our job today?"

"We're flying the last ship, as usual. If anyone goes down, we'll assist."

Mac pointed at Hobo. "Maybe we won't have to do anything."

Wright nodded. "One can only hope."

When they arrived at the little airstrip, Barkley landed on the center line at the end of the runway. The other four landed on the edges, two on each side. That made it easier to enter a V formation when they lifted off for departure. A captain walked down from the S3 tent and told them shut down. He explained the lift had been postponed for a couple of hours. Mac got out and began to look around at some of the soldiers. Wright asked, "What are you looking for?"

"Those two NCOs who approached us last time."

"You won't find them. Part of the reason Blame got a shorter sentence was he gave up the names of his contacts at the firebases. If you really want to find them, you'll need to fly to LBJ."

When Mac moved back to the helicopter, he noticed a small crowd had gathered around Hobo. He could tell by the way his tail was wagging that Hobo loved every minute of it. He smiled as he watched. The men reminded him of his friends back home in Georgia with their hunting dogs. Later, the S3 stuck his head out of the tent and made a small circle with his right hand; signaling Barkley to crank. Everyone acknowledged, and all five aircraft began the startup procedure. In no time at all, four of them were running, but, the lead aircraft's blade slowed to a stop. Wright turned to Mac and said, "You've got the controls. I'll go see what's wrong."

When Wright came back, he explained, "Barkley can't crank his aircraft. He's got a weak battery, and he's afraid he'll get a hot start. We need to give him ours and call Bear to get us a battery out here."

Mac replied, "Take the controls and let me go see." He quickly walked over and had the copilot get out. He climbed into the seat, looked up at the overhead console, and pulled out one of the circuit breakers. Then he pulled the starter switch and held it. The engine began to turn over, faster and faster. With his right hand, Mac pushed the circuit breaker back in, and the engine came alive. He rolled on the throttle and yelled over at Barkley, "Take the controls!" Then he got out and walked back to Wright's aircraft. Everyone stood there with their mouths hanging open.

When Mac got his helmet back on, Wright asked, "How in the hell did you do that?"

Mac grinned in satisfaction. "It's a maintenance officer's secret. I'd tell you, but then I'd have to kill you."

"This is payback because I wouldn't tell you about Dant, right?"

"Payback is a bitch," Mac responded.

The grunts quickly loaded, and Barkley came on the radio, "Let's get this show on road. On the go."

All five aircraft lifted at the same time. Mac marveled at how they seemed be to as controlled as if one pilot were flying them. As the formation turned, each one maintained exactly the same distance from the others. It was obvious that all of them had their AC at the controls. He recognized skill when he saw it and knew at that moment he was seeing absolute perfection. There was total silence on the radio, both inside and out. Until today's flight, Mac had never seen how good Bravo company's pilots really were. Most of them were just kids, but they showed flying abilities way beyond their years. The first radio call after takeoff was from the Cobra pilots assigned to cover the insertion. Barkley acknowledged their presence and released them to fire their rockets for cover. About one hundred feet from the LZ, Barkley gave the outside door gunners permission to fire the machine guns. In Mac's ship, that was the crew chief. Like Mac, the right door gunner could only sit and watch the show. The other aircraft was only forty feet away from them when they hit the ground. Mac had a ringside seat to watch how the young soldiers quickly took up defensive positions. He was close enough to see their wide-eyed stares, brought on by their apprehension and fear. As the aircraft broke ground, Mac realized that, whereas he was going home, they were being inserted to experience only God knew what. For the first time since arriving in Nam, he felt guilty for having such a safe job.

When the formation climbed to about fifteen hundred feet, the ACs turned the aircraft over to the copilots. No outside radio calls were made, but it was obvious to everyone in the formation what had happened. No matter how hard each tried, he, like the other copilots, did not have the skill to hold the tight formation the ACs had done so easily. The harder he tried, the worse it got. The best description he could come up with was the one his IP from flight school had always said—*The formation has gone to hell.* He kept waiting for Wright to say something, but he remained silent, just looking out at the countryside as they flew. Suddenly Wright commented, "You know, people used to come to Vietnam for vacation and safaris. I wonder if they'll ever do that again."

Mac couldn't think of a response, so he remained silent; it had been a rhetorical question anyway.

CHAPTER 29

The mission loads seemed to slow down toward the end of the month, due to the standing down of the 1st Cav and their units transitioning to the 222nd Battalion. Any information on what would happen to Bravo Company seemed elusive. The maintenance loads were lighter, so they all had a lot of free time to worry. Barney and Mac tried to pick Rock and Papa-San's brains on what was being said in NCO circles, but unfortunately, they were just as clueless.

On one of these slow days, Major West's driver approached and directed Mac to report to the major. When he arrived, Wright met Mac at the door and said, "One of our aircraft went down."

Major West had both captains come into his office. "Mac, I need for you to be the investigator for the accident and head out to the site. This couldn't have happened at a worse time. The 1st Cav headquarters closed down, and we haven't officially been attached to the 222nd aviation yet. The mission commander isn't sure if he was shot down or if it was pilot error. Captain Wright said he'd fly you out there. Do your best to determine the cause. I'll report whatever findings you come up with."

The driver took both of them to the aircraft, where Wright's crew chief and gunner were already onboard. It was almost an hour's flight to the accident site; and all the way there, Mac worried it might have gone down because of something his maintenance had failed to do.

When they arrived, Mac was shocked at all the activity on the ground. Wright made a wide circle to give them a closer look. They could see an engineer platoon already cutting down smaller trees next to the aircraft. The wreckage was located about fifty feet from the open area. There were still two helicopters left in the middle of the opening. Wright picked the best location he could and landed next to them. They quickly shut down and made their way over to the crash site. When Mac came around the underbrush into a clearing he was stunned at what he saw: the tail boom was twenty to thirty feet up in the fork of a huge tree. It was as if a giant had snapped it off the helicopter and placed it there for safekeeping. It appeared to be as damage-free as it had in the revetment this morning before takeoff. The fuselage lay on its right side at the base of the huge tree. The ground was stained a brownish-red, and Mac commented to Wright, "Looks like a lot of blood."

Wright said, "I understand two of the passengers were killed. The door gunner was Medevaced, but he only had a broken leg. He was the only crew member to get hurt."

Mac shook his head. "That's pretty amazing." He worried that he wouldn't be up to the task assigned him. But when he moved to the rear of the aircraft, those worries vanished, and he sighed in relief. He saw the problem immediately. When the tail boom had been twisted off by the tree, it removed the sheet metal that was covering the tail rotor drive shaft. The burnt metal and grease he could see was a clear indication that the number one hanger bearing had seized and come apart. Experience told him that when the drive shaft disconnected, the tail rotor stopped. He'd been taught in flight school that when a Huey was above forty knots of airspeed, it streamlined and didn't need much pedal control. As the aircraft slowed to land, the tail rotor was needed to offset the torque of the engine. The entire body of the aircraft wanted to turn the same way the rotor turned. Putting pitch in the tail rotor blade with the pedals stopped this action. When the pilot lost tail rotor control, he wasn't able to stop it from spinning. Mac could only imagine how scary it would be—even if you pulled power to try to get back up to forty knots, that action would only result in the aircraft spinning faster because of the increased torque. He simply couldn't understand how they had survived.

Wright had gone around the opposite side and asked, "Have you figured it out yet? Thank God I wasn't in this one. Both pilots were only nineteen. If they'd been old farts like us, they would both have been killed."

"You're right about that," Mac replied. He pointed to the hanger bearing and said, "There's the culprit. From the burnt grease, it looks like it's been failing for a little while. The pressure from the torque on the last mission probably caused it to snap. When I get back, I'll have Pappy check all of the aircraft for any signs of this."

As they were talking, another aircraft landed. They walked over to see who it was. Barney waved them down. "Mac, I've got the gear to rig it to be slung back."

The rest of the afternoon was spent rigging the fuselage and removing the tail boom from the tree. When the engineers started climbing the tree and tying off ropes, it was like watching a circus act. Everyone was fascinated with their skill, and it was nearly dark before they all left.

There was no unit ceremony in April; in fact, no one even mentioned Bravo Company was no longer in the 1st Cav Division. The highlight of the week was the arrival of four 67 N crew chiefs, two new medics, a mechanic for the motor pool, and a first lieutenant for aircraft maintenance. Rock and Papa-San blindsided Mac at breakfast with their plan for the new replacements. They wanted him to have a promotion ceremony at the day's maintenance meeting. One of the new replacements was a SP5 who had been a crew chief for A Company, 227th Battalion, two years before. They agreed he should be given a helicopter without coming to maintenance. With the crew chief hurt in the crash of 7-8-1, Blame being jailed, and one crew chief DEROSed, the flight platoon needed three new crew chiefs. Mac asked, "Who should they be?"

"Whitehorse and Smitty." replied Rock.

"What about Ensley?"

Rock looked at Papa-San. They had planned to hold off with their next suggestion, but since Mac asked, they had to come clean, "We want Ensley to take over the PE team when Tom DEROSes next week. Ensley's all for it. Is that okay with you, sir?"

Mac laughed. "Hell, yeah. Maybe we can keep him busy for a change."

Papa-San said, "We've got another problem. Pappy DEROSes next week, but he doesn't want anyone to know about it. He's sworn us to secrecy, so please don't tell."

The news about Pappy hit him as hard as when Dixon had left. Pappy, Dixon, and Rock were the reasons Mac had been able to make good on his promise of providing fourteen birds per day. The breakfast group knew how the news would hit Mac, so they kept silent and drank coffee while he processed it. Minutes later, he looked over at Barney and requested, "Why don't you go get the new lieutenant and bring him to the maintenance meeting?"

Without another word, the group stood and walked to the maintenance area.

When Barney and Lieutenant David Lillard finally showed up, Mac began. He quickly took care of the aircraft status and then announced, "Two of our team members are getting promoted. Whitehorse, Smitty, get your butts up here, front and center."

When they got in front of his desk, Whitehorse came to attention. Seconds later Smitty did the same. Mac pulled open the center drawer of his desk, retrieved something, and moved to stand in front of Whitehorse. "I can't have you two leaving maintenance out of uniform. I can see both of you are missing your crew chief wings." When he began to pin on their wings, Ensley began to clap. Mac held up his hand for silence. "Congratulations to the both of you. You earned it. Someone else earned a promotion as well. Tom Sawyer, come forward. I understand you'll be DEROSing next week, too. What are your plans?"

Proudly, Tom responded, "Because Papa-San helped me get my airline maintenance certification, I'm going to work for Delta Airlines."

"Tom, I'm impressed. If I ever fly Delta, I'll look for you." Mac turned to the group and said, "When you lose one good leader, it makes room for another to grow. Ensley has accepted the challenge to be PE team leader." Mac stuck out his hand to Ensley and said, "Congratulations, I expect good things from you."

Ensley stood there, grinning proudly, "Me, too," he replied.

Mac walked back around behind the desk. "Before we leave, I'd like for you to meet a new addition to the team—First Lieutenant David Lillard, the new test pilot, so be nice to him. Let's go to work."

As everyone moved outside, Lillard whispered to Mac, "Sir, I don't know how to do a test flight."

Mac chuckled and told him, "Neither did Barney or I, until we took a course. Let's go see Bear in operations and get you set up. You came at a perfect time. When I first got here, the company commander had me fly every type of mission the pilots get. By doing that, you know what they are going through, so I recommend you do the same. In a couple of months, you'll be running the show. Trust me, that's not when you want to be learning new lessons. But the first thing we need to do is get you set for the three-day test flight school at Phu Loi run by 15TC Battalion. We're lucky they stayed here when the 1st Cav headquarters went back to Texas."

As the three men walked out of the maintenance area, they noticed several men surrounding Papa-San. Barney whispered, "Looks like his night school has some new students."

Mac recognized one of the men in the crowd: Morgan. He laughed to himself: *New teeth, new ambitions.* They continued on toward operations, and as soon as they were out of earshot, Barney asked, "Where'd you get those crew chief wings?"

"Captain Miller has a drawer full of them."

Captain Wright was walking toward them without his flight helmet and vest. Mac called out, "Hey there! Are you lost?"

"Nah, came looking for you." He stopped briefly to say something to Barney and Lillard then came up to Mac and said, "I put Lillard in Dant's old room. He'll be rooming with Lieutenant Royce, who just made AC and needs a copilot."

Mac could see Wright was talking as fast as he could, so he raised his hand and stopped him, "You didn't walk all the way down here to tell me about sleeping arrangements. What's wrong?"

Wright slowed down, "Savage received a letter from Dixon's fiancé. He was killed at Fort Rucker last week. He was transitioning into the OH-58 and the tail boom separated from the aircraft in flight and killed him and the IP. Apparently someone had made a hard landing and didn't write it up in the logbook. I thought you'd want to know."

Intellectually, Mac knew what Wright had said, but he just couldn't believe it. "Pilots are supposed to get killed in Nam; not a little accident in Alabama." He started to pace in circles as the others just watched, not sure how to respond. In desperation, Mac asked, "You're joking, right? He's getting married this Christmas."

No one said anything. Slowly they began to resume walking down the road. When they got to the company area, Barney and Wright were prepared to spend the afternoon in the bar; however, when Mac got to operations, he began to explain his plans for the lieutenant. Barney and Wright watched in awe at how he had suppressed his feelings and become all business.

April turned out to be a month of change. It began with Papa-San's certification class doubling in size. Unfortunately, everyone being busy left Rock out in the cold. Mac noticed it didn't take him long to solve the problem, though, and he was pleased to see him develop a friendship with Staff Sergeant Thomas from the 2nd flight platoon. Pappy, Sawyer and a specialist from avionics DEROSed. It seemed situations beyond his control were systematically destroying Mac's well-oiled maintenance machine. It was like the seniors on the varsity team had graduated, and he needed to find a way to get the others to step up and take their place. The one light at the end of the tunnel was Ensley, who hit the ground running. He constantly challenged the other PE team leaders; and as a result, he kept the maintenance flow chart above water. Of course, Ensley's success was making him even harder to live with for the men. As his confidence grew, so did his sarcasm. They brainstormed on how to get back at him with a series of practical jokes, but their plans were frustrated when they discovered he could take it as well as he could dish it out.

The last day of the month, 7-8-1 left Bear Cat. Mac noticed others seemed as sad as he was to watch the helicopter being hauled away. A small group of guys gathered around, discussing where they would take it. Mac didn't want to get involved, so he headed for the mailroom. He was expecting his monthly letter from his grandmother, but to his surprise, he found three others as well. One stood out—it was longer and wider than the others. He could see it was from the artillery branch and ripped it open to discover his new orders. He was slated to attend airborne school en route to the 82nd Airborne Division at Fort Bragg, North Carolina. His report date for the Fort Benning Airborne School was August 14, 1971. At first he was excited, until he realized he had committed himself to jump out of a perfectly good aircraft. He wondered what his daddy would say about that.

CHAPTER 30

Mac thought he had seen everything Vietnam had to offer, until Rock informed him of an event that struck fear in the hearts of every soldier, whether overseas or throughout the United States—an IG inspection. Rock was furious and kept mumbling, "My God, don't they know we're fighting a war over here? Why do we need an inspection? If we fail it, do they send us home?"

"Are you absolutely sure you heard it right? An IG inspection?" Mac was skeptical.

"That's what Top said—that the team would be here at the end of the month. The first sergeant wants all unauthorized equipment gone before then. Sir, I guess you and Captain Barney will lose your aircraft."

Mac smiled. "That's okay. I never felt right flying it anyway. Do we have anything else I need to worry about?"

"Just Ensley's mule. You know, our problems are easy compared to those of the supply sergeant. For the last six or seven years, all of the supply sergeants have taken advantage of any aircraft that went down or any enemy fire that came even close to our area. They'd submit paperwork to the division property book section that some of the stuff they'd signed for had been destroyed, and used any enemy activity to clean up their shortages. But from what he told Top, he still has some of the stuff, and there's no way he can account for it if we get an inspection."

"How about our guys?"

"You and Captain Barney don't need to worry about a thing. Papa-San and I have everything on our hand receipt."

Mac immediately relaxed; he remembered Barney's comment when he first met Rock—that Mac and Barney just needed to stay out of their way—and boy, how right he'd been. That evening in operations, Wright was waiting for him as usual. Mac asked, "You got a mission for me tomorrow?"

"Yeah, but it's not with me. You'll be Mr. Petersen's copilot. I've got to get ready for some damn inspection. Let's go to the bar. I seem to remember I owe you a drink."

Mac didn't remember the bet, but he wasn't one to turn down a free vodka and 7-Up. A couple of pilots had made their first trip into Cambodia and were celebrating by buying drinks for their buddies. The atmosphere in the bar was like a party. When Mac and Wright found a table, they were quickly joined by Tex, who was feeling no pain—and the volume of his voice proved it as he loudly proclaimed, "Boys, it looks like they're calling it quits on this war and sending me home. Have one on me."

Several hours of free drinks later, Mac realized he'd better call it a night. When he stood up to go, Wright said, "Not so fast! You still have to tell me how you started Barkley's aircraft. It's driving me crazy."

"That's why you're buying? You thought if you got me drunk, I'd spill my guts and tell you my secret."

"Well, did it work?" Wright asked.

"Oh, why not? You know the battery powers two things when it starts. First it has to turn the starter, and second, it fires the igniters. They take a lot more power from the battery than the starter does. My trick only works if the battery is just weak; it won't work when it's dead. First thing I did was pull the circuit breaker for the igniter plugs, so all the battery had to do was turn over the engine with the starter. When I got it up to thirty percent, I turned on the throttle to dump the fuel at the same time I pushed the igniter circuit breaker in. It started. The biggest threat is having a hot start, so you can see why we just do that in an emergency."

Mac almost laughed when he looked up at Wright. He looked so disappointed as he said, "Ah, hell, I thought it was magic. I knew it took more power for the igniters; I could have done that."

"You'd be surprised at the number of people that don't realize what they know until someone else makes it obvious. Well, now that you know you know, I'm going to bed. I have a mission in the morning."

Mac had flown with Mr. Petersen a few times before. He was a quiet guy from Fort Bragg, North Carolina, and the son of a career army NCO. On the way to the firebase, Mac said, "I have news. Pete, you won't believe where I'm going. I got my orders last week, and after airborne school at Fort Benning, I'm being assigned to the 82nd Airborne Division. Isn't that your Dad's old unit?"

"Yep, he retired when I was in high school," Petersen replied. "He owns a bar about three miles from the main gate called Pete's Place."

"What a perfect name. How long did he serve?" Mac asked.

"Thirty years. They gave him permission to stay longer, but his knees wouldn't let him jump anymore. He says when you're too old to jump, you should just drink. He had two combat jumps."

Mac said, "Sounds like you're really proud of him."

"I am now, but he was a real bastard when I was a kid. I've got two older brothers who knew just how to push his buttons. He caught the oldest one smoking marijuana with a friend on the roof of our house. The only reason he caught them was they were dumb enough to invite my other brother, James, up to smoke with them."

The entire crew had been listening in fascination, and the crew chief asked, "What did your old man do?"

Pete hesitated, then he laughed and said, "I guess it's okay to tell it now. He threw my brother and his friend off the roof of our house."

A long silence followed. No one knew what to say. Finally the chief asked, "Did they get hurt?"

"He broke my brother's wrist and sprained his ankle, but his friend didn't get off so lucky. It broke his right arm and three ribs."

"No way! Did your dad get in trouble?"

"Not really. When the ambulance took them to the hospital, they found two bags of drugs on them." He shook his head and continued, "For some reason, that subject never came up again. I have no idea what happened afterward."

Mac was curious. "Where's your brother now?"

"He's an instructor at Fort Benning's airborne school. If you're lucky, you won't see him."

Mac made a mental note to look him up as he asked, "What's his name?"

"Frank A. Petersen."

"Great, wouldn't want to have to avoid every Petersen at Fort Benning."

"When you get to Fort Bragg, stop in and see my dad," Petersen told him. "You can tell him I don't think he's a bastard anymore. Ask him to pull out that special drink from his freezer, and the two of you can have one for me."

Mac asked, "Uh, what's the special drink, or do I really want to know?"

"My mom is Italian, from a little town called Sorrento. They special-ize in liquor there called *limoncello*, and you will swear it's the nectar of the gods. Only really close friends get to sip the yellow gold."

"Well, you've convinced me. I can't wait to get there and try it now."

Pete reached over, flipped on his radio, and called for clearance to land. After shutting down, he said, "Captain Mac, I'll go see what the mission is." He got out and walked up the hill toward a bunker. Mac got out to stretch and walked around to the side of the aircraft to chat with Whitehorse. "Well, old buddy, how do you like being a chief?"

Whitehorse grinned. "It's okay, but I really miss the guys."

"I bet you mean Ensley."

"Yeah, he was always doing something to make us laugh. Don't get me wrong, being a crew chief is a great job, but…"

"It's a lot lonelier than you thought it would be, right?" Mac finished for him.

"Yes, sir. While you were talking to Mr. Petersen, I learned more about him than the entire time we've been flying together. I didn't realize we had so much in common. You know, I feel the same about my father. His being chief made my life hell. I had so many rules and standards to live up to, it was crazy—but I have to admit, now I'm glad."

Mac sympathized, "Having a strong father isn't always easy. Okay, now please tell me. What's the secret of the rain dance? You have no idea how long I've been waiting to ask you this."

Whitehorse ducked his head with a grin and said, "Well, my father explained it to me by saying you just keep dancing until it rains. Until today, I just thought it was a joke, but now I realize he was telling me to persevere. Not quitting will help me achieve my goals, so you just keep dancing."

Mac said, "Whitehorse, you're already sounding like a chief to me. I'm proud I got to know you."

Whitehorse turned away, opened the cargo door, and pulled out some C-rations. "Sir, would you like some of this fruitcake?"

Mac realized he must have hit a nerve, and things were a little awkward until he saw Pete returning, riding on a mule. Pete called out, "It's a resupply mission. Chief, help them load the supplies."

It was obvious this was a new task for Whitehorse. The men were loading the supplies like it was a truck. He remembered his mission with Woody and stepped forward and suggested, "You might want to put the water bladders next to the transmission wall and the rations behind the seats for a better CG."

Pete overheard him and said, "Sounds like this isn't your first rodeo."

He graciously accepted the compliment and said, "Yeah, another pilot taught me that."

"Captain Mac, crank her up. You fly, and I'll take care of the radio. They're located someplace southwest of here."

Mac and was thrilled to be flying and not just taking over to relieve the pilot on the mission. When Pete made contact with the men on the ground, he saw the needle on the console move to the left. He just eased his direction to the left until the needle centered. Pete saw his correction and smiled to himself; obviously Mac knew what he was doing. After flying for a while, the men on the ground called, "I hear you. You're nearly overhead."

Mac looked at the needle; it was off course the width of the needle to the right side, and he realized the wind had pushed him slightly off course. Just as he centered the needle, Pete pointed, "There they are, straight ahead. Damn, this must be a group of new guys. Look how small that hole is."

Mac looked down and countered, "At least it's bigger than one of our revetments."

Pete cautioned him, "Not by much."

Mac slowed the airspeed and pulled more power than needed, then came to hover over the newly made hole in the jungle. This wasn't a place for settling with power. He stayed at a hover until he felt he was completely in control of the aircraft. Whitehorse came over the intercom, talking to the door gunner, "Bobby, keep your eyes open. The pilot needs us to guide him."

Mac was sure the gunner knew his job, but he was relieved to hear Whitehorse giving the guidance, just in case. He began to slowly descend into the hole, and as he did the chief would direct him to move his tail five feet to the right. After that correction, he'd descend another few feet, and the process continued until he was within ten feet of the ground. A soldier then appeared and began to give hand signals. He had his arm stretched out to each side motioning for him to move down a couple of inches. Mac began to relax a little, as the soldier seemed to know what he was doing. When the aircraft was about a foot and a half off the ground, the soldier just dropped his hands. Mac pushed down on the collective and settled to the ground. As he did, he heard a sickening crunch from the belly of the aircraft. He didn't need to be told—the soldier had set him down right on a tree stump, and a big splinter had punched through the sheet metal. Woody's warning on his first hover-down came back: *They think this is a flying truck. If you don't watch them, they'll land you on a stump.* Pete put his hands over his face, "Captain Mac, I've gone nearly a year without any damage, and now you've ruined my record."

"Pete, it's not your record. I screwed it up, and I'll fix it."

"Sir, you know what I mean."

"I understand you're disappointed, but wait until my maintenance crew hears about it."

Whitehorse spoke up, "Sir, I'm looking at the bottom, and it's not leaking any fuel."

Pete thought for a moment and then suggested, "Let's get this stuff off the aircraft and get home before it does."

Everyone was quiet on the trip back to Bear Cat. Just short of the airfield, Mac asked, "Pete, do you still want me to have that drink with your dad?"

"Yeah, and tell him now I understand how he felt when we boys screwed up."

Pete started to land at the fueling point, and Mac stopped him, suggesting, "Don't refuel until we can check out the damage. Try to land in a revetment as close as you can to maintenance. I'll take care of the write-up, and you can do your thing at operations. I'll see you later in the bar."

Pete looked at him. "Drinks are on you."

"Fair enough."

When Mac walked to the shed, he noticed 4-4-3 in the first maintenance tent. He couldn't decide if he should ask about it or just pretend he hadn't seen it, but once he entered, the decision was made for him. Rock greeted him with, "We decided to keep the tail boom intact and only remove the components we have paperwork for. We should have it gone by tomorrow. How'd your mission go?"

"Not so good. I did some damage to the belly during a hover-down. I need Papa-San to check it out for me."

Immediately Rock could tell the captain was stressed—he'd never asked Papa-San to do anything before. "Don't worry, sir. I'll check it out myself, and it should be an easy fix. Why don't you take the list over to operations?"

"I can do that. I'll see you guys in the morning."

At oh-four-hundred, Rock greeted Mac with the news, "The damage was just sheet metal. The fuel tank was clean. The sheet metal guys released it last night. It's a standby ship."

"Thanks, Rock," Mac said. "I think it will be a while before Pete asks me to fly with him again. He made it pretty damn clear I'd ruined his record on damaged aircraft."

"Sir, don't you always say if you don't screw up, you're not doing anything?"

"Leave it to you to throw my words back in my face."

Rock grinned. "Isn't that why you keep me around?"

Mac changed the subject. "By the way, do you have your orders yet?"

"I've had them for months, sir. I'm going back to Fort Eustis, to my old job."

Mac looked at him, trying to gauge Rock's mood. "How do you feel about that?"

"That's what I agreed to when they agreed to let me come over here. It got harder and harder to send my students when I'd never been. Now I feel like I can be a good instructor to them."

"Rock, I just assumed this was your second tour."

"Boss, if it's okay with you, you can just keep that under your hat."

CHAPTER 31

Ensley's mule was the topic at breakfast. Rock and Papa-San tried to give it to every unit on post, but with the threat of units standing down, no one would take it off their hands. After tossing around ideas, Papa-San finally asked, "Captain Mac, do you think you could get Captain Wright to take it to one of the firebases?"

Mac frowned. "He's already got more equipment to get rid of than he can handle. I don't think he's flown a single mission since we heard about the inspection. One of his additional duties is company supply officer.

Barney shook his head and commented, "You know those additional duties have a way of jumping up and biting you in the butt. I remember I had nine of them when I was a second lieutenant. One of them was material readiness officer. I was required to turn in a report once a month on the operational status of the company's equipment. When I asked SFC Petty, he told me not to worry and that he'd take care of it. I would just sign the form each month, and he'd turn it in. Then one month he went on emergency leave, and I had no choice but to do it myself." He hesitated and then looked around the table and grinned.

Rock couldn't stand it and had to ask, "Well, what did you do?"

Barney said, "I did what all smart lieutenants do. I asked the first sergeant to help me."

The group erupted with laughter. Barney was always making everyone else the butt of his jokes, but this time the joke was on him. Mac laughed and looked around, seeing all different ranks and experience, but he knew that for the first time in his career, he was working with his peers. He waited until the noise subsided and then asked, "Any suggestions on what we do with the mule?"

Rock asked, "Are you making a parts run to Phu Loi today?"

"Yeah, around noon. Why?" Mac replied.

"Have you picked out which aircraft you plan to take?"

"No; do you have one in mind?"

"You always cross the river northwest of Bein Hoa, don't you? If you had a sling load, you could push it off over the river, and no one would ever know," Rock suggested.

Mac grinned. "This was your plan all along, wasn't it?"

"Well, I can't take all the credit. Papa-San came up with the sling-it-out part, and I came up with the river."

"Boys, it looks like old Mr. Ensley is losing his ride."

When they got to maintenance, Mac realized there were a lot more people involved, because they already had it rigged and ready for him right next to an aircraft rigged with a hook. Evidently, he'd been the last to know. The meeting was the shortest the group had ever had. When Mac walked to the aircraft with his helmet, he announced, "Guys, I'm making this trip by myself."

Rock joked, "No witnesses, huh?"

Mac said, "Something like that. Now, let's get this show on the road." When he came to a hover, Rock moved to hook him up and then moved to the side. Mac was a little nervous. The two transmission containers he'd slung in over the last couple of months had about the same flight characteristics of the fifty-five-gallon drum filled with water he had used in flight school. The mule wasn't round like those containers, and he was worried the flat bed of the mule would do some strange things. Just as he'd thought, as he began to fly the wind caused the mule to spin and try to fly. By adjusting his airspeed, he discovered at fifty knots it stayed steady, but at that speed he only felt comfortable flying thirty feet above the ground. Even then he never felt comfortable enough to take his finger off the release button on the cyclic. It took him almost forty-five minutes to get to the river. Raised in the mountains of Georgia, he'd learned while fishing for trout in the creeks and streams that the deepest holes were always in the bends. The sharper the bend, the deeper the hole. He was sure that would apply to the rivers and streams in Vietnam as well. He finally found the place he was looking for. The river made an almost ninety-degree turn to the left and was half as wide as the rest of the river. He pushed the release button and felt the drag of the mule go away. He made a sharp right turn to see the results but was only able to see a splash as it hit; it immediately sank deep into its watery grave. With a rush of adrenaline, he turned toward Phu Loi, still at thirty feet. He called the tower, requesting clearance to 15 TC pad. They came back with, "You're clear, no traffic."

He thought he saw the perimeter, so he popped up to a couple of hundred feet. He didn't recognize anything and quickly realized he'd flown more to the west than he'd intended. He was over Firebase Zion. He felt like a fool and quickly dropped back to thirty feet, turned northeast, and began a slow climb to fifteen hundred feet. He thought he'd corrected his mistake with no one the wiser when he got a call from the tower requesting his location. He advised he'd been on a maintenance check, and his ETA was five minutes. He couldn't believe his rookie mistake and was relieved he'd made this flight on his own.

A small crowd was waiting when he got back. Ensley was standing in front, and he walked over as Mac landed between the revetments. Once he was close enough, Mac yelled, "Get in, I need to refuel before I put it away."

Ensley liked being Mac's crew chief, and he was smiling as he crawled in the helicopter. Once they refueled, Mac returned to find the crowd still waiting for them. Everyone was curious about the mule, and he couldn't help but feel a little guilty that he'd just dumped a valuable piece of equipment in the river. He hadn't felt this bad since he used to steal watermelons from his neighbor's field. He knew if he'd asked, the neighbor would have helped him pick it out, but it was just a little bit more exciting to eat it without having to share the bounty. He truly believed God had punished him for doing it by giving him dysentery for a day. He found himself holding his breath, wondering what his punishment would be for dumping the mule. Everyone was laughing and joking about the event, and even Papa-San wanted details on how it had occurred. Time passed so quickly, they were all surprised when aircraft began returning from their daily missions. Mac asked Barney, "When does the lieutenant get through test flight school?"

"I'm not sure. He lives in the lieutenant's hootch, and I think they believe he's just another pilot. He was flying every day with them until he left for Phu Loi."

"Maybe that will be good. Rock and I had a tough time building up trust with the pilots when we first arrived."

Barney laughed. "Haven't seen them buying either of you any drinks now."

"I hear you, but I'm just too short to care," Mac replied with a grin.

At breakfast the company supply sergeant came in and asked Rock and Papa-San to come sign the new hand receipts he had prepared. As they walked back to maintenance, Barney told Mac, "I told you they'd keep us out of trouble." Once they had all assembled, Barney asked Mac, "I can't believe it took this long to just sign a hand receipt. Do you think something's wrong?"

"I have no idea, but if there's a problem, there's no one better to fix it," Mac said calmly.

Later, Rock and Papa-San drove up in a deuce and a half. Mac looked at it and asked Rock, "What do we need that for?"

"We don't need it at all—that's the problem. According to the supply sergeant, we have one more than we're authorized. Our deuce and a half's serial number is not on the division property books, so we've got to get rid of it before tomorrow's inspection."

Suddenly Mac was concerned. "You know our helicopters won't pick up a deuce and a half. How do we get rid of it?"

Rock grinned evilly, "How about us going over to the PX? I need some razors and shaving cream."

Mac had worked with Rock way too long to even think about questioning his motives. He just climbed into the truck. It was just a short drive across the post to the PX. Rock picked a spot near the rear of the parking area, got out, and took the lock and chain that was used to secure the steering wheel with him. Army trucks don't have ignition keys, so the chain is how they're secured. He stuck the lock in his pocket and threw the chain into the bed. Mac was watching him in amazement. Rock looked over and said, "How about getting some ice cream first? It's been a long time since I've had any."

Beginning to get the plan, Mac smiled and said, "Yeah, I guess we can do that."

Once they finished with their ice cream, they went to the PX. Like most soldiers, they walked the aisles to see what new items were available. As they left, Mac looked at his watch and realized they'd been inside for over an hour. They walked across the parking lot toward the truck, and Mac realized it was no longer there. He turned and looked at Rock. "You knew this would happen, didn't you?"

"If I had to guess, I'd bet someone did the same thing once before, and that's how we got it in the first place. Are you ready to walk home, sir?"

Mac laughed. "Lead the way, Merlin. You've dazzled me once again."

CHAPTER 32

It had been a month since the IG inspection. Mac smiled as he recalled how Rock had handled the two NCOs who inspected the maintenance shop. As he'd answered their questions, he took on his former persona of instructor. He had all the school solution answers, and they were impressed to learn that Bravo Company had a DS detachment that had overcome the problem of weak or failing engines. The icing on the cake had been when he had the two NCOs join Ensley's team as they completed their PE. One of them was so caught up with their performance that he failed to make any notes. The IG senior NCO's out brief to Mac was, "Sir, you have one hell of a team here." As he recalled the remarks, he realized they'd come a long way from just having one flyable bird. He walked outside and noticed Sergeant Thomas and Rock standing there, like they were waiting for him. Just like every other day, Rock said, "Sir, if it's okay, we're going over to get a ham sandwich." Normally Mac would just nod his approval, but today he decided to join them.

"You know, I've heard about this sandwich for so long, I'm craving one too. Think I'll go with you," Mac said.

Rock whirled around and looked at Thomas. It was obvious they were caught off guard by Mac's comment. Rock stuttered, "Are you sure, sir? They're not like the ones back in the States."

"I get it. I know the Vietnamese don't know how we make sandwiches, but I'm sure it will hit the spot."

Rock grinned and said, "Sir, now don't you forget. You asked to come with us."

After a short walk, they entered the PX lot, where the deuce and a half had mysteriously disappeared. Mac looked at Rock and gave him a secret smile as they walked across the spot. Rock led them toward a little shop next to the main PX. As they sat down, Rock said to the Vietnamese waitress, "We'll have three ham sandwiches."

She grinned, went behind the counter, and quickly returned with three beers—Hams beers. Rock just gave Mac a poker face, and Mac grinned. "I get it. Just make sure you don't get your sandwiches too early in the day," he said.

Rock said, "You can trust us, sir."

"You know what's really scary? I absolutely do."

CHAPTER 33

It had finally arrived—the day Mac would sign out and leave Bravo Company 229th, his home for the past ten months. Over the last month, he had taken a lesson from Pappy: no one had known Pappy's DEROS date, and he'd been able to go about business as usual. Mac wasn't quite that lucky, though, as he'd only made it until the previous day. There would be ten more days until Barney would DEROS, and he was the one who had put two and two together. Confirming it with Captain Miller was all he'd needed to do. Miller was the awards and decorations officer, and Miller knew everything about everybody.

When Barney confronted Mac, he swore him to secrecy. He was the rating officer on Barney's OER, so he had a big stick to use against him. Barney reasoned the men would just find out from someone else; and Mac smiled, because he knew Rock would DEROS in five days, and Sergeant Thomas would DEROS three days later. They would be the ones having to deal with the good-bye parties. His plan had worked so far; however, when he went to the orderly room to sign out, the first sergeant directed him into the commander's office. There he was welcomed by Major West, Captains Wright and Miller, and Dancing Bear. West smiled and said, "Thought you were going to get away before we noticed, didn't you? Well, buddy, this isn't our first rodeo. You need a little more lettuce on that shirt pocket. Captain Miller, what do we have for him?"

Miller stepped forward. "Sir, I have orders he'll receive fourteen air medals, another ARCOM, and…oh, yeah, you also earned a DFC for pulling one of Charlie Company's crews from a hot LZ."

Major West took charge. "Mac, it's a real privilege to pin this medal on your chest. Is it true you and Ensley didn't even have a pistol onboard?"

Mac hurried to explain, "Sir, it's such a pain in the butt to come to the arms room and check out a weapon for every test flight."

"Well, congratulations. You're living proof good soldiers don't always do the safe or smart thing. If any of you need any more proof, Mac will be leaving us and going to the 82nd Airborne Division. You're supposed to fly them, Mac, not jump out of them." Everyone burst out laughing. After a quick handshake with each, the party dispersed. Soldiers have a tough time saying good-bye.

As the jeep drove by the maintenance area on his way to the 90th replacement, Mac could see a couple of his PE teams going about their work under the new leadership. The jeep ride was a little more exciting than he'd expected. It was his first ride through the countryside and Vietnamese villages. He had observed hundreds of them from the air, but today he was riding within three feet of their front doors. When he made eye contact with the locals, he wondered what they thought of the American riding through in his khaki uniform. At the 90th replacement, he picked up his duffle bag and briefcase. The driver didn't even turn off his engine, just said, "See you later, sir," as Mac stepped to the side. With that remark, he realized he was no longer a Killer Spade pilot. After he signed in, the worst part began— waiting. *Everyone jokes about how being in the army means to hurry up and wait, but it's not funny when you're the one actually doing it*, Mac thought. He stored his belongings and walked into the day room. It had been a year since he'd been there, but absolutely nothing had changed. He recognized two of his OCS classmates at the same poker table. Brown had been in his sister class in OCS and two classes behind him in flight school. Mac approached and said, "Charlie, you were at that same table when they took me down to the 1st Cav. I certainly hope you've been winning all year."

Brown didn't miss a beat, "Things were a little slow around Christmas. Where'd they stick you?"

"Bravo Company, 229th."

"They gave me gunships, ARA Cobras. Pull up a chair."

Mac flashed back to the old games in the bar, where players tried to buy the pots. These guys looked like hardcore players, trying to intimidate the new meat coming in-country. He looked around for a chess game but was disappointed none were to be found. A nap might make the time pass more quickly. Unfortunately, all those mornings on the flight line at oh-four-hundred had trained him not to sleep in, especially on his last day in Nam. So he joined group of new arrivals in the mess hall. They looked absolutely exhausted; throughout history, the fear of the unknown had kept a lot of men from sleeping. Once they realized he was leaving, he had their complete focus, and they bombarded him with anxious questions. An entire year had gone by, but their questions were the same as the one the young soldier had asked on the flight over. They were pleased when he told them the 1st Cav Division had moved back to Fort Hood, Texas. It was a sure sign the war was winding down. He saw no reason to tell them a lot of their units were still here, doing the same missions.

After breakfast an old master sergeant, reminding him of Papa-San, had everyone going to Ton Sun Nhut Airport fall into his formation. He didn't need to ask twice. Mac was amused; he hadn't seen a formation fall in so quickly since his first week in OCS. The longer he was in the army, the more he realized everything remains the same. One does what one has to do to survive. The ride back to the airport was the same route, but he saw the countryside with new eyes. Before, he hadn't noticed most of the bridges had been rebuilt on the old ones that had been destroyed. He now noticed women, children, and old men. Where had all the young men gone? When the bus arrived, they were issued tickets and told to check in their duffle bags. Next to the entrance was a huge box with *Amnesty* written on it and a warning that this was the last opportunity to turn in unauthorized items. Below was a list of about fifty things. It became fun for him to watch some of the soldiers' reactions. They'd try to nonchalantly walk by the box, but after passing it, either their consciences or fear kicked in, and they'd come back, open their bags, and pull out pistols, grenades, bullets, survivor vests, and anything else that looked dangerous. It seemed seeing the freedom bird sitting there, waiting for them, reminded them the most important thing was having the ability to climb onboard and go home. As Mac watched, he could see the change in their attitudes, and most of the duffle bags became a lot lighter.

As they boarded, they passed up the first available seats and seemed to move on to locate the seat they'd held on the trip over. Mac moved down the aisle until he felt comfortable and took an available window seat. He decided to slip off his low-quarter shoes and was interrupted by someone asking about the empty seat next to him. The soldier asked, "Sir, do you remember me?"

Mac looked up. The soldier didn't wait for him to respond but continued to explain, "I sat next to you on the flight over here last year."

The man in front of him appeared to be several inches taller, but Mac knew that wasn't possible. He looked at his chest for a name tag, but couldn't help but see all the ribbons on the other side. He said, "Yeah, I just didn't recognize you with all of those medals."

The soldier grinned. "I see you've got a lot of 'I was there medals' yourself." The scared young man Mac had flown over with had been replaced with a strong, confident soldier. Mac could see in his eyes that whatever he'd gone through had prepared him for the remainder of his life, and he would never let fear slow him down again. He asked, "Would you like the window seat on the way home?"

"No, sir; this seat was perfect on the way over, and I think it'll do just fine on the way home."

When the plane began to taxi to the runway, everyone got quiet. It lifted off and turned toward the east. Moments later the pilot came over the speakers, "Look out the windows, guys, that's the ocean. You're going home." The plane erupted with cheers and laughter. When the noise level decreased, the soldier asked Mac, "Sir, do you play chess?"

VIETNAM WAR FACTS

During the official Vietnam era—from August 5, 1964, to May 7, 1975—9,087,000 military personnel served on active duty.

A total of 2,709,918 Americans served in uniform in Vietnam.

Vietnam veterans represented 9.7 percent of their generation.

Two hundred forty men were awarded the Medal of Honor during the Vietnam War.

The first man to die in Vietnam was James Davis, who died in 1961. He was with the 509th Radio Research Station. Davis Station in Saigon was named for him.

There were 58,148 soldiers killed in Vietnam.

Of those killed, 17,539 were married.

Of those killed 11,465 were under twenty years old.

Five soldiers killed in Vietnam were only sixteen years old.

The oldest man killed was sixty-two years old.

As of January 15, 2004, there were 1,875 Americans still unaccounted for from the Vietnam War.

Ninety-seven percent of Vietnam veterans were honorably discharged.

Ninety-one percent of Vietnam veterans say they are glad they served.

Seventy-four percent say they would serve again, even knowing the outcome.

Vietnam veterans have a lower unemployment rate than the same nonveteran age groups.

Vietnam veterans' personal income exceeds that of the same nonveteran age group by more than 18 percent.

Eighty-seven percent of Americans hold Vietnam veterans in high esteem.

There is no difference in drug usage between Vietnam veterans and nonveterans of the same age group.

Vietnam veterans are less likely to be in prison—only one-half of 1 percent of Vietnam veterans have been jailed for crimes.

Eighty-five percent of Vietnam veterans made successful transitions to civilian life.

(*Source*: All statistics are from Veterans Administration Study).

COMMON MYTHS DISPELLED:

Facts

- Two-thirds of the men who served in Vietnam were volunteers. Two-thirds of the men who served in World War II were drafted. Approximately 70 percent of those killed in Vietnam were volunteers.
- Of those killed in Vietnam, 86 percent were Caucasians, 12.5 percent were black, and 1.2 percent were of other races.
- Servicemen who went to Vietnam from well-to-do areas had a slightly elevated risk of dying, because they were more likely to be pilots or infantry officers. Vietnam veterans were the best-educated forces our nation had ever sent into combat; 79 percent had a high school education or better.
- The average infantryman in the South Pacific during World War II saw about forty days of combat in four years. The average infantryman in Vietnam saw about 240 days of combat in one year, thanks to the mobility of the helicopter. The average time lapse between wounding to hospitalization was less than one hour. As a result, less than 1 percent of all Americans wounded, who survived the first twenty-four hours, died. The helicopter provided unprecedented mobility.

- The average age of the 58,148 killed in Vietnam was 23.11 years. (Although 58,169 names are in the November 1993 database, only 58,148 have both event date and birth date. Event date is used instead of declared dead date for some of those who were listed as missing in action.)

GLOSSARY OF VIETNAM

TERMINOLOGY

AHB – assault helicopter battalion

Airborne – refers to soldiers who are qualified as parachutists

AO – area of operations

Arc Light – code name for B-52 bomber strikes along the Cambodian-Vietnamese border. These operations shook the earth for ten miles away from the target area

Article 15 – section of the Uniform Military Code of Justice. A form of non-judicial punishment

ARVN – Army of the Republic of Vietnam; the South Vietnamese Regular Army

Battalion – a military unit composed of a headquarters and two or more companies

Bird – any aircraft, but usually refers to helicopters

Body Bag – plastic bag used to transport dead bodies from the field

Bronze Star – U.S. Military decoration awarded for heroic or meritorious service not involving aerial flights

C-4 – plastic, putty textured explosive carried by infantry soldiers. It burns like sterno when lit and was used to heat C-rations in the field

CG – center of gravity

C-Rations – combat rations. Canned meals for use in the field. Each usually consisted of a can of some basic course, a can of fruit, a packet of some type of dessert, a packet of powdered cocoa, a small pack of cigarettes and two pieces of chewing gum

Charlie – Viet Cong, from phonetic alphabet for VC, Victor Charlie

Cherry Juice – hydraulic fluid

Connex Container – corrugated metal packing crate approximately six feet in length

Det-Cord – explosive that looks like rope used to daisy-chain claymores

Donut Dolly – women from the American Red Cross

Elephant Grass – tall, sharp-edged grass found in the highlands of Vietnam

EOD – explosive ordinance disposal

FOD – foreign object damage, trash on the airfield

Frag – offensive fragmentation hand grenade, five second fuse

Hook – short for a CH-47 Chinook

Huey – Bell UH-1 helicopter

Indian Country – area controlled by Charlie

Jesus Nut – large nut which holds the rotor blade on rotor shaft of a helicopter

LBJ – Long Binh Jail, the Army stockade in Long Binh

Log Bird – resupply helicopter, usually a Huey

Low Boy – a tank transporter, also called Dragon Wagon

LZ – landing zone (note that some were Fire Support Bases and had names)

Mad Minute – random firing of all perimeter defensive weapons to discourage infiltration and test weapons

MPC – military payment certificates; script issued in lieu of dollars

Napalm – thickened gasoline

RPG – rocket propelled grenade, Soviet made

Short – very little time left in country

Six – radio call sign of a unit commander

Snake – slang for a AH-1 Huey Cobra attack helicopter

Web Gear – canvas belt and shoulder straps used for packing equipment and ammunition on infantry operations

XO – executive officer, the second in command of a unit

YARDS – affectionate GI term for Montagnard

Made in the USA
Charleston, SC
16 June 2013